PUSH
AND PULL

To Helen,
Love conquers all.

Love,
Diane
(12/8/2018)

PUSH
AND PULL

DIANE RIVOLI

COVER ILLUSTRATION BY JOSH RIVOLI

Also by Diane Rivoli

LICENSE – A NOVEL (2015)
A prequel of sorts, *License* ends 4 years before *Push And Pull* begins. Major characters become minor and minor characters become major.

EVERY MOMENT IS A POEM, EVERY POEM A SONG (2016)
A companion piece to *License*, this collection of 36 poems includes 19 poems first seen in *License* in addition to 17 others.

For Matt and Juan

She was starting to think that maybe, just maybe, the very handsome Jay was gay.

Excerpt from *License – A Novel*
by Diane Rivoli (2015)

CONTENTS

Chapter 1
YOU CALLED, MY LOVE?

Oh, the glory of the morning! Jay stood on the front porch, yawning and smiling into a bright blue April sky and basking in the sun. Basking - A misnomer. It was what he was trying to do, hoping to do, in that pool of sunlight, but what he was really doing was shivering there in his husky-man t-shirt and jeans, lured out coatless on a promise of warmth the sun couldn't keep. Husky - another misnomer. No way was he fat. It was more of a 'football player build' kind of thing.

How different yesterday had been; twenty degrees warmer and he had almost baked on the sun-warmed bricks like a pepperoni-topped pizza in a wood-fired oven. Today frost whitened the windows on the cars in the driveway and clung snow-like to the grass in the yard.

But morning was morning - a fresh start to a new day, and a weekend day at that. There would be no coffee sloshing around in a travel mug today, no rushed bowl of cereal as everyone hurried off for work or school. Adrian was cooking breakfast. The allure of sizzling bacon was wafting through the open screen, the clatter of pans, the chopping of knives. That was one of the things Jay loved about Adrian - the thoughtfulness and care his sweetheart took preparing those special weekend breakfasts.

Jay smiled again and breathed deep of the morning, enjoying the cool rush that filled his lungs, exhaling faux smoke into the brisk air, then he flicked the lighter and filled his lungs with what he had really come out on the front porch for - The glory of his bad habit; a long and smoky toke of tar and nicotine.

He held the smoke captive, savoring his first drag of the day, before releasing it in a lazy stream through pursed lips.

Up and out the smoke waltzed, coupled with his breath. Jay watched as it meandered, rooting for it to reach the mulberry tree in the center of the yard, but the smoky dance lost steam and dissipated well before it arrived.

As hard as he had been cheering the wavering tendrils on, Jay hardly noticed now that they had never made it there. His thoughts had taken up where the smoke left off, drifting up into the tree's spring bud covered branches, imagining the berries that would hang there, heavy and sweet, come summer. Berries that he would pluck and pop into his mouth till his fingers and teeth and lips and tongue were stained red. Like a kid again when he and his buddies had gorged from the wild mulberry tree that grew in the clearing behind the deserted log cabin in Ellison park, sticking out their tongues to see whose had gotten the reddest, and chasing each other around the streets of his small-town home of Croakers Norge, screaming and lurching like zombies, with the berries' pseudo blood dribbling from their juice stained lips.

It was the sight of the mulberry tree standing ripe with fruit next to the For Sale sign six years ago that had sealed the deal and prompted him to buy this house over all the others he had dragged his then eight year old daughter, Mina, to see. A touch of home when he was far from it, a reminder of carefree times when all he had to worry about was not diving too deep into the brown waters of Shuck Pond and dodging clumps of mucky mud that he and his friends scooped up from the bottom and flung at each other with glee.

Nostalgia wandered through Jay's head – Peter, Johnny, Gerry, and Mark, clear creeks and mossy stones, cattail-lined swimming holes, garter snakes in fish tanks and caterpillars in jars. And then there she was, Khaki Campbell, smiling at him from under that wild mulberry tree as she hung from its low branches; waving at him from the worn wooden dock that jutted out into Shuck Pond just before she ran to the end and cannonballed in, her knees drawn up to her chest, the sun gleaming off the smooth silk of her hair; cheering from the bleachers when he sent the pigskin spiraling across the football field; lying warm beside him in the cool evening grass discussing the stars, her voice soft in reverence of the night '…must have been stoned out of their minds. Cassiopeia's like, only four stars. Even if you drew a line between those stars, there's no way it comes out looking like a woman. The little dipper's the only constellation that makes sense.'

Khaki, with her bright colors and black hair… She had always known… And she had whispered in his ear…

Suddenly nostalgia imploded. Jay's drifting thoughts scattered and flew. Adrian was calling him from the house. He crouched down, stubbed out his Newport 100 in the frosty grass, grabbed the morning paper off the step and hurried into the house.

"You called, my love?" Jay asked, grinning, as he tossed the paper on the kitchen table.

"Yes," Adrian replied, intently chopping something into bite size bits on a bamboo cutting board. That was another thing Jay loved about Adrian; even that simple word 'yes' was like a song, wrapped as it was in a Colombian accent. "I've got meat and potatoes all over my hands," Adrian continued, "and I forgot I wanted an onion too." One final chop-chop and Adrian finally looked up, deep set brown eyes smiling at Jay from under curved, dark brows. "Would you mind grabbing me one? A small one."

"No problem. Anything for you, my darling. What are you making?"

"I came up with the perfect use for the leftovers from the pot roast last night. I'm making roast beef hash to go along with our bacon and over easy eggs. Or would you rather have scrambled?"

"Either/or, as long as there's no veggies."

"LOL. Veggies are good for you."

"You know I don't like things that are good for me. Except for you."

"How do you know I'm good for you?"

"How do I know? Because you try to make me eat veggies. Because you put a smile on my face and a boner in my pants! What could be gooder for me than that?"

Jay walked over with the onion, deposited it on the granite countertop and put his arms around Adrian, nuzzling kisses into the nape of his sweet one's neck and pressing the firm bulge in his pants hard against the slender globes of Adrian's backside to demonstrate just how 'good' good was.

"Ooooh…," Adrian breathed, low with desire. Then suddenly, "Jay!" warning him away as slippered feet shuffled into the kitchen from the hallway bringing with them a blank-faced and dopey-eyed Mina.

Mina's not quite awake morning face burst to life in an instant - a grimace of disgust. "Eeeeew! Dad! Is this the first thing I have to see when I get up in the morning? You and Adrian having sex!"

"Having sex? We were just hugging," Jay countered as he moved away from Adrian, trying not to look guilty as charged, and headed for the coffee pot.

"Yeah. Right. I bet if I hadn't come walking in you would have been having sex. You've always got your hands all over Adrian. I never saw you and Mom doing this sort of stuff."

"It's called affection, Mina. Something I'm sad to say your mom and I didn't have. All you saw us do was argue and scream at each other or try to ignore each other completely," Jay began judiciously, losing his sensibility at the last moment and storming ahead, "Did you like that better? Do you want me and Adrian to start doing that too? Scream at each other all the time?"

"You know that's not what I mean. You know it!" Mina accused, her voice climbing with each word. "And maybe it would be better. Maybe I don't want to see two …."

"Hey Mina, guess who I heard was going to be playing at the Downtown Armory next weekend?" Adrian interjected, excitement hanging on the words, hoping to grab Mina's attention and yank them all back from the looming precipice, "That local band you like so much. Surf Shifters! And they even played one of their songs on the radio yesterday. You know, that one with the great beat. BaBam BaBam BaBam." Adrian started humming, trying to remember the tune, boogieing in place, and thumping to the rhythm.

"LOL. You mean Maze Shifters?" Mina laughed at Adrian, but her hostile face began to soften. "I already know. It popped up on Facebook last night. Some other band was on the schedule but they had to cancel so they got Maze Shifters instead." The angry line of her mouth became a smile. "They are so hot. OMG!" Brightness twinkled in her widening brown eyes. "Beth's gonna ask her parents if she can go. Can I go, Dad? It would be so awesome." And then she was dancing along with Adrian, gyrating her hips and waving her arms to Adrian's mimicked beat, as the disheveled frizz of her chestnut hair bounced around her head.

Relief flooded over Jay. And gratitude. Adrian always had a way of lightening the mood, smoothing over the rough surface that Jay and Mina constantly grated up. Another thing he loved, another reason why Adrian was his sweetheart.

He filled his mug with hot coffee, anxious for the soothing warmth it would bring, and stood grinning as he sipped, watching Mina and Adrian bop and sway.

***

What was the matter with him? A father should be the voice of reason and maturity. Instead, he fed Mina's teenage frenzy. Fed it? He actually joined it! He acted more like a 14-year-old than she did. If it wasn't for Adrian…

Jay sat in a booth at Betty's Pantry, spearing ketchup laden French fries and nibbling on them from the end of a fork. He'd

5

had to leave the dancing twosome and the roast beef hash and his caffeine fix behind when the phone rang calling him into work. Big accident in the parking garage by Falcon Ridge Hospital. Channel 20 wanted photos for the evening news.

Most of the time, Jay loved his job. Following human interest stories and capturing exuberant, happy faces at festivals, concerts, and sporting events; that put a zing in his own step. His co-workers were great too – people he looked forward to seeing every day. They even got together outside of work from time to time. And he counted Mike Chatelain, Channel 20's Account Executive, and Dixie Andrews, the Director of Creative Programming, as two of his very best friends. He'd even been a groomsman in their wedding - four years ago this coming July.

But being interrupted in the middle of a meal or a show, or a fuck, and having to rush off to photograph misfortune and anguish? That was something he could do without.

This time though, he was almost glad he'd gotten the call. The sunny mood that had quelled the storm could have been a decoy, lulling him into a false sense of security. The issue he did not want to address might have come sneaking back in to roar in his ear. And besides that, he had avoided Mina's plea to go to that Maze Shifters concert. No doubt she would have started to dig in and hound him for an answer about that.

"Well, it looks like that didn't hit the spot at all did it, Jay?"

Jay jumped a little, startled. Sheila, the waitress, was standing by his booth, looking down at his empty plate and beaming. He looked up at her and stared, looked down at his plate and stared at that, then looked up at Sheila again. Didn't hit the ...? Then, the fact that she was teasing him finally sunk in.

"Oh, it really was terrible, Sheila. I could hardly stomach it," Jay teased her back. "That's why I come here all the time, for the bad food. Hey, what's for dessert? Got any of that chocolate bread pudding today?"

"Oh, that bread pudding was to die for, wasn't it? But sorry, there's none to be had today, Hon. If you've got a hankering for chocolate we do have a delicious looking chocolate cream pie today. We've got lots of nice pies – apple, pecan, lemon meringue, brambleberry. And we've got…"

"Did you say mulberry?"

"No, not mulberry. Brambleberry. It might be something like mulberry though. You wanna try it?"

"Is it homemade?"

"Homemade?" Sheila stood there with her hands on her hips, rolling her eyes. "Look out the window, Jay. Does it look like the time of year for fresh berries? There was frost on the ground this morning. The crust is homemade."

"Yeah, all right. What the hell. I'll give it a whirl."

"Coming right up."

The pie was crappy, not at all up to the Pantry's usual standards. Too sweet and more gel than fruit. But Jay ate it anyway, and as he ate his mind drifted again to where it had been that morning – to his carefree youth back in Croakers Norge. Carefree - That was just nostalgia talking. His life had never truly been carefree. Too many times he had felt alone even when he was with a group of friends. He had felt lost, scrabbling for answers, trying to pull himself along a straight line that kept buckling and twisting and turning. And he had felt like a liar, which ate a hole into the pit of his stomach because lying was against his religion. But not lying would have been even worse.

He was shoveling the last bite into his pie hole when he glanced up and just caught a glimpse of a waitress with straight black hair rushing into the kitchen holding a tray piled high with dirty dishes. Something about that hair, the way the light shone off it, the curve of her nose, the jut of her chin.

Jay nearly choked on his pie, grabbed his cup of coffee to wash it down and scalded his tongue. Sheila had just refilled it from a freshly brewed pot and was standing there staring at him again.

"You all right there, big boy?"

7

"Yeah," Jay croaked, coughing and gagging. He reached for his water glass, took a big gulp and then let his tongue rest in the water for a moment to cool the burn.

"Is that a new waitress I just saw going into the kitchen, Sheila? She looks like someone I used to know. Is her name Khaki?"

"No, sorry to disappoint, but it's Katie."

Chapter 2
WHERE HAD ALL THOSE YEARS GONE?

There must be fifty ways to leave your lover, but telling them outright that this was the end wasn't one of them. Sheila was going with the slip out the back, Jack plan.

'See you later, Sheila,' Jay had called out to her on his way out the door, but unless she ran into him at The Groundhog Garden Store or Hickory's Food Mart, it wouldn't be at Betty's Pantry.

Today was her last day. And she hadn't told Jay. She hadn't leaked the fact that she was planning to leave waitresshood behind to any of her regulars. The last thing Sheila wanted was anyone making a fuss over her – leaving a bigger than usual tip tucked under their plate or jumping up out of their seat to hug her and hand her sentimental farewell cards or goodbye gifts. How would she wipe her eyes when her hands were busy holding tumblers full of lemonade or cola or chocolate milk? How was she supposed to see when her lenses got all fogged up?

The thing was, she really was going to miss them; handsome Jay with his hearty appetite and wide, easy smile, Gus the dog groomer, petite Angela with her German accent, the wavy haired guy who always left her a five dollar tip with a chocolate kiss sitting on top, old Mr. and Mrs. Forbes who came in nearly every morning at precisely 9:00 for a cup of tea and a slice of warm pecan pie. She'd even miss that joker with the tattoos and the constant frown who complained about everything.

And now she would never find out what happened to the Newfoundland at the dog groomer's that the dog's owner had never returned for. She'd never hear Jay tell any more stories about that daughter of his that he was so proud of.

But it just couldn't be helped. Carrying those heavy trays loaded with stacks of dirty dishes, trying to maneuver around tables and chairs while juggling plates of biscuits and sausage gravy, Reuben sandwiches and beer battered fish fries – it was just getting to be too much for her to handle. By the time the end of the day rolled around, she was barely able to lift her legs high enough to climb the steps onto the homeward bound bus.

Sheila couldn't quite figure out how or when it had happened, but somehow she had gotten old. Well, not old really. Certainly not as old as Mrs. Forbes. But that semblance of youth that had always seemed to hover about her had finally disappeared.

Where had all those years gone? Wasn't it only yesterday that she was a fine young thing in her thirties, waiting tables at the Ayrault Tavern? She had a dozen tables in her section and she remembered what every single person had ordered without even writing it down! She whisked in and out of the kitchen with pitchers and platters and plates and fended off unruly over indulgers with nothing but a glare and her quick wit. And maybe, if still required, a slap on the hands.

Now she was twice as old, waiting on half as many tables, scribbling people's orders down with a pencil. She didn't whisk now, she plodded, with her feet clad in sturdy, thick soled nursing shoes. And who would want to slap her butt or try to cup her bosom now?

Well, maybe if she was still at the Ayrault they would. If some guys were drunk enough, they'd try to cop a feel of anything that belonged to a female body, no matter how wrinkled or plump or gray that female body might be.

And at Betty's Pantry, whether Sheila was young and beautiful or old and gray, no guy would have tried anything like that anyway. Betty's was a respectable place; families brought their children there, and the strongest drink on the menu was espresso roast coffee.

But the fact of her dwindling abilities wasn't the only reason Sheila had decided to retire. Mainly it was because her Gordy needed her.

A bitterness had lodged into the set of his jaw. He looked down and saw the crack that the rough winter had birthed in the cobblestone walkway but not the crocuses that bloomed yellow and purple and white along the edge. He looked up and saw the half broken branch drooping in the sycamore but not the glory of the sun in a cloudless blue sky.

Even worse was that she had glimpsed the banished ghosts of another life peering out at her from the piercing blue of Gordy's eyes. She had heard him raging at that crack in the sidewalk as if were an enemy's face. She had watched him bolt for cover under the kitchen table when air pockets in the crackling fireplace logs had exploded like the staccato pop pop pop of gunfire.

"Hey, Sheila, you've got that faraway look in your eyes again." It was Katie, the new girl, pausing beside her with a pot of coffee, ready to make the refill rounds. "Was that another one of your regulars?"

"Yeah. Jay. Comes in at least once a week. Really nice guy. Always telling me about his teenage daughter's escapades. Never heard him mention a wife though. You know…" Sheila was about to mention that Jay had asked about Katie and thought she might be someone he knew. But there was something about the way Katie was staring at the door that Jay had recently exited… "…you better get going with that coffee, Katie," she said instead. "I see some antsy faces looking this way."

"True that. I'm on it." Katie grinned, raised the coffee pot in a salute and headed for the first table on the left.

Everyone had ghosts that came back to haunt them from time to time. And Sheila would wager that Katie had quite a few

11

of them. That was something else Sheila would never find out about. Today was, after all, her last day.

Katie was on her own with this one.

Chapter 3
A DUCK BY ANY OTHER NAME…?

Technically, Khaki Campbell couldn't be called a gypsy. But she was light and flighty, like an unattached feather, and since she was named after a duck, this made perfect sense.

Her parents, Denny and Becky, were proud of the unique name they had given their first born. They stuck out their chests like strutting barnyard kings whenever anyone asked its origins.

What a day it had been! The sun full out in a brilliant blue sky. The air warm with just a hint of autumn chill. And they were having the greatest time wandering through the poultry barn at an old time Agricultural Faire, captivated by the Rhode Island Reds and Leghorns, the Muscovies and Bantoms and Jersey Giants, when pregnant Becky had been taken with the olive green and creamy tan of a sleek Khaki Campbell.

'Denny!' she had called to her husband excitedly, 'come over here and look at this duck. Isn't it beautiful? And oh my god, can you believe it? It's called a Khaki Campbell. It has our last name. This has got to be a sign.'

And so Khaki Campbell had become, not only a breed of duck, but the name of a girl as well.

When Khaki thought of Croakers Norge, the small hamlet from whence she came, she thought of green and blue and brown. She thought of the smooth moss covered stones that lined the bed of Feverfew Crick and of the mud that squished up through her toes from the bottom of Shuck Pond.

She never thought of the boy she left behind or how the sun sparkling from the creek's dancing waters had reflected back on her from his green eyes. She never thought of his strong arms lifting her, dripping and laughing, from the water when she slipped on the smooth stones. And she never thought of how moist his eyes became or how his lips had quivered when she told him she was leaving Croakers Norge - because he hadn't wanted her anyway; not in the way she wanted him to.

Still, even though he was never on her mind, she knew he had tried to bend to the mold and failed and that he had ended up flying from Croakers Norge the same as she had, grappling for stability on wings that were tattered and frayed. But she also knew that he had mended those wings, finally accepted the truth of himself, and settled into life. That he was in love. And that he was happy.

And knowing this about the boy she never thought of made Khaki happy too. It warmed her insides and made her smile. A smile that grew and lit up her eyes until tears dimmed the light and washed the smile away.

"Let me take you," she had whispered in his ear so many times. "Let the night calm us down."

But he had never let her.

And the night never did.

So Khaki had packed her bags and gotten her ticket, and flown over Croakers Norge higher than any other Khaki Campbell ever had, looking down as if from the vantage point of a god at the small village nestled in a verdant hollow, its edges tickled by long, thin fingers of mirrored gray/green and surrounded by a wider blue swath that was Oatka Creek.

All the years of her life flashed before her as she looked out the window of that high flying airplane and she felt like she might lose her balance and go toppling over; falling down, down, down through the blue sky back towards home, scrabbling for a purchase on the wispy clouds that floated there like the creamy white innards of a cattail let loose on a breeze.

Then the plane banked and turned and Khaki swallowed to clear her ears and she was left exhilarated and defiant, with only a hint of the memories she had gathered over her nineteen years still swimming in her eyes.

14

And that moist hint of memory was of him, standing on the outside of the airport barrier with her parents waving goodbye, his mouth a straight line that wavered and crashed when he tried to make it smile.

He was her best friend. He had known her promises were false. He had known this was the end.

That was fifteen years ago. And she hadn't talked to him or seen him since. Until now, trying to peer at him over the top of a menu as she passed it to a customer or from around a stack of dishes piled high on a tray.

There he was. Still the same after all these years. Jay.

But Khaki was not still the same after all those years. She was not even Khaki at all. She had soared and floated, crumbled and crashed, hopped and skipped and tripped. But first, she had landed.

It was Education 101 that came into focus as that highflying plane descended and touched down those fifteen years ago. The doors opened and out spilled Khaki with her dorm room assignment and meal plan. But the wind caught her again after only one semester and carried her away, following the path of least resistance and an ad online that read 'Roommate Wanted'.

She filled out the accompanying questionnaire, hit send, and a few hours later the reply came – 'We are pleased to say that you have met or exceeded our initial Roommate Criteria Test. The Compatibility Interview is next. Please choose a date and time from the selection below.'

"Can I help you?" the young man that answered Khaki's knock on the door of that four-bedroom city duplex had asked.

"Isn't this 31A Douglas Street? I'm supposed to meet a Hank here at noon."

"Well, I'm Hank but some guy named Khaki is supposed to show up at noon. Did he send you instead? Are you his girlfriend?"

"No, I'm not his girlfriend. I am Khaki."

Khaki had never liked her name. She had complained to her mother about it many times. And her mother had tried to justify her faulty name choosing abilities by making Khaki feel proud instead of upset; shown her pictures of the beautiful duck she was named after, compared it to being named after a flower like Lily or Rose.

But anyone could see it wasn't the same at all. People knew that lilies and roses were flowers. No one knew that a Khaki Campbell was a duck, beautiful or otherwise.

'Lily' and 'Rose' brought to mind the beauty of nature in whites and yellows and pinks and reds. They made you think of sweet fragrances floating on a summer breeze.

'Khaki' bought to mind combat and frantic faced soldiers and that indeterminate shade of pukey tan/green. 'Khaki' came gagging out of the mouth like dry crackers were stuck in your throat.

And now this. A hint of things to come. If there were no box to check 'male' or 'female' in on a form or application, people could get the wrong impression. No one could be sure if she was a boy or a girl. 'Khaki' - a name as indeterminate in gender as it was in shade.

The other two guys that Hank shared the apartment with had all gathered round now too, staring with surprise at the person standing on their doorstep with the curvy shape and coral pink jeans that they had expected to be of the male persuasion.

They had all laughed then, at themselves, not at her. Offered her a beer and the room and the promise that they wouldn't try to peek through the crack in the door when she was in the bathroom. And they had mentioned an option that Khaki had never considered before.

The next day, Khaki had gone to the Social Security office and filled out the forms. Khaki Campbell ceased to exist.

She was Katie Campbell now. 'Katie' was feminine and bright. 'Katie' lit upon the lips like a smile.

Chapter 4
WHATEVER WILL WE DO?

There was the rise and fall of cheekbones and animated hand gestures. There were upturned lips. There were bright, lively eyes alternately wide open or slightly squinted with crinkles at the corner. Well, the left eye anyway. Jay could never tell anything from Adrian's right eye. It was always stuck at half-mast, locked into a perpetual lazy wink by the radiation treatments that had blasted away at Adrian's cancer ravaged lungs.

Jay had never seen the love of his life with both eyes open wide. They'd only been together for a little over three years now and the invading monster had been vanquished for more than ten. So whatever those turbocharged words were that came jetting out of Adrian's mouth, the meaning must have been on the happy end of the excitement scale. Jay just couldn't figure out what that meaning was. And the rocking beat of the music that was coming from behind Mina's closed door didn't help either. The Maze Shifters no doubt.

He cocked his head and tried to concentrate, to watch the words as they formed - the shape of the lips, the reveal of the teeth, the position of the tongue.

"You know that .... Mina ... go to? I told her .... and her friends............. I hope ....Shifters........be fun ....them too."

But it was no use. Adrian always talked too fast when there was excitement in the air. And that was the problem. When the words came cartwheeling and somersaulting out of Adrian's mouth drenched in that Colombian accent, they didn't always land right in Jay's ears.

Jay shook his head, grinning, and laughed. And then he coughed, the gurgling kind that came from his lungs and then bubbled up into his throat. He really should give up smoking. A fleeting thought that dissipated faster than a tendril of smoke from the end of a glowing butt.

"You're talking too fast, Hon! What's that you said? Something about Mina?"

"Come on Jay, you mean you didn't understand a thing I just said?" Adrian frowned, slightly vexed, reined in the excitement and started over with exaggerated slowness, making the words walk instead of letting them run. "Okay, you know that Surf Shifters... I mean, Maze Shifters concert we were talking about before you had to leave? I told Mina she could go. Well, what I really told her was that we'd take her. They're a really great band. It'll be so much fun."

Elation had returned by the end of the retelling but then a cloud seemed to cross Adrian's face, throwing a shadow on the smile. "I'm sorry. Have I overstepped my bounds? I probably should have waited for you. But Mina was so excited and I thought for sure you'd say yes. I hope you don't mind."

"Adrian, listen, there are no bounds here. We've been together long enough, you should know, we're a family, all three of us. You pick up Mina after band practice every Thursday and take her to soccer meets. You help her when she's stumped on her math homework. In my mind you're as much her parent as I am."

"Hearing you say that, it makes me feel so good. It gives me wings! I do think of Mina as my daughter. I love you both so much."

Adrian reached for Jay's hand, raised it to trembling lips and kissed it softly. Jay leaned in, put his own lips on their joined hands, and little kiss by little kiss, inched them along until his lips and Adrian's lips were joined as well in another gentle kiss.

18

Jay straightened up then, his face still washed with the lingering tenderness of love when Mina's rocking music struck a chord (had it gotten louder?) and opened wide his love-struck eyes.

Jay began to chuckle. "I've got to know. What did Mina say when you told her we were going to the concert with her?"

"OMG!" Adrian laughed. "You should have seen her face. She wasn't too happy about it. She wanted it to be just her and her friends. But I told her it was either my way or no way."

"It would have been 'no way' in more ways than one. Not only 'cause we wouldn't allow it, but because neither would the Armory. They have an eighteen and over policy unless accompanied by an adult."

"Good to know. Oh, how could I forget this? I almost didn't tell you! Mina's going to babysit for Mike and Dixie's twins tonight."

"She is? I saw Mike and Dixie both at work yesterday. Neither one of them mentioned needing a sitter for tonight."

"It was a spur of the moment thing. One of their neighbors invited them to go to Karaoke Nite at Temple Bistro and Brew. Mike's picking Mina up at six. So it looks like it'll be just you and me tonight, Babe." A mischievous little smile danced across Adrian's face. "Whatever will we do? Got any ideas?"

***

"You know what I've been thinking about a lot lately?" Jay asked pensively as he poured wine into Adrian's glass and then drained the last of the bottle into his own. "This girl that I grew up with. Black hair, blue eyes... Her name was Khaki Campbell."

Jay swirled the wine in his glass, gazing entranced as the cabernet caught the candlelight like flickering rubies in its depths. He brought the glass to his lips and then suddenly set it back down, unsipped, chuckling and shaking his head as he remembered. "I used to call her Quacky."

"Was this girl your friend?"

Jay grinned, "Not when I called her Quacky, she wasn't." He slugged down his wine in one gulp and reached for another bottle from the wine rack. "You know why I called her Quacky?"

"Let me guess. Hmmmmm. Hang on, this might take me a while... because Quacky sounds like Khaki?"

"Think you're smart do ya, huh? Wrong. It's because she was named after a duck. Yeah, look it up. A Khaki Campbell is a kind of duck. I overheard her mom telling my mom the whole story about them naming her after this duck they saw at some fair. I couldn't wait to spread the word. So next school day, when Khaki came walking by, we all stuck our hands up into our pits and started flapping our arms like wings and waddling around and quacking like ducks and pointing at her and laughing."

"What a bad, bad boy you were," Adrian mock scolded, shaking a finger at Jay. "The poor kid. Did she start crying?"

"She laughed at first. She had no clue what the hell we were doing. We were ponly in first grade. I don't think she even knew she was named after a duck." Jay paused, gazing again through his newly filled glass at the wavering candlelight. "But we made sure she figured it out."

"Is that why you've been thinking a lot about her lately? You're feeling sorry for having been somewhat of a bastard and you're looking for atonement?"

"No, that's not it. Believe it or not, somehow we became best friends. All the way through grammar school and even high school. Yeah..." Jay grinned, a laugh erupting suddenly as he threw back his head. "I remember this one summer, we were like nine years old, and me and Khaki were checking out this new track of houses they were building behind the high school. It must have been a Saturday. No workers were there. Anyway, dumb little kids that we were, we jumped into a basement that had been dug out; nothing but a big cement-walled rectangle in the ground. It was like a treasure chest down there – pieces of wood, loose bricks, tools and nails and tubes of caulk. Even a

20

half empty pack of cigarettes and a lighter. Lit one up and had my first toke. Khaki dared me to do it. And then while I'm there coughing my brains out, she sticks a caulk gun down my shorts and pumps brown caulk all over my ass. I got her back though, scooped that shit out of my shorts and smeared it all over her head. OMG." Jay guzzled more wine, memories sparkling in his green eyes.

"And you're telling me this was one of the good times?" Adrian asked incredulously, sipping while Jay guzzled.

"Hell yeah! We were screaming and laughing and chasing each other around that basement, till she tripped on a hammer and went flying. Scraped up her palms and her knee when she landed; right in a corner that smelled like piss. Of course she wanted to go home after that. That's when we knew how dumb we were. There were no stairs built yet. There was no ladder. It was easy to jump in but it was too deep to jump out."

"So what did you do?"

"First we panicked, then Khaki cried, then we yelled for help, then we piled up stuff against the wall that I could stand on with Khaki on my shoulders and finally, after tipping over at least ten times, Khaki was able to pull herself out. She threw down a bunch more bricks for me to pile up and finally I made it out too. It's a good thing I was tall."

"Your parents must have grounded you for life after that."

"Grounded me? My parents never grounded me. It's the strap I would have gotten, if they'd ever found out. We went down to the creek, stripped naked and washed all the dirt and blood and caulk out of our clothes, hair and butt cracks. Yup. That was the day I smoked my first cigarette and saw my first naked girl." The brightness in Jay's eyes faded a touch then. "For what it was worth," he added. "Like I said, I was only nine and well... We talked about everything, you know, me and Khaki. And what we didn't talk about, she still knew. But then... I think she wanted more... Even though... You know what I mean."

"Yeah, I know." The quiet empathy of the words suddenly bubbled into a snigger as Adrian reached to collect the two empty wine bottles and instead nearly knocked them to the floor. "Whoa! Don't worry, I got them. They didn't get smashed. But I think I did. I think I'm hungry too. Are you hungry? Want some cheese and crackers?"

"Do I ever say no to food?" Jay followed Adrian out to the kitchen, grabbing the crackers from the high cabinet over the stove while Adrian rummaged around in the fridge for the cheese. "You know, I swear I saw her at Betty's Pantry today when I stopped there for lunch."

"Saw who?"

"Khaki Campbell. They've got a new waitress. Name's Katie. From the side she looked just like Khaki."

"OK. I think I've heard enough about this Khaki Campbell now. Should I be jealous?"

Jay set the crackers on the counter and moved in close to kiss Adrian's moist, warm lips. He carefully removed the brie and cheddar from Adrian's grasp with his left hand and set them on the counter beside the crackers while he drew Adrian closer with his right hand, running the tip of his tongue softly across Colombian lips, coaxing them to open, thrusting his tongue inside to cavort with Adrian's.

"You don't have to be jealous of anyone," Jay whispered. "I love you. You're the only one I want."

Slowly Jay began undoing the buttons of Adrian's shirt, from top to bottom, his tongue following, darting along the path of bare skin that was exposed by the parting fabric, feeling Adrian thrill beneath his touch. When he reached the belt, he pulled the shirt loose, pressing his hand hard then against Adrian's crotch.

He felt it there, as he knew he would, bulging behind the zipper his anxious fingers fumbled to undo - Adrian's manhood, as erect and rock hard as his own.

Chapter 5
WHO'S GONNA KNOW?

What were they doing in there? Mina didn't even want to know. Except she did. She got the glass she kept on the floor of her closet behind her tall boots and held the open end up to the wall. The bottom end she held to her ear.

It was from an old Three Stooges episode stored on a clunky VHS tape that Mina had learned this trick. Her friend Bethany's dad had two whole shelves of the ancient things lined up on a bookcase in the basement right next to the entrance to his 'man cave'.

Mr. Cash had found her and Beth there one rainy Saturday afternoon pointing at the white boxes of tapes with their heads tilted to the side, trying to decipher the scribbled writing inked on the spines. He came ambling over with his hands in his pockets and a big smile on his face, mistaking their pointing and giggling as interest in his prized collection instead of what it really was – making fun of it and thinking he was a dork.

He had recorded all the movies and shows on those tapes from the TV when he was a kid, he told them - Ghostbusters, Big Trouble in Little China, Short Circuit, Star Trek-The Next Generation. But his favorites were the Three Stooges tapes.

It was one of those that he pulled off the shelf then, stuck it into the prehistoric machine he still kept around to watch them on, and roped her and Beth into watching it with him, so they could 'watch and learn what real comedy is all about, girls. Just like my Dad did for me when I was your age. He passed the Stooges torch to me and now I proudly pass it to you.'

The Stooges torch? Seriously? Mina had to clamp her mouth shut so she didn't laugh and shout 'How dorky' right out loud. She didn't laugh at the Three Stooges though. Where was the comedy in watching three pea brained idiots bumble around, burn holes in people's shirts with a hot iron, and smack each other in the head over and over again? She didn't even smile. Not once.

But Mr. Cash couldn't stop laughing; with his mouth wide open and his eyes crinkled shut. And when he had to leave for an appointment before the episode was over, he could barely drag himself away. He handed Beth the remote so they could 'Stay right here and watch the rest without me, girls. Don't laugh too hard!' And then, just before he rushed out the door, he looked back and winked at them with this goofy gleam in his eye and chortled 'Be kind, please rewind!' As if they'd know what some nerdy slogan from way back in the olden days meant.

They could hardly wait to press eject. But just before they did, there was the stooge named Moe holding a glass up to a wall and listening to the secrets being whispered on the other side. And a scheme had hatched in Mina's brain.

That night she had stood in her closet with the glass pressed to her ear, holding her breath, certain that it wouldn't work but somehow it had.

Her dad and Adrian always tried to be so quiet. They didn't want her to know they were having sex. But she knew anyway. The quiet itself told her. It got thick and heavy and it burrowed into her ears begging her to listen.

Mina knew it was wrong. Just like she knew it was wrong to have friends come over while she was babysitting too. But that hadn't stopped her. Oh, no. She had told Matt to show up at the Chatelain's at 8:30 anyway.

Eddie and Michaela were nearly asleep when she laid them in their cribs at 8:00, lulled into a half doze by her gentle rocking and the Taylor Swift, Maroon 5 and Maze Shifters songs she sang to them in quiet slow motion. Mina loved rocking the twins. They would get all snuggly in the crook of her arms and suck their thumbs. And Mina would feel all snuggly too with the rocking and the warmth of their little two-year old bodies pressed against her. Sometimes she almost drifted off to sleep along with them, catching herself at the last minute with her chin falling to her chest. It was total peace.

Unless it was one of those nights, just like this night, that she had told Matt to come over. Then nervous excitement took over and a tinge of guilt crept in and pinched her belly. And she was in a hurry to get the twins all tucked in and their bedroom door closed before Matt arrived.

Mina had left the front door unlocked so that Matt could come in without having to ring the bell and at 8:30 there he was. Only it wasn't just him. Matt had Brad with him; the wormy-faced gnome he worked with after school at the hardware store.

"Matt!" Mina hissed, "What's he doing here? It was only supposed to be you." Mina didn't think twice about hurting Brad's feelings. He already knew she hated him.

"Chill, Mina. One friend, two friends. What's the difference? Who's gonna know? Me and Brad'll still be outta here by ten, just like you said." And then Matt had tried to kiss her, as if she would want to kiss him now, with Brad leering at them.

Mina turned her head and shoved him away angrily.

"What the fuck. You don't have to be a bitch about it."

Matt's eyes were blazing now. The night was falling apart. And the babies were sleeping in the room just down the hall. Mina knew she had to take control, drop her anger and make Matt forget his, move things back into the safety zone.

"I'm sorry, Matt." Mina softened her voice, forced her face into a little smile. "It's just that I was looking forward to it being only you and me." And then her fake smile blossomed into reality. "Oh yeah, you know what? The Maze Shifters are going to be at the Armory next weekend. And I'm going! With Beth and Clare. You want to come too?"

Wormy-faced Brad had walked into the kitchen while she and Matt were talking about the Maze Shifters. Mina heard him in there, screwing around, opening cupboards and drawers and the fridge. He came back out with a bag of potato chips and a tall, ice filled glass of cola and plopped himself on the couch.

"Don't tell me you actually like those douchebag Maze Shifters," Brad said, ripping open the bag and stuffing a chip in his mouth. "And I bet you're not going with just your friends. Little twats like you have to have an adult there to hold their hand at the Armory. Are you going with your daddy, little girl?"

"What do you care?"

"I don't fuckin care. I just wondered." He stuffed another chip in his mouth and gulped from the glass. "You know, I heard your father was an SP."

Mina knew she should have ignored him. There was a look in his eye that screamed ambush, danger. But Mina plunged in anyway.

"An SP? What's an SP?"

An evil grin spread over Brad's face. "A shit packer. You know. He sticks his dick where…."

Mina's face burned hot and red. "Shut up. Just shut up!" She spat the words. It took everything she had not to scream them.

Brad laughed with malignant pleasure, took another gulp from his glass and reached into the bag for more chips. Mina lunged at him, control lost, arms flailing, grabbing at the bag to wrench it from his hands and ripping it instead, sending potato chips hurling out in all directions.

The glass that Brad had just set back down on the coffee table teetered and rocked before it tipped over, rolled to the edge and fell to the floor, a trail of cola following in its wake, splashing as it hit the hardwood floor.

"You asshole," Mina glared at Brad, ignoring the dripping cola and the puddle that spread and crawled along as it grew.

Then she turned the venom in her stare on Matt. "You're both assholes. Why'd you tell him my dad was gay, Matt? It's none of his damn ass business."

"I didn't tell him your dad was gay," Matt defended himself. "All I told him was that you had two dads."

"Assholes! I want you out of here. Just get the hell out."

"Well, uh… you want us to help you clean up the mess first?" Matt, at least, still possessed some kind of a sense of chivalry.

The gnome had no such sense. "Fuck that. I'm not helping the little twat clean up the mess. She made it."

"I don't need any help. Just get out. Get out now." She shoved Matt hard in the back, forcing him towards the door and glared at Brad who sneered at her as he followed Matt out.

Mina shouldered closed the door and rammed home the lock, her heart too loose, her stomach too tight, knowing something wasn't right; something more than the everything that wasn't right already. It was the smell. She'd been pushing the thought to the back of her mind as inconsequential, probably just a stink oozing out of Brad, but when she finally rushed into the kitchen for the roll of paper towel to clean up the mess, she saw it on the counter where Brad had left it - the open bottle of Captain Morgan's Spiced Rum.

It took her an hour to sop up the rum and sweep up all the chips. She used a baby wipe she tiptoed into the twin's room and took from the box on the changing table as a final step to clean the tackiness off the tabletop and floor; grateful that the floor she was trying to clean without leaving a trace was hardwood and not carpet. The evidence of her transgressions, she stuffed into a plastic bag and carried out to the garbage tote by the side of the garage, pushing it to the bottom under the other bags that were already there.

Captain Morgan was winking at her when she went back into the kitchen to rehang the roll of paper towel and wash the glass that, luckily, had not broken. And before she searched the cabinets for the empty spot that the bottle of rum called home, she poured a little of the dark liquid into the glass and took a swig herself. It burned on the way down and she tried to spit it back out. But then a warmth spread through her and she finished what she had poured into the glass instead.

She had been so cold.

Hours later, the sound of the key turning in the backdoor lock jangled in her ears and Mina bolted upright on the couch. She must have fallen asleep. The TV droned with the end of some movie she couldn't even remember the beginning of, but the other events of the evening blared out, something she couldn't forget, stuck to her memory with pushpins and highlighted in florescent orange. She glanced around quickly one last time, took a deep breath, closed her eyes as she let the breath back out, and opened them again to smile at Dixie and Mike as they came walking into the room.

"Hi," Dixie whispered and sat down on the couch next to Mina, "sorry we were out so late. The time kind of got away from us. How'd it go?"

"Great. Eddie and Michaela are always good for me. I tried to teach them hide and seek." Mina chuckled softly. "But they did it all wrong. I'd count to ten and yell 'here I come' and when I turned around, there they were, right behind me. They jumped up and down and laughed and then they screamed 'Ga chew'. They're so cute."

All three of them were chuckling softly now as Mina recounted her evening with the twins. Dixie's eyes were sparking so bright, motherly love written all over her face. And she kept looking at Mina too, with something like love or pride or trust or faith, a certainty perhaps, that she had left her beloveds in the most capable of hands.

And the guilt that Mina had lost for a moment as she got caught up in the story of Fun With Eddie And Michaela clawed back into her heart and twisted her stomach into a knot.

"Did you have any trouble getting them to bed?"

"No. No trouble at all. I rocked them in the chair and sang them lullabies and they fell right asleep."

'and then Matt and Brad came over,' Guilt jeered from the pit of her stomach, 'and we argued and rum spilled all over your floor and I even drank some.'

"Did you see the treat I left for you in the fridge?"

"The special slice of pizza? With the ricotta and roasted red peppers? Yeah! It was awesome. Sooooo good. It was a really big piece but I ate the whole thing it was so good."

'and I went into your bedroom and imagined you in there naked, with Mike naked on top of you, a man and a woman, making love on the bed. I opened a lacquered wooden box on your dresser and looked at every pin that was inside. And then I put them all back. Except for the rooster pin. I put that one in my purse.'

"Well, I better get you home," Mike said as he grabbed his keys off the counter. "You always do a great job, Mina. We really appreciate it."

He reached into his back pocket for his wallet and handed her two twenty-dollar bills, the same look on his face that had shone on her from Dixie's face earlier. Respect, or admiration even. His smile was so warm.

"Thank you." Mina smiled back. But she couldn't look Mike in the eye. And her heart was beating way too fast.

The house had been quiet and dark when Mike dropped her at her front door, waiting in the driveway till he saw that she was safely inside before he pulled away; the only light came from the low wattage bulb her father always left on over the kitchen sink so she could see when she got home late from babysitting. And it was late – 2 A.M. Mina had actually thought her dad and Adrian were sleeping. But then she caught the barely audible sigh and the throaty moan. And she had gotten the glass.

And now she stood there in her closet, her brain mired in confusion, her left hand holding the glass securely against the wall and her ear, her right hand buried in the hot pulsing wetness between her legs, not sure who she hated more – her father or herself.

Chapter 6
WHERE WAS...?

Eddie and Michaela were napping. And Dixie was sitting in her 'home office' staring, not at her computer screen or the pile of papers on her desk, nor at the messy state of the bedroom that her office occupied the corner of, but out the window at the noontime sun, beguiled by the profusion of pink that graced the front yard atop the flowering Robinson Crab.

She and Mike had planted that crabapple tree together, the summer before they got married - on the day they got engaged actually. It had flourished in those 5 years, rocketing from a scrawny sapling barely any taller than Dixie to the fifteen foot pink crowned queen that it was today.

A glorious tree on a glorious day. But it was Monday and she was supposed to be working. Mondays, Tuesdays and Thursdays were the days Dixie got to work from home. And she did work. But usually not on anything related to Channel 20 or creative programming.

But daydreaming was not the culprit here, preventing her from getting her job done. Daydreaming was actually Dixie's biggest asset. Her mind wandered, unhindered and free, seeing everything and nothing, until inspiration erupted in a flash of light, settled into a warm glow and took shape in the form of her next whimsically entertaining human interest piece.

So, the problem was not that she WAS daydreaming, but the WAY she was daydreaming. Instead of her mind wandering hither and yon while the twins napped, it stayed tuned to the same channel – WTWINS. Either that or she ended up falling asleep herself, with her head thrown back and her mouth wide open.

A thought had started hovering in her brain lately. Every time it approached, she scooted it away and refused to let it land. But it was becoming ever more insistent and she was going to have to hear it out. It was this - her ability to work from home might be reaching the end of the line. The older the twins got, the harder it was to do anything besides take care of them. They napped less and were active more. They wanted to run and jump and romp. They wanted to crush flowers and taste dirt and pick ants off the sidewalk and roll them between their fingers.

And she wanted to run and jump and romp with them. To teach them to smell the flowers, feel the dirt, leave the ants and just watch them as they scurried and swarmed. She wanted to...

Suddenly a light went on in Dixie's head. Inspiration came swooping in, singing at the top of its lungs.

She could incorporate the twins and her job into one mix. Load Eddie and Michaela into the stroller and do a piece on people at the village playground. Talk to the kids digging in the sand and swinging on the swings. Talk to the parents or grandparents or sitters that sat watching the kids or slid down the slide behind them. She'd arrange for Jay to meet her there to take candid photos and shoot some footage.

And here was another great idea. A way to keep the work from home plan in place. When summer vacation started, she could have Mina come over on Dixie's stay at home days. She'd ask Jay what he thought about it at the playground. Mina could....

The light bulb dimmed. Part two of Dixie's utopian plan turned sour. There was another thought she hadn't let land today. She'd kept it circling, not allowing it to close in. But it hit the runway now, jouncing wildly as the breaks screeched and squealed.

Something had gone on here over the weekend. Their faith had been breached. And when the tangled hints were combed through and smoothed flat, they all seemed to point in one direction – to Mina.

***

Who knew how things happened sometimes, especially with toddlers in the house. Dixie had found two spoons in the garbage pail once. She had found a crumbled cookie under Mike's dresser and a saucepan lid under the changing table. She hadn't felt the need to launch an investigation to determine just how it was that they had gotten there.

So when Dixie opened the cupboard Sunday morning to put the olive oil bottle away that she had left out on the counter to remind her to refill it from the big jug she kept in the pantry, she didn't think twice when she found the bottle of rum in the olive oil's spot. She just cocked her head and thought 'how curious.'

And when she didn't see any sign of the twenty ounce bag of potato chips that Mike had picked up on his way home from the barber, along with a gallon of milk and a loaf of bread, she only thought 'I can't believe Mina actually ate all those chips.'

Then, Mike came in the house with a question mark shadowing his face, holding something in the palm of his hand. "Look what I found on the front porch. Cigarette butts! Where the heck did they come from?"

They had both stood there, shaking their heads and shrugging their shoulders.

"The wind?" Dixie suggested.

"A classless salesman, pissed off that we weren't home to answer the door?" Mike offered. "Or maybe it was you," he grinned, "doing a lousy job of hiding the fact that you've taken up smoking."

"Yeah, right." Dixie grinned back. "Maybe it was Eddie. By the way, have you been drinking rum?"

"Drinking rum? Why would you ask me that?"

"I found the bottle of Captain Morgan's in the wrong cabinet."

They stared at each other and shrugged their shoulders again.

"Huh," they both said.

But a seed of misgiving had begun to sprout.

When Dixie found Michaela sprawled flat on her belly between the coffee table and the couch, her eyes fixed on something underneath, and her tongue pressed to the floor, she had to investigate.

"What are you doing, Michaela? Don't lick the floor. It's dirty. Is something under the couch? What do you see?"

"See tay tip."

Dixie crouched down and peered under the couch with Michaela. Sure enough, there were potato chips under there. And a spicy aroma that reminded Dixie of pumpkin pie – cinnamon and cloves. Dixie went to brush the chips out from under but instead of sliding out over the smooth hardwood, they broke into pieces at her touch, most of the chip tacked to the floor by some nearly dry liquid - the source of the scent, the reason for Michaela's tongue licking the floor. A puddle of rum.

And the spout began to grow.

A little later, when Dixie opened the black lacquered box on her dresser to put away the bugle blowing fairy pin she had worn to karaoke the night before, something else seemed amiss.

It wasn't like she had OCD. She didn't compartmentalize her pins and organize them by size, shape and color. She just set them down into the box and closed the lid. But there was something off in the way the pins laid in the box this day. Their disorganization was too organized.

She started picking up the pins and looking at them, one by one – the delicate rose pin that her parents had sent her just last week for her twenty sixth birthday, the glass bead and feathers pin that Mike had surprised her with one day for no reason at all except that he loved her, the macramé pin she had found at a garage sale, the Cloisonné balloons, the decoupage tea kettle….

But where was her favorite? The pin that had started her collection; the one she had gotten at Fitzpatrick's Diner on the day she left home to head off on her own? It wasn't in the box. It wasn't still pinned to any of her blouses or scarfs or purse straps either. Her brightly colored rooster pin was missing.

She found Mike at the kitchen table with the twins, crayons and coloring books strewn between them, his page neatly filled in between the lines, their pages filled with scribbles and crisscrossing wavy lines in Dandelion, Fern Green and Celestial Blue.

"Mike, have you seen my rooster pin?"

Mike looked up from the beach scene he was coloring: Tangerine poised over the stripes on the Emerald sand pail he was bringing to life, the bright smile in his eyes fading at the sight of the clouded distress in hers.

The chips, the rum, the butts, the pin.

She and Mike had taken all those puzzle pieces and lined them up, rearranged them, looked at them upside down and sideways. But the same picture kept popping up over and over again; the one they didn't want to see and could scarcely believe - Mina, partying with friends (how many?) at their house (had she done this before?), endangering the twins, violating their home and their trust.

But Dixie couldn't loose the feeling that they still hadn't gotten it right. Maybe the puzzle pieces fit the picture, but the picture didn't fit Mina. The only thing they had really gotten right was that something was wrong.

Chapter 7
IS EVERYTHING ALL RIGHT?

Jay wasn't one to sing the Monday blues. Monday was just a day, like any other day. A day to live his life. And life was good. Mostly.

But something about this Monday was chafing at him, messing with the balance of his yin and his yang, making him wish he could have stayed in bed with the fleece blanket snug and warm around his head.

He slid the front seat of his Kia Sorento back a bit for more legroom while he waited and took a deep drag on his cigarette. He held it in, savoring it, feeling the smoke swirl in his lungs, filling every nook and cranny, before it billowed back up through his throat and floated over his tongue and his teeth. A few tendrils escaped through his nose (and maybe even out his ears?) before he finally exhaled, blowing a cloud of smoke out onto the dashboard to skitter across the windshield and finally drift out the open window. Across to red Infiniti parked beside him it floated, caressing the car's sleek lines with ghostly fingers, before scattering in the breeze over Betty's Pantry. It left a slight sense of calmness behind to swirl in Jay's brain, smoothing the sharp edges of his unease.

Anxiety had started to gnaw that morning, when Mike had popped into the break room at the same time as Jay did (on purpose?) and they both headed for the Keurig machine.

"Morning Jay. Like minds, huh. Go ahead, you go first." And Mike stood aside as Jay stuck his dark espresso roast k-cup into the holder and pressed green for go. "Hey, you know what I was just thinking about?" Mike continued as the water dribbled into

35

Jay's mug, "Betty's Pantry. Isn't Monday the day they always have the Smorgasbord Vegetable Soup special? I love that stuff. Want to join me for lunch? I've got a meeting with Citizen Tire at twelve-thirty. How about we meet at Betty's at one-thirty? The lunch crowd will be thinning out by then and we can have the waitress's undivided attention."

There was nothing odd about Mike asking Jay to meet him for lunch. They were friends, and that's what friends did. And because it wasn't odd, that's exactly why Jay knew that it was odd. Odd in the way that Mike asked it. Mike's mouth was smiling, but the accompanying gleam in his eye had been at half-mast, and hints of a hidden agenda kept slipping out from under his tongue.

"Well, I wouldn't know anything about vegetable soup, but how can I pass up an invite for lunch at Betty's Pantry? Sounds great." And Jay had smiled too but a question mark had substituted for the accompanying gleam in his eye and anxiety had pricked at his gut and begun its slow crawl.

Because Mina had been acting oddly this Monday morning too. She had sat at the kitchen table with her mouth pinched together like a wrinkled prune, nibbling on her bagel and sipping at her juice instead of scarfing and slugging and texting and primping and rushing out the door with her books nearly falling out of her unzipped book bag.

"Is everything all right, Mina?" he had asked.

"Everything's fine."

"Are you sure you're feeling okay? You look a little peaked."

"I'm fine."

"You might be coming down with something. Maybe I should…"

"Dad! Stop! How many times do I have to tell you? I'm fine. Everything's fine."

And she had pushed away from the table, grabbed her book bag and walked out the door to the bus stop – hair a mess, teeth unbrushed, not even a good-bye.

Jay could have chalked this up to typical teenage moodiness exaggerated by the Monday back to school blues (or maybe it was her time of the month) if not for the fact that Mina had been acting un-Mina-like on Sunday too.

She'd passed on Adrian's famous peanut butter and chocolate chip pancakes at breakfast, there was no gushing about the antics of the twins she had babysat the night before, and even talking about the upcoming Maze Shifters concert hadn't livened her up. She had barely opened her mouth all day.

Except when Jay had been getting a glass out of the cupboard and made some simple comment. "I could swear we had more glasses than this. I wonder where that tall blue one is. Are they all in the dishwasher?"

Then Sunday's uncommunicative Mina had nearly jumped down his throat. "Why are you asking me? You think I know where every glass in the house is? Why don't you ask Adrian? Maybe Adrian broke one."

It could be that he was mixing his signals, adding together incongruous elements that had nothing to do with each other. And Jay really hoped that he was. But somehow he knew that he wasn't. There was a common denominator between brooding Mina and ambiguous Mike. Saturday night.

Jay spotted Mike's black Nissan pulling into the parking lot then. He took another quick draw on his cigarette, stubbed it out in the tray, plastered a smile on his face and went to greet Mike, unease picking and nagging at his already shaky composure.

Was it a coincidence that Mike had steered them to the last booth in the row? The one farthest from the entrance and farthest from the swinging kitchen doors, the one with the least chance of them being interrupted or of anything they said being overheard? Jay didn't think so.

At least they were sitting in Sheila's section. Except it wasn't Sheila that was standing there spouting off the day's lunch specials. It wasn't Katie the new girl either, that Jay had been hoping to get a better look at. It was rode-hard and put-away-wet Rayanne, with her hair piled on top of her head like a flashback from the fifties; The only waitress at Betty's Pantry that Jay didn't care for. She never smiled and she never remembered to tell the cook he didn't want lettuce and tomato on his sandwich.

"....and today's sandwich special is ..." blah boring, blah bland, blah, blah, blah. Rayanne's monotone leached the appeal from every dish. "...on kimmelweck, so do you need a few more minutes?" She didn't even pause between sentences.

"Yeah, I would say we need a few more minutes." It was Mike that answered, exactly the same way that Jay was about to, with barely controlled irritation chopping at the smile he was trying to keep on his face.

"Okay, sure, I'll give you a chance to look at the menus and then stop back." But Rayanne didn't leave. She stared for a moment. First at Mike, then at Jay. Was she hoping they would jump to a decision under the tawdry glare of her black eyeliner? Where the heck was Sheila?

Jay raised his eyes heavenward and shook his head when Rayanne finally walked away. And there was Mike doing the same thing. Their eyes caught and they grinned at each other. Jay almost wanted to laugh out loud. They didn't have to say it. They knew they were both thinking the same thing – 'what a piece of work'.

"Maybe she's having a bad day." That was Mike, always giving people the benefit of the doubt.

"Nah, I've had her before. She's always like this." Jay shook his head again, smiling, feeling somehow like a weight had been lifted from his shoulders. The wonders of a smile, a laugh, and good old camaraderie. Maybe he was making something out of nothing after all. "Lucky for us she's not the cook. Are you going to get the soup?"

"Did she mention a soup special? I think I might have dozed off while she droned."

Jay laughed again. He was even starting to feel hungry. "Well, let's see, they usually have the specials listed in the menu too. Yeah! Here it is, Smorgasbord Vegetable Soup – a chicken based broth chock full of celery, carrots, onions, zucchini, escarole, fennel, and pastina."

"That's definitely what I'm getting. What about you?"

"What about me getting the soup? Definitely not. Maybe if they strained all the vegetables out of it and just left the broth and the pastina. The roast beef sammy with horseradish mayo sounds good."

"Now we just need the waitress to come back."

"That's one thing about asking for another minute. One minute seems to turn into ten. And with Rayanne..."

But then there she was. "So what'll it be?" Still dull as ever, sans smile, plopping and sloshing two glasses of water down on the table in front of them accompanied by a thick slice of aggravation.

It wasn't Rayanne's fault. Somehow the irritation she had left them to peruse their menus with had transformed into joviality and whisked them into an alternate universe. Mike had no grim tidings hiding behind a fake smile. There was no reason for Jay's stomach to be clenched into a tight ball. They were just two friends out to enjoy a nice lunch and each other's company. But now Rayanne's return to take their orders sucked them back.

"I'll have the roast beef sandwich special and fries," Jay said, trying to hang onto the smile that was fading fast as he watched Mike scowl and pull a wad of napkins from the black metal dispenser at the end of the booth to soak up water that had sloshed out of his glass when Rayanne plopped it down.

Mike looked up and their eyes caught again, only this time his scowl had left his defenses wide open. 'Hidden agenda' sat there completely exposed. "On second thought, skip the fries. I'm not really that hungry."

Jay didn't know what he had really expected Mike to say - 'Mina lied...', 'Mina hit...', 'Mina ruined...'

39

But when Mike finally opened up, what he did say was none of those things. "Jay, I've got to tell you, I'm worried about Mina."

It was worse than Jay thought. Anxiety reached in and wrung his stomach dry.

Chapter 8
CAN I BE HONEST?

A drian snipped off the last of the spent peony blooms and watched it's wilted and browning petals flop down into the pail on top of the others. He knew from experience that if he left them to fall from the stems on their own, the disk at the base would turn black and moldy and threaten the health of the entire plant.

There was no denying that experience was a good teacher. Experience had taught him that if you mixed the batter until just combined and then let it rest for five minutes before you spooned it onto the hot griddle, your pancakes would be both fluffy and spongy and beg you to top them with butter and maple syrup and eat as many as your stomach could possibly hold.

Experience had taught him that if you were headed south on Main Street at four P.M. on a weekday, you'd better turn left at Chestnut, then right at Triad and catch Main Street again well past the Bordello Wine Company bottling factory. Sorry was the driver that didn't and got caught in the rushing crawl of the just released first shift.

But there was one thing that experience had pressed upon him in ways large and small that, for his own sanity and happiness, he did his best to ignore and pretend he did not see - that once perfection had arrived, it wasn't long before the splendor would start to fade.

It made sense for flowers and for fruit. But in relationships? Just coincidence, he told himself. A presumption that had no basis in fact and no reason to be true. But here he was, in a house that was a home, sunlight streaming through the windows, lilac, crabapple and honeysuckle drifting on the breeze; living with a wonderful man and his sweet daughter, everyday so happy the smile never left his face. And so much in love! Jay's kisses lifted him to the clouds. When they made love, it was ecstasy coursing through him, through them both – hot, pulsing, rock hard.

Perfection.

And now experience's lesson had come to taunt him again.

Perfection falling apart. Despair fraying the edges, confusion and failure ripping at the seams.

At least in the garden he could try and forget his woes; get carried away by the colors and the scents and the warmth of the sun on the back of his neck.

He dumped the once white peonies onto the compost heap, reached for the watering can to fill it from the spigot on the back of the house and started his watering rounds.

And there was his neighbor waving to him from over the picket fence. "Hey Adrian! Beautiful day isn't it?"

He was never so glad to see her smiling face. "Hi Mrs. Vandenbunder." Adrian waved back, emptied his watering can into the terra cotta planter filled with purple, white and red petunias on the bottom step leading up to the deck, and walked over to the fence to chat. "Yes, it is gorgeous. I'm in heaven here."

"'Mrs. Vandenbunder'," she scoffed, shaking her head and sighing. "There you go again. I've been telling you since you moved in to call me Annie."

"Yes, I know. But Jay introduced you as Mrs. so that's what I'm used to."

"And he's another one. Calling me Mrs. Vandenbunder," Annie scoffed again. "It makes me feel old. So anyway, Mr. Adrian Maura," Her eyes sparkled playfully as she emphasized the 'Mr.' and the 'Maura', "I see your clematis is loaded with blooms again this year. What do you do to get it to so beautiful? Mine looks half dead. It's all woody vines and hardly any blossoms."

"Oh, it is beautiful, isn't it? I love the purple. But I don't think 'cause of anything I do. Well, I do put a good dose of fertilizer on it early in the spring but mostly I think it's just luck. I'm no expert."

"Oh come on. Look at your yard. Everything's beautiful. I see you out in it all the time. You must know what you're doing."

"I weed it, I water it and I wing it."

"Well, you wing it better than I do. Seriously, I'm thinking I might steal out in the wee hours of the morning and dig up some wildflowers from the side of the road. Yellow buttercups, white daisies. Have you seen how pretty it is along Latta Road right now? And last September with the Queen Anne's lace and chicory blooming all white and blue. It was gorgeous!"

"But you know, those wildflowers are all weeds."

"Beautiful weeds. And weeds grow like crazy. Just what I need. But with my luck, even weeds wouldn't do good in my garden. Anyway, what I really wanted to talk to you about was that Carl and I would like to take you and Jay out to dinner. As a thank you for helping me film those YouTube videos."

"You don't have to do that Mrs. Vandenbunder," Ooops, 'Mrs.' again! Adrian winced and shrugged in apology. 'Annie' just didn't feel natural sliding off his tongue. "We were happy to help you. And besides you already gave us a gift card to The Groundhog Garden Store."

"I don't care. We want to take you out to dinner too. Are you free this Saturday?"

"I'll have to check with Jay first and then I'll let you know. How's your book doing?"

"Okay, I guess." Annie's bright face dimmed. "I had such high hopes. Somehow I really thought those videos would spur sales. You know, reach the multitudes and pave my way to a best seller. But honestly, they don't seem to have generated any sales at all. Probably because the only people watching the videos are my friends and relatives and they already have my book! The multitudes still don't know I exist. Nothing I try seems to work. And I try so hard." Fine lines that Adrian had never noticed before fanned out from around Annie's eyes and mouth. A frown did not suit her.

"Bummer," he sympathized, his face falling too easily along with hers, and then he jumped right back into a smile to pep her back up. "I loved your book. It's like a dance with words. And the end! I was crying all over."

"Thanks." A dab of a smile appeared and then faded again. "But, it's just that…"

"You're not thinking of giving up are you? You can't do that! You've got a great book. You've got to keep trying. Keep trying and keep writing."

"Well, you know, actually I have started another book."

"Really? What's it about?"

"Top secret." Her bright face was back. "But enough about me and my book. What's up with you guys? How's Mina? School's probably almost done for the year, isn't it? She must be looking forward to those lazy days of summer."

"No lazy summer for her this year. She's going to be babysitting a few days a week for friends of ours. Two-year-old twins. And then Jay signed her up for a summer soccer day camp on the days she's not sitting."

"Wow. That'll make for a very a busy girl."

"Yes." Adrian's face fell again. He paused, pursed his lips tight together, closed his eyes and sighed. He looked at the ground and then back at Annie. Should he tell her? He decided to go for it. "Can I be honest? Jay's been taking Mina to see a therapist. He found out she was steeling and doing other bad things and it was because her head was all mixed up. It's the therapist that thought it would be good for Mina to be involved in lots of activities this summer. Keep her busy and her mind occupied."

"My goodness. I had no idea. Is the therapist helping?"

"I hope, but I don't know. Mina never talks to me anymore. She used to be so sweet and now… And Jay… He puts the blame on himself for all of this I think, but sometimes I feel he's blaming me. Everything is tension... I think maybe Jay doesn't want me here anymore."

"I can't believe he'd be thinking that at all. I've seen the glow he gets on his face when he looks at you. You two have a great relationship. All three of you do. Mina too. Listen, it's really tough on a parent when things go wrong with their kids. I know! You want to swoop in and protect them and right all wrongs but when it's something beyond your control, it just eats you up inside."

"Yes, I know this makes lots of stress for Jay. I understand this. I try to help, at least to give him someone to talk to but I feel he pushes me away. The way he looks at me now.... It's different... I don't know..."

"You're not thinking of leaving are you? It's like you just said to me, you can't give up on a good thing just because you've hit a rough patch. Relationships aren't always sunshine and roses. I know all about that too."

"I don't know what I am thinking. Jay, and Mina, they mean everything to me."

"Well, have you talked to Jay about this? Told him how you feel? That's what you need to do. You can't keep it all bottled up. You need to talk to him! Maybe he has no idea how much this is affecting you. Things will work out, Adrian. Just hang in there."

"Thank you Mrs... Annie! For the good advice. I didn't mean to lay all this on you."

"You didn't lay anything on me. That's what friends are for. And listen, don't forget to ask Jay about Saturday. It'll be good for you to get out and enjoy yourselves. Especially now. Some good food, good conversation, some wine..." Annie paused, winking at Adrian and smiling slyly. "Maybe it'll set the mood, rekindle the flames. And oh, tell him we're planning on going to Seasonings Steakhouse. That'll entice him. The menu's all about the meat. And I know how much Jay loves the meat."

Suddenly Annie's eyes opened wide. Her mouth became a round O in a blushing face. What had she just said? And then

45

Adrian caught it too. They stared at each other, round O's changing into smiles, smiles widening into grins.

How they were laughing as they parted and waved goodbye.

And just like that, Adrian felt carefree and happy again walking away from the picket fence and into the house, still smiling and chuckling at Annie Vandenbunder's unintentional faux pau. Laughter had a way of lightening the mood, chasing troubles away so you forgot they were there.

Mina had her head in the fridge, surveying its contents when Adrian came in from the back yard. And with his troubles out of sight, out of mind, he saw the sweet girl he had looked on as a daughter for the last three years standing there, the one that was always happy to see him, the one that jumped in the car excited and breathless when he picked her up after soccer and started right in telling him about the kick she had blocked or the goal she had scored or how she had seen this boy she liked watching her from the bleachers.

He forgot about the new Mina. The sullen and silent one that sat stone faced on the seat next to him when he picked her up now, the one that threw dirty looks at him if she wasn't ignoring him completely.

"Hey, Mina! Looking for something to eat? There might be some leftover peanut butter pancakes in there." Adrian walked over to the fridge while he spoke, drying his hands on a towel, and peered over Mina's shoulder to see if he could spot the pancakes, safely sealed in their cellophane wrap.

The slap across his face came hard and fast.

"You're not part of this family!" Mina screamed. "And I don't need your help!"

Her arm swung out to slap Adrian again and he grabbed her by the wrist to stop the blow.

And just like that, all those troubles that had been leaching the joy from his life for the past six weeks came charging back from around the corner where they had been hiding, reinforced, blazing red with the shock and sting and the scratch.

Chapter 9
WHAT THE HELL'S GOING ON HERE?

EMERGENCY - COME HOME NOW he had texted Jay. And now Adrian waited for the worried phone call he was sure would come asking him what was wrong.

How many times had she screamed it as she struggled to pull herself free of his grasp? "You're not part of this family. You don't belong here. I don't have to listen to you. You're not my father."

Each time it sunk deeper and deeper into his heart, hurt more than the slap she had unleashed with all her might against his face.

It was only out of self-defense that he did it, gripped her wrists so tight and dragged her to her room. It was not his place to use force on this girl. She was not his daughter, as much as he had liked to think that she was. And what would he do if she didn't stay in her room until her father came home like he told her to? Please God, don't let him have to find out.

But Jay was Mina's father. And Mina was Jay's daughter. And what was Adrian? The one you loved and left when the going got tough? Nice to have around for a while but if it came to pick and choose the one you'd boot out the door? Should he start packing his bags now?

The phone had barely made a sound when it was in Adrian's hand.

"Mina se ha ido balísticos. Ella me dio una palmada en la cara y me gritó que yo no soy parte de esta familia. Ella está en su cuarto ahora…"

"Adrian! You're…."

48

"...pero si ella sale y empieza a pegarme de nuevo, no sé qué va a pasar. No puedo controlarla. Ella...."

"I can't understand you, Adrian, you're..."

"...es tu hija. Es necesario tener cuidado de esto. Nada..."

"...speaking in Spanish. Adrian, stop. Speak English!"

"La maldición del dios. I am so upset. I am saying Mina's gone ballistic. She slapped me in the face. She's screaming at me that I'm not part of this family. She's staying in her room now but I don't know what will happen if she comes out and starts hitting me again. I can't control her. She's your daughter. You need to take care of this. Nothing's been the same since you found the glass in her closet. Mina's been looking at me like I'm a shit. You don't look at me at all. If no one wants me here, what the hell am I doing staying in your house? I'll wait till you get home and then I'm gone. I gave up so much to come here, to be with you. I don't need to put up with this."

There was silence on the other end of the line.

"Jay? Are you there? Did you hear..."

"All right, just calm down. I'm on the way. I'll be there in five minutes. Don't go anywhere. Do you hear me, Adrian?" Composed warred with frenzy in Jay's voice, before becoming a quiet plea, "I don't want you to go." And then he hung up.

Fifteen forever minutes later, Jay stormed through the front door - concern, distress, and anger all flashing in his eyes and careening across his face. "What the hell's going on here? Mina!"

The bedroom door down the hall opened first a crack and then Mina flew out, her earlier rage diluted with tears, her eyes flashing like her father's but with a strange combination heavy on the defiance, laced with repentance, and scented with fear.

"Did you slap Adrian in the face? Did you scream at him that he wasn't part of this family? He treats you like a goddamned princess. He takes you shopping and braids your hair and helps you with your lines for the school play. He laughs with you and dances with you and even holds your hand when you're sick. And you do this?"

49

"I don't care! He's not part of this family. You and me are the family. You're my father and Adrian's nothing. Adrian doesn't belong here."

"I don't know what you got going through that head of yours but you better get something straight right now. Adrian is part of this family. And whether you want him here or not doesn't matter. I want him here. He's my partner, Mina, and I'm gay, and that's it. None of that's going to change. Do you understand me?"

Mina just stared at her father trying to hang onto rebellion, but the defiance in her eyes was losing ground, drowning in a wash of fresh tears.

"You've got the best thing that anyone could ever ask for here," Jay continued, his voice tempered now by the wavering pools that were his daughter eyes, less unbridled anger and more controlled concern. "A wonderful family. Two people that care about you and would do anything for you. Two people that love each other. So what if we're both men. So what? That doesn't make what we have worth any less." Jay sighed then. A sigh so deep Adrian thought he might suck all the air from the room. His anger was gone now and all that was left was an exhausted resolve.

"I know things haven't always been easy for you, Mina. I know you have issues and I know you think it's all because of me. But your life is your life. And mine is mine. Not always good and not always bad. You know what I see when I look at my life right now? I see you - smiling and calling out goodbye to me as you rush out the door for school, running full blast down the soccer field behind the ball, making yourself a sandwich and spreading that peanut butter on that bread so thick." A hint of a chuckle bubbled behind Jay's lips. "I see Adrian slipping grated carrots into the meatloaf mix when he thinks I'm not looking, trying to get me to eat my veggies, and standing on the deck squinting in the bright sun with his sunglasses on top of his head." There was tenderness in the eyes Jay rested on Adrian now. He chuckled again, even quieter than before. "I see all three of us screaming on the roller coaster at Seabreeze with our arms raised above our heads and laughing together at some movie on TV with a big bowl of popcorn on our laps. I see happiness and I see love. And I feel so blessed." Jay paused and glanced again at Adrian, a barely visible smile passing over his lips.

It was one of those moments. Seeing that smile, listening to Jay talk, love, more than he had ever felt before, surged up in Adrian. Seeing love flicker back at him in the tenderness of Jay's eyes sent warmth sluicing through his veins, flushing away the depression that had held his heart squeezed in a vise for weeks, anointing the pain and turmoil of the afternoon like a salve.

Joyful tears misted his eyes and he blinked to clear them, to refocus his attention back to what Jay was saying to Mina.

"What do you see when you look at your life, Mina?" Jay was asking her, his voice still quiet and contemplative at first, but Adrian could hear the sharp edge of anger creeping back in, chafing more and more at each word. "I can't understand why you don't feel blessed too. I can't understand how you can have slapped Adrian. I can still see the red lines of your fingers on his face! And how you can stand there and tell me you don't care about all the things he does for you. That we both do for you. I love you, Mina. Nothing's going to change that. But right now, I am so disappointed in you."

"I'm sorry. I'm sorry. I shouldn't have hit Adrian. I'm really sorry." All the tears that had been pooling in Mina's eyes spilled over now. There was no defiance left: only a plea for forgiveness and a longing to be wrapped in her father's strong arms and absolved of her blame.

But Jay stood with his arms crossed over his chest, unwilling to take her in, raising his eyebrows and shaking his head, inclining it in Adrian's direction. Mina followed Jay's lead, turned her red rimmed eyes on him, looking from Adrian to the floor and back again.

Adrian had no doubt that Mina knew what her father wanted her to do. And she should have wanted to do it too. Her apology should have come flying from her lips. Instead she hesitated before reluctantly shuffling towards him, her eyes downcast, looking at anything and everything but him.

"I'm sorry, Adrian. I never should have slapped you and said what I said. I really didn't mean it."

Her words were stiff. The shame and the plea she should have looked at him with were missing from her eyes. And what Adrian thought she really didn't mean was that she was sorry.

But Adrian took her in his arms anyway; told her that he forgave her. And he meant it with all of his wounded heart.

The cry of battle had left them exhausted. Adrian went to the fridge to try to get some kind of a dinner together but he couldn't grasp how to connect the dots between eggs, cranberry juice, lettuce, kale, okra, onions, milk, beer, a piece of fish, American cheese slices, and peanut butter pancakes and compile them into a meal. Jay pulled a couple cans of chicken noodle soup out of the cupboard but how to get the soup from the can to the pan was a mystery he couldn't seem to solve. Mina dragged herself from her room, where Jay had sent her to 'think, really think, about the life she had and what it meant to her', to set the table; setting out plates but forgetting the napkins and silverware.

They ended up ordering a pizza and trying to make small talk but nobody ate much and they said even less. Their feelings were still too raw.

Later, after Mina had gone to bed, Adrian and Jay sat together on the slat-backed glider bench at the far side of the deck, wrapped in a blanket to keep out the chill of the not quite summer night, and let out what they had kept locked up for too long.

"I told Mina that she'd better get it straight that we're a family. But I don't think you get it either, Adrian. 'Your daughter', you said. 'Your house', you said. Mina is our daughter. This is our house. I love you, Adrian. You're the best thing that ever happened to me. But if you can't get that straight in your head, I don't know if this relationship is going to work."

"You don't think I've got that straight? I told you before I think of Mina as my daughter. And this house, this is my home, our home. But ever since you found out what Mina was doing.... And then you found that glass..... You weren't talking to me or touching me. I thought your love was gone. My stomach was turned inside out. And then Mina turned on me.... I felt like I was dying inside. How could I think anything was 'ours' when I thought everything was gone?"

"I wasn't paying attention.... I didn't even realize. I was upset. I was angry. The only thing on my mind was Mina, worrying about her, wishing I could just snap my fingers and make everything right, feeling like.... like I had failed her. Failed the most important job of my life."

Their despairs and insecurities, their hopes and desires, their fears and their passions - all escaped in whispers into the moonlit sky. Renewal was what shone back down on them; understandings reached in the beating of their two hearts, love strengthened in the clasp of their two hands.

Chapter 10
YOU MEAN…?

Did she hear someone call her name? Sheila paused in her perusal of the New Guinea impatiens she was contemplating and glanced around the Ground Hog Garden Store.

How she loved this place. Every flower you could imagine and even those you couldn't, every color of the rainbow mixed and mingled and combined, gracing tables and floor space and hanging overhead. She breathed deep, clearing her senses, drawing in the fragrances of beauty and potting soil.

But had someone called her name? She didn't see anyone she knew. Maybe it was just those hot pink New Guineas trying to get her attention. The salmon colored ones had drawn her over to the hanging baskets first, but the hot pink might go better against the wood tones of her house. Or how about the yellow calibrachoa? Or the white…

"Sheila!"

Someone was calling her name! And there was Jay from the diner striding down the aisle towards her; the broad smile she remembered from her waitressing days brightening his face.

"Oh, for heaven's sake. Jay! It's so good to see you. How've you been?"

"Missing you. Nothing tastes as good without your smiling face delivering it to my table. You didn't even say goodbye."

"What can I say? I just didn't want a fuss."

"Who would've fussed? I would have just tethered you to one of the stools at the counter and not let you leave."

Sheila laughed. Of all the things she missed about working at Betty's Pantry, it was probably heartthrob Jay's lively banter that she missed most of all.

"Isn't Katie taking good care of you?"

"Katie? She's not taking care of me at all. Every time I go, I get Rayanne and service with a frown. No matter where I sit. I think it's a conspiracy."

"Ah, Rayanne," Sheila nodded her head sympathetically. "She's a tough one but give her a little time. She'll warm to you. That's funny though. Katie was supposed to be my replacement and besides that, I kind of thought…"

Sheila let the rest of the sentence trail off. What she had kind of thought was that maybe Katie did know Jay. Jay had only been joking about a conspiracy theory but what if it was true? And if Katie was hiding a secret and keeping her distance, Sheila had no business stirring the pot.

But she could see that Jay was only giving the conversation half of his attention now anyway. The rest of his attention, along with a gleam in his eye and an ever widening smile was on a teenage girl heading towards them pushing a cart loaded with a bounty of yellow, orange and red marigolds, white begonias and a flat of tomato plants.

Could this girl be Jay's daughter? She looked a lot like him - tall with a large boned frame and wide shoulders. She had the same high cheekbones on a round face, the same shade of chestnut brown hair. Except Jay's chestnut hair was smooth and straight and hers was kinky. Except Jay's skin was a vanilla bean milkshake …

"Sheila, this is my daughter, Mina."

… and his daughter's was a coffee frappe

"Well now, Mina. It's so good to meet you. I used to wait on your dad at Betty's Pantry. He was my favorite customer. And you were his favorite topic of conversation. He told me all about your soccer games and school plays. You played the Reverend Mother in the Sound of Music last year didn't you?"

"Yeah." She smiled and it was the same smile as her father's too, but fleeting and on the shy side, and with slightly fuller lips.

Sheila asked her if she was enjoying her summer vacation and what grade she'd be in come fall but what she really wanted to ask was if her mother was still in the picture. Had her father and mother been married? Did she spend lots of time out in the sun working on her tan or was her mother really a black woman? Not that it made any difference. She was just curious. It was such a surprise. Something Sheila would never have expected.

Jay stood smiling down on them with fatherly pride and affection soft in his eyes, sometimes joining in to flesh out Mina's bare minimum answers. But Sheila couldn't help noticing that Jay's smile and the soft affection in his eyes were not always aimed at Mina. He seemed to be looking over Mina's shoulder at someone else. And the only someone else there was a Hispanic man that Sheila had seen walking down the aisle next to Mina's cart. Sheila had thought it pure coincidence, had expected the man to keep on walking when Mina stopped, intent on his own flower hunting pursuits. But he had stopped too. And he was smiling and chucking and nodding his head along with their conversation. And now Jay was looking at him like…?

"…was never my strong suit either, so Adrian helps her out with that. Oh, you know, I never introduced you. Sheila, this is my partner, Adrian."

His partner? You mean hunky Jay was…? She had no idea! Not even an inkling. He never told her. But why would he? Did she think he should have just blurted it out with his order - 'I'll have ham and swiss on sour dough, hold the tomato, hold the lettuce and, by the way, I'm gay'?

She didn't want it to happen. She tried to stop it. But she was too late. She felt the smile sinking on her face. And she plastered it back on. She felt judgment passing like a dark cloud over her eyes. And she smiled even wider. She was open-minded. She was a liberal thinker. She wasn't prejudiced. Was she?

'I hope Jay didn't see that look on my face', she thought as she shook Adrian's hand with her over compensated smile. *'Please don't let him have seen it.'*

***

He saw it. That hard look of uncomfortability with a trace of disapproval that bit off the upturned edges of Sheila's smile and narrowed her eyes. It only sank her face for a moment before she bobbed back up to the sunny surface, sputtering and flailing to regain her jarred composure.

Jay couldn't fault her for it. He was no flaming fag. He had no blush of the feminine on his cheek. It was just a complete shock to her system. At least Sheila tried to cover it up, looked embarrassed even that the look had landed on her face in the first place.

Not like his mother. It was nothing like the hand she had smacked across his face nearly four years ago when the words 'I'm gay ' had finally dared to disengage themselves from his lips and traveled to her ears. Nothing like the frigid eyes she had glared at him with or the mouth she had cursed him with or the back she had turned to him as if he had ceased to exist.

She'd had no idea either. She'd pulled grit encrusted, half dead caterpillars and moth's wings out of his grubby little boy pockets. She'd spanked him for teasing the hell out of his sisters and hiding their sanitary pads in the basement. She'd looked on with pride and shared a wink and a knowing little smile with his dad when flirty cheerleaders flocked around him after a high school football game.

But her wink was illustrating a falsehood. What she thought she knew was all wrong. Maybe Jay didn't sashay or wear eyeliner and silk scarves. Maybe he didn't giggle with his sisters and have an interest in fashion magazines. But, as much as he tried to convince himself that he did, he had no interest in those cheerleaders either.

In kindergarten, instead of having a crush on Mrs. Towersey, like his friend Joey did, he'd had a crush on Joey's father. While most of the guys were jerking off lusting after their hot (and she was hot!) eleventh grade English teacher, Miss Mead, fantasies about the industrial arts teacher, Mr. Wickham, gyrated and swelled and pumped through Jay.

He tried to quash those thoughts, shove them down into a deep hole and tamp down the dirt so no one, especially himself, could find them. But they always tunneled back up, orgasming in his dreams and working their way out to the surface.

And he started to wonder why he was toiling with this secret. Why not just let it all hang out? Would it really matter to his friends and family? He was still the same person either way, wasn't he? Damn straight he was. And he'd start coming clean where love was the strongest, in the comfort of his own home. To be able to be one hundred percent himself! He couldn't keep the smile off his face. He was lighter than air. It felt like freedom.

His mom and dad were snuggled together on the couch watching a movie when Jay came striding in, his smile a little hesitant now, a touch of nerves guzzling some of his confidence, but still determined to liberate the truth. The truth never made it out.

What his parents thought the movie they had rented was going to be about, Jay didn't know. But it was just at that very moment that they did find out what *Brokeback Mountain* was all about. And that TV screen had gone black so fast. They both looked like they might vomit. It was words that they did end up puking out – faggot, obscene, homo, sin, queer, indecent. And it was Jay that ran to the bathroom sick, the malice in those words churning and roiling inside him.

And he kept on digging and burying and tamping and hiding and trying to live a life that others expected him to live for the next thirteen years.

But now? He let everything hang out. He wasn't going to hide who he was or who he loved. He wasn't going to pretend he didn't know Adrian or introduce him as his 'friend' or his 'neighbor'. And if someone was offended by it? If someone didn't want to know him because of it? He said 'Fuck 'em. God bless and have a nice day'.

***

"...from Colombia," Adrian was telling her in response to her question.

"Really. Well, I just love your accent." Sheila replied, smiling. Not the over-stretched lips stuck to dry teeth smile she had started with, but a real smile.

This Adrian was personable and easy to talk to. And after the shock of the initial bombshell and the upset of that unfortunate look flashing across her face, Sheila was relieved to be settling back into her normal self again. Well, maybe she was still a tiny bit flustered, and talking a little too fast and asking too many questions and exclaiming a little too loudly but...

Suddenly Jay, who had been quietly watching and listening and smiling over them as they spoke, was laughing and putting his arm around her shoulders and giving her the biggest hug. "I just love you, Sheila! You know, if I go to Betty's Pantry now and you're not there, I'm going to miss you even more than I did before. Can't you come back? Maybe work just one day a week? We can have a tryst, you and me; lunch every Wednesday. What do you say?"

Sheila looked up at Jay, overflowing baskets of petunias and impatiens hanging above his head; his daughter standing behind their cart of dreams for a summer of beauty, looking alternately bored and embarrassed when her eyes weren't locked on her purple cell phone; his partner standing right beside him, their hands nearly touching.

This was the real Jay. A Jay that was different than the one she thought she knew, and yet the same. A Jay it would always be her pleasure to know.

Chapter 11
DID THIS MAKE HER A STALKER?

Did this make her a stalker? She had moved to the same town and gotten a job at a restaurant he frequented. And now, as she had been doing once a week (at least) for the last few months, Katie was driving down Cliffshore Way, slowing when she approached the sage green ranch with the dark green shutters and ivory front door.

She knew the exact position of Jay's house on the street by heart now - on the left, at the end of the curve, just after the gray colonial with the row of boxwoods bordering the sidewalk. And she knew the point at which she should start lightening the press of her foot against the gas pedal to get the most gawking time and the least chance of inciting road rage in another driver who might happen to be behind her.

The first time she had made her way down Cliffshore Way, peering out the driver's side window as she searched for the house with 391 over the garage or next to the front door, the sudden blaring of a car horn had sent her heart lurching up into her throat and her bladder threatening to evacuate.

She'd slammed on the brakes just as a car came up on her left and whizzed past, the driver laying on the horn and throwing her the finger. To the jackass's credit, he had probably tapped on his horn a few times to nudge her from her crawl before he lost all patience and restraint. But her ears were already full of the loud thumping of her heart and she couldn't hear anything else.

By the time she had settled down, she found she'd driven all the way through and out of the neighborhood. 391 Cliffshore was still an unknown, far behind her. And her brain felt like it had seized up; a useless blob stuffed into a wire mesh cage - hard thin wires pressing in and pinkish brain matter bulging out between the open squares.

Several days later, with a flimsy composure loosely draped over her shoulders, she tried again. The house looked cozy and well kept. There were bushes under the front windows with pots of yellow flowers in between, and a tree in the yard that tickled her memory but she couldn't place it.

It was always Katie's intention to stop, to ring the bell next to that ivory door and watch Jay's face when he saw that it was her. But his car was never in the driveway (of course, it could have been in the garage). And the lights were never on (of course, it was broad daylight).

Of course she could have stopped hiding behind a menu at Betty's Pantry and shown her face, gone up to Jay with contrition and hopes of forgiveness floating in her eyes and laid an explanation on his table along with his order.

And of course she could have called him. Katie could have sent her mom over to Mrs. Hendershott's house on a recognizance mission, as she had done many times in the past, to nonchalantly slip in an inquiry as to her son Jay's cell phone number along with the small talk.

But, of course, she didn't do any of these things; because she was chicken, or more precisely, a poultry of a different persuasion. Katie was Khaki and Khaki was what she had always been – a duck, the one lacking a backbone that always flew the coop.

Chapter 12
HOW COULD HE NOT?

Ebony Jade Randolph.   Jay still thought about her sometimes. How could he not?   Mina was a young woman now and, from the side, she looked just like her mother, his ex-wife.

Ebony Jade Randolph. It was what she took with her Nikon N80 that had first grabbed his attention - The fur coat of gray/green and black mold on the forgotten sandwich, the writhing mass of mucus white maggots feasting on dead robin, the unflushed tampon, wavering tendrils leaching out from it in menstrual red.

Her gaunt and grizzly had stood out in sharp contrast to the sun shimmers and zoomed in scrutinies of the other photography students that hung on the wall outside 271 Newhouse Hall. They screamed and clawed at you, they made you want to look away at the same time as they made you want to look more closely, and Jay Hendershott had wondered, as he hung his own sparkling gems of light dancing on sea spray and frolicking carousel horses, what went on inside Ebony Jade Randolph's head when she snapped them.

Ebony Jade herself was svelte and fine, with eyes the color of ripe figs and smooth, nut-brown skin, unmarred by freckle, blemish or scar, except for one tiny mole to the left of her mouth, a beauty mark, like that of Marilyn Monroe. And Ebony Jade had strong, equine legs that raced her down the track, blazing to take the finish line.

Jay had found himself mesmerized by the detonating photos Ebony Jade took, entranced by her flawless skin, awed by the long stride of those perfect legs. And Ebony Jade ended up taking not only the finish line with those perfect legs of hers (feet at the bottom and...), but running off with Jay's virginity as well with what lay at the top.

And after the surge and the explosion, after the heady rush had waned, Jay felt like he had just told the biggest lie of his life.

But Ebony was soft and warm, deep and dark; and somehow, Jay found himself coming back for more.

And Ebony was bright and intense and passionate, her laugh turned dusk to day, her eyes shot fire or glimmered like stars; and six months later, Jay found himself on bended knee, opening a small velvet box before her.

And six months after that, he was standing at the front of Apostle Baptist Church watching Ebony Jade Randolph walk down the aisle to meet him.

Ebony had never looked more beautiful than she did that day, with the delicate netting of black and white pearls shimmering in her short, dark hair and threaded into the bodice of her cream colored wedding gown. Jay's tuxedo had been black, his shirt white, his vest and tie the same cream as Ebony's dress.

Black and white was the theme, garbing the entire wedding party, adorning table settings, bobbing in balloons floating about the ceiling. Black and white was a statement, a testament - to hewing barriers, forging unions, mingling opposites, and freeing souls.

If hewing and forging had simply meant cutting the thorns from the stems of white roses and bundling them with black satin, if mingling and freeing had referred only to untangling the black and white balloons that had gotten twisted in their black and white ribbons, maybe there would have been a few less RSVP's marked 'unable to attend', fewer uncomfortable smiles and stiff handshakes.

But most of the brown and pink faces that had come together for this black and white wedding had their glasses raised in cheers and celebration.

"Jay, Jay, Jay. Congratulations boy!"

"Ebony, you are so gorgeous. I just love your dress. And Jay, what a fine looking young man he is. Where are you two going for your honeymoon?"

"Are you sure you're old enough to be married? I can't believe it. Seems like last time I saw you, you were just a toddler in diapers."

"Congratulations, Jay and Ebony. You make a beautiful couple. And you're going to have the most beautiful babies. Those mixed race babies are always the most beautiful. I've always said that."

"I never figured my sister would marry a white dude. I don't know what she sees in you. Ah, but you know I love you, bro. For a white guy, you're all right."

"Jay! Congratulations. I gotta tell ya, that's one good lookin' wife ya got there. And feisty! Ya think you're gonna be able to handle a wild cat like that, Jay?"

"What a beautiful ceremony that was. I'm so happy for you Jay. For the both of you. I'm kind of surprised you didn't wait till after graduation though. Unless... I hope you don't mind my asking... I can't tell by looking at her or anything but... Is there a bun the oven?"

A shotgun wedding? How many people besides Aunt Tina had thought that? The speck that would become Mina wouldn't start percolating for another few days - The best souvenir a honeymoon could offer.

Love. It was all about love. Love was the reason for popping the question. Love, and the impetuousness of youth, the reason for the short turn around from proposal to wedding march. Love and…

…and taking advantage of the situation before the dazzle began to fade….and doing what was expected of him while he could still convince himself that it could work.

Taking advantage. Had he taken advantage of Ebony too? Not consciously, but looking back, Jay figured that he probably had. He had used her to follow the footsteps his parent's thought a man should take, but with a twist. If he had to suppress who and what he was and do what they expected of him, why not pay it forward and make it hard for his parents to do what he expected of them – accept the wife he had chosen.

Oh, it wasn't that his parents didn't like Ebony. His mother hadn't even flinched when he brought her home for dinner that first time, with her ripe fig eyes and nut-brown skin. "I hope you like pot roast, Ebony Jade. It's my specialty! Ebony Jade. That is such a beautiful name," she had said, her smile warm and welcoming.

"So, you're on the woman's track team. Are you a sprinter? You know, I ran cross-country when I was in high school," his dad had said, impressed with Ebony's achievements and proud of his own.

They had no problem accepting his black friend. But a black friend and a black girlfriend are two different things. And a black girlfriend and a black wife different yet again.

It had taken three stiff shots of Black Velvet for Clark Hendershott to lose the stiff handshake he had offered when well-wishers slapped him on the back in father of the groom congratulations. It had taken a lively song spun by the DJ and half a bottle of white zinfandel for Beverly Hendershott's forced half smile and stony eyes to give way to something that in any way resembled happiness during the mother/son dance.

Expect. Accept. Suppress. Obligation. The wrong reasons to build a relationship.   The wrong words to anchor a marriage.

But he had loved Ebony, hadn't he?   He called her his gazelle and his gemstone in the halcyon days of fresh-faced romance. It wasn't until later - when he couldn't keep his eyes from straying to the hunky guy at the hardware store; when he couldn't get it up for Ebony Jade unless he fantasized about what lay bulging behind the zipper of said hunky guy's jeans - that things began to sour.

After that, he had called Ebony Jade Randolph... different things.

Chapter 13
WHAT KIND OF A MOTHER...?

Where was the harm in appreciating a nice tight butt? The guy wouldn't know she was ogling his behind. Unless he had eyes in the back of his head.

Beverly Hendershott allowed herself the pleasure of the view a moment longer before quickening her pace, closing the gap between herself and the object of her ogling affections to take care of the job at hand.

"Excuse me. Can you help me?" she called out.

"Certainly, what can I do for you ma'am?" he of the sexy butt asked as he stopped in mid-stride and turned to face her.

So what if she was old enough to be his grandmother? Her heart adrenalized at the sight. He was even sexier from the front than from the rear. And such blue eyes.

"Ma'am?"

"Oh, um, yes, um... I was just wondering if you could tell me where I could find the mailboxes and some new house numbers?"

"The mailboxes would be at the end of aisle five, and the house numbers... Well come on, just follow me, I'll show you."

"Okay. Thanks!" she said, smiling. '*It would be my extreme pleasure*!' she thought, smiling even more.

"Are you looking for a pole-mounted mailbox or one that attaches to your house?"

"One that attaches to my house. I just got vinyl siding and the old mailbox and house numbers are probably thirty years old."

"Yeah, no sense putting those back on. What color's your new siding?"

"It's called wicker. It's a beige tone. The house used to be dark gray so this is a big change for me. And the shutters were white but now they're a chocolatey brown. I'm going to paint the front door boysenberry - a reddish purpley color."

"Cool. Sounds like it's going to look really nice. Well, here's the mail boxes. The four on the left are the house-mounted type. And the house numbers are one aisle over, to your left. Is there anything else I can help you with?"

"Do the mailboxes come with everything I need to mount them?" She had already spotted this information printed right on the side of the box. But she hated to let him go.

"Let's take a look."

His arm brushed against her as he leaned in to grab one of the boxes. Beverly could have moved out of his way and given him more room. But she stayed put. He felt strong and smelled masculine and she liked it. She imagined that he was probably gentle and attentive to the desires of a woman too. And she liked that even more.

"You're in luck. Looks like they do." He smiled at her as he pointed at the box and read out loud, "All hardware included."

"Oh good." She was nearly breathless with the titillating beat of her heart. "Well, I'll look these over and figure out which one I want. And you say the house numbers are the next aisle over?"

"Yup, that's right. Over to your left."

"Okay. Well, I guess that's all I need. Thanks so much for all your help."

"No problem. Good luck with your house!"

He smiled again, such a warm smile, and Beverly watched him head off past the door bells, door knobs and angle brackets. There was just something about a man with tight fitting jeans, a hot butt, and a tool belt.

Her husband had always had a hot butt too. Two firm globes, skin as soft as a baby's ass under a spattering of fine dark hairs. She used to give them a squeeze when he was getting out of the shower and sometimes, maybe even an ooh la la kiss.

And he'd turn his front to her instead, another firmness sprouting from his dark nest and reaching past his belly button. "Squeeze here, Honey Baby," he'd say, grinning and waggling. Or, "This is the place your sweet lips really belong, Baby Doll."

And she'd grin too, more than glad to oblige.

At the end, that hot and sexy butt of his had hardly even existed. It was a scrawny thing, just like the rest of him. Skin draped over bone that he held together by pure will power until he finally gave in and took God's hand.

She'd been missing him for almost ten years. Hadn't even dated once in all that time. Hadn't even thought about sex. Not much anyway. But lately the subject had been on her mind, titillating her more and more. And now here she was, infatuated with some young man at the hardware store. He'd been so patient and kind with her. But who was she fooling? He probably thought she was a doe eyed ditz.

Maybe it was time she started showing some interest in the widowers at church who'd been trying to get her to notice them. David was very nice. He had a good sense of humor and was always making her laugh.

And she had always liked Herb. He managed the pancake supper every fall and the flea market every summer.

Either one of them would make fine companions, if companionship was all she was looking for. But what if she was looking for a little sumthin' sumthin'? David appeared to be overly fond of fried foods and second helpings. And Herb was even heftier than David. With age and weight against them, would they be able to rise to the occasion? For that matter, after all her years of inactivity, would she still know how to slip into something more comfortable?

But there was no sense in thinking about these things right now. In ten days she'd be boarding a plane headed to upstate New York for a two-week visit with her son and granddaughter.

Actually, Beverly had originally planned on driving. It would have only taken seven or so hours. But one day when she opened her mailbox, there sat a big envelope in the most beautiful shade of green. Inside the envelope - a greeting card. Inside the greeting card - a ticket for an airplane. 'Dear Mom, You'll arrive a lot quicker on a plane. More time for us to spend together and less time for me to worry about something happening with you driving all that way alone. Can't wait to see you! Love, Jay and Adrian and Mina.'

Beverly was ashamed to say that she hadn't seen Jay and Mina in over three years. She was even more ashamed to say that she had never seen Adrian – the one her son lived with, the significant other, the partner, the…(it was still so hard for her so say it) the MAN her son loved - at all.

When Jay first sprung the news on her she had talked to Adrian on the phone though (screamed was what she had really done) accusing him of walking with the devil, brainwashing her son, and blaspheming love. Hate had sizzled on her tongue and shot through the telephone line and she hoped it was sharp enough and hot enough to obliterate the person holding the phone on the other end of the line, erase the fact of their existence from the lives of those she loved and make things normal again.

But hate didn't sit right with her and she had turned to the lord. He had always been such a comfort to her, especially after her husband died, and she had prayed to Him for guidance with this too. Immorality and damnation was what He had thrown at her instead, and as time passed something about this didn't sit right with her either. It ground into her soul till it was raw. It felt exactly like hate.

What kind of a mother would stare through her own son as if he didn't exist? What kind of a mother would toss the roses he had sent her for her birthday in the trash? What kind of a mother didn't accept her own child for what they were?

Now she intended to do what she should have done three years ago – embrace her son for the wonderful man that he was and had always been and give him her blessing. And if this didn't sit right with God? She'd recommend that He search His own soul, maybe chew a couple of Tums. The minty ones were refreshing but Beverly would probably recommend the fruity flavored antacids to the lord. There was just something about all those rainbow colors.

Chapter 14
THE LAST TIME?

"**Y**ou know what I think today might be? I think it's Be a Sucker and Help the Homeless Day!" the oaf with the Frankenstein forehead was saying to the guy across from him, grinning at his own wittiness and stirring the third packet of sugar into his coffee. "Yeah, I seen three of 'em this morning. One at the Culver Road exit, one on the corner of Park and Dahlia, and one near the bank. Holding up their cardboard signs and trying to look needy. Needy my ass. They probably got better jobs than me and do this on the side for extra cash!"

Katie set the triple decker bacon, ham and turkey club with a side of onion rings and another side of mac and cheese in front of his double oaf chins, thinking how she'd like to have a little 'accident' and let the bowl of bubbling hot mac and cheese slip from her fingers and spill onto his polo shirt covered gut. It would never make it to his crotch though, where she really wanted it to go. Not with two hundred pounds of beer belly hanging over and hiding it from view.

"Did you say it was help the homeless day?" Katie asked, smiling sweetly. "I can tell you're just devastated that you couldn't help them out. But you're one lucky guy, aren't you? If you somehow found your self homeless, you wouldn't need any help seeing that you've got a built in supply of energy all stored up that can even keep you warm and double as a mattress." She blinked her eyes at him, her face a mask of innocence.

He stared at her, head cocked, mouth hanging open while his wheels turned. And then he matched her smile with one of his own, laughing as if he understood what she'd said. As if being homeless was some kind of a joke. As if he could understand anything with a brain that was probably as weighted down and wrapped in fat as the rest of him.

Suddenly there was Rayanne, hurrying towards her and humming *'Get ready 'cause here I come'* as she passed behind. This was the pre-designated signal; the one that meant 'He's here. Hold the menu in front of your face, turn your back towards the door, head for the kitchen. In other words – hide'. But Katie already knew. She had seen Jay's silver Kia Sorento pulling into the parking lot through the window too, over the dome of the oaf's stiff haired head.

This time though, Rayanne added a little something extra to the pre-designated hum - the sharp jab of her elbow into Katie's side and an angry glare. "In the kitchen!" she hissed through clenched teeth, inclining her head towards the swinging doors and then stomping off towards them herself.

"Enjoy your lunch," Katie said brusquely to the oaf and his buddy before darting to the kitchen herself and shoving open the doors.

It was compulsion that made her do it, glance over her shoulder as she shoved. She had to see. Had he come in yet? Where was he going to sit? Was he smiling? Was he…. and there he was, Jay, the object of her obsessions, looking right at her.

Her heart leapt into her throat! But it was only his face that was aimed in her direction. His eyes were looking at something off to the side. If he had been looking straight ahead, he would have seen her. Their eyes might have caught. And then what? What would she have done? What…?

She rushed ahead, the doors swinging closed to safety behind her. And conflict in front.

"That's it!" Rayanne hissed again, trying to lock her anger into a whisper. "I'm tired of this shit. Don't you think I'm busy enough without having to run interference for you? What the fuck do you think I am?"

"Oh come on, Rayanne. He hardly comes in anymore. Just once a week. It used to be more like three times."

"I don't give a shit how many times he comes in. I don't give a shit if you're standing right in front of him when he comes walking through the door. If he sits his ass in your section, you're gonna wait on him. I'm not gonna do it anymore."

"I can't do it. I'm not ready!"

"Not ready? Ready for fuckin what? It's been months. If you don't wanna see this guy, then quit."

"I do want to see him. I'm just not ready. It's complicated."

"Complicated. All right, explain it to me then. Explain to me why you can't go up to him and say 'It's been a long time' or 'You piece a shit' or whatever the fuck it is you wanna say."

"It's because... Well, he was... I just..."

The swinging doors flying open interrupted Katie's stuttered non-answer and there was Betty flying in behind them. "Girls! Is there a problem here? You should both be out on the floor. Jay came in and was sitting there unattended. I gave him his water and a menu. He's one of our regulars and already I've noticed he's not coming in as often as he used to. Is there something going on here I should know about?"

"I'm sorry, Betty. It's all on me. I held Rayanne up complaining about my boyfriend," Katie blurted out, taking all the blame, hoping Betty would believe her, hoping Rayanne would keep her own mouth shut and not expose her lie, or even worse, her entire Jay-avoidance scheme.

"Save it for after hours. Folks come in here expecting good service and good food and I expect you to give it to them. Now get back out there and give the people what they came for."

Betty pushed open the doors and all three of them walked out, Betty heading towards the register, Katie towards the larger dining room and the young family that had arrived while she was detained, and Rayanne, bless her, heading towards the booth across from the counter that held Jay, shooting Katie a dirty look before she was out of sight and mouthing 'this is the last time'.

The last time…

… that Rayanne would run interference for her with Jay.

… that Katie would wait on anyone at Betty's Pantry if she followed her heart's desire and threw an icy beverage into the clueless, Neanderthal face of Mr. No Help for the Homeless, who was dangling his last onion ring like a worm over his mouth as she passed by, ready to snag it with his flappy lips.

The last time…

Three words she had once joined to anxious questions that had defined and controlled her life - 'Is this the last time I'll find something to eat?', 'Will this be the last time I'll sleep with a shelter over my head?', 'Is this the last time I'll have a clean glass of fresh water to drink?'

Katie could hardly remember now why it was that she had she gone to Arizona. A quest for adventure and newness perhaps. To spread wide her duckling wings in the eternal warmth and sunshine of an almost other worldly place.
But it had not gone well. She had trusted too easily and been duped. And she found herself on the streets secured to nothing but emptiness – empty hands, empty pockets, empty stomach. Homeless.
Homelessness was brown. Not rich, fertile earth brown. Not sepia or chestnut or copper. Not cocoa, russet, or bronze. It was scorched, bone-dry brown. It was grit that crunched between your teeth and made you spit brown. It was the only color Katie could see brown just before she couldn't see anything when the thundering winds of the haboob had hurled the rage of the Sonoran Desert at her; needle sharp bullets of sand and dirt, stinging her eyes, clawing her skin, forcing themselves up her nose and between her lips, polluting her air.

Even homeless, without the aid of any personal device ownership, she had known the haboob was coming. The urgent tones of its imminent arrival leaked out from the open windows of cars as they sped for safe moorings, interrupted play by plays on TVs tuned to the sports channel at open air bars, waiters and bartenders hectic in their preparations to hunker down, shouted out from the mouths of people suddenly launched into escape mode, racing for shelter, urging her to do the same.

But Katie didn't move. She just stood there watching the people, the cars, everything dashing by. And then it was quiet. The streets empty except for her and the gusting winds that were becoming steadier with the darkening sky.

If there was ever a time she should have run, it was now. Instead she faced into the wind, her hair whipping behind her head, her bare arms stretched out like a saguaro cactus, her toes instinctively curled down gripping the bottom of her sandals as though to root herself in place.

She was strong and brave. Stronger than any storm. And she had the balls it took to survive. If she could beat this, she could beat anything. And if it turned out she couldn't? Let it take her then. There was no one to care anyway.

It was thoughts of Croakers Norge that had first flooded over her when the brown wall swept in, stealing light and color, lashing and tearing and grating its brutal violence upon her. The cool blue of fast rushing streams. The lush green of spring grasses. The sweet red juice of summer berries.

Next she thought of death because the storm was much worse than she had ever imagined it could be.

And then there he was, a shirt wrapped and tied around his face, his eyes squinting through a narrow gap, struggling to see through the grinding burn of the sand, struggling against the fury to get to her, struggling to grab her under her arms and pull her to safety.

And she thought to resist him but she had nothing to resist with. And she tried to cling to him but she had nothing to cling with. He dragged her, limp and nearly lifeless, into the shoe store across from where she had made her stand. He saved her life.

Her knight in sand buffed armor had insisted on calling an ambulance for her, even though she insisted she was fine. She was glad he didn't believe her. With every labored breath, her scoured lungs ached and rattled.

The hospital had insisted on calling her parents, even though she insisted she was no child. But the hospital won because she was still covered under their health insurance. So much love in her mother's hug, protection in her father's strong hands. How the tears had flowed.

Her parents had insisted that she come back to Croakers Norge with them, and, being homeless, how could she insist on staying behind? Home. It sounded like heaven.

Except that it wasn't. She slept in her old room but the pink walls were now beige. A butterfly print duvet lay over a different bed and lacey butterfly pattered curtains fluttered in the window.

She drove down Vector Road expecting to see the field where she used to play tag and baseball but the open spaces and weedy grasses were gone. A row of houses stood in its place with manicured lawns and blacktopped driveways.

Her parents had uprooted the overgrown red-berried hollies from the front of the house and replanted with boxwoods. Mrs. Gorely next door had died. The old gazebo in the village square had been torn down. Her friend, Mary, was off following the path of academia. Nancy was married, with two toddlers, and had moved to nearby Rookton. Kim's schedule was always booked solid with a busy career and a fiancé. And Jay..... Of course Katie had already known that he was gone. His absence was like a hole in her heart.

Croakers Norge was and would always be her hometown. But it was no longer home. She only stayed six months, long enough to recoup her health and a modicum of financial security working the breakfast shift at the Koffee Klatch and evenings at the upscale Grove House, before she was leaving Croakers Norge again.

And as she was pulling out of the driveway in the used Ford that her parents had helped her buy, smiling and waving from the drivers seat, all she could think about was the last time she had left, smiling and waving at Jay, how straight had been the line of his mouth, how it had wavered and crashed when he tried to smile back.

The last time.

Rayanne was right. She had let this drag on way too long. She had come here to see Jay, to make apologies and offer explanations… Hadn't she?

The problem was, if she couldn't even explain it to herself, how was she going to explain it to Jay?

Chapter 15
WILL YOU?

Katie was exhausted. Not the kind of exhausted you get from working too hard or being up way past your bedtime, but the kind that happens when it's too loud to see, too dark to taste, too bitter to smell, and stress pulls the minute hand in the wrong direction and the day never ends.

Twice the young mother had to remind her to bring that glass of chocolate milk she had ordered for her pudgy-cheeked little girl. She'd given the family of four's lunch bill to the single guy that had gotten nothing but a cup of coffee and a sweet roll. She served a grilled cheese sandwich instead of a cheeseburger, French dressing instead of ranch.

Her brain was a sieve, everything leaking out, except one long strand grappled to her gray matter, firing off the same message again and again – That's it. Can't hide anymore. Can't keep putting it off. Have to do it. Have to talk to him. Time's up. Have to do it. Now.

Finally her forever shift was over. Finally she was home, yanking off her clothes, climbing into bed, dragging the blanket over her head to block the light of the still bright early summer evening sun and pressing the pillow against her ears, praying that it would muffle her incessant thoughts and the overly loud beating of her heart. But sleep would not come. Her eyes were wide open under her closed lids. Can't hide anymore. Time's up. Time's up.

She threw off the blanket, paced the floor, and then she was pulling on her jeans, grabbing her keys, and driving down

Cliffshore Way, slowing at the end of the curve, and staring out at the sage green ranch in which he lived.

The garage door was open and Jay's Sorento was inside. The ivory front door was open to let in the summer breeze. And her heart was pounding so fast she thought she might pass out. Her foot hovered over the accelerator ready to press it and run.

And then the tree in the front yard caught her eye, the one that always tickled her memory but she couldn't quite place. Elongated raspberry-like fruits hung thick and heavy from the tree's leafy branches, dark and ruby red - Mulberries.

Croakers Norge. Ruby stained lips. Smiling eyes. Starry night skies.

So much wasted. So much missed. So much to make up for.

Katie pulled into the driveway, got out of her car, and up to the front door of 391 Cliffshore Way she went.

***

Jay was excited, with a big dose of nervousness mixed in. After all the times he had reached out to her only to hear silence and then a click on the other end of the line, to find cards in his mailbox that looked suspiciously the same as cards he had sent out but with 'return to sender' scrawled in contempt across the front, she had finally reached out to him. And today was the day.

He swished the mouthwash, spit into the bathroom sink and then smiled into the mirror, checking his look to see what she would see, as if the mirror was him and he was her – his mother.

Had anything changed in the four years it had been since she'd seen him last? His hair was shorter. And he sported an eternal five o'clock shadow now. Possibly he was a few pounds heavier but that was because of all the extra calories that got added when Adrian snuck stuff like grated cauliflower or mashed zucchini squash into his recipes.

But the biggest difference between him then and now was that he had lost that gaunt look he always thought he'd had around his eyes. The look you get when the answers don't fit the questions and life doesn't fit you. He had a joie de vive about him now. A sparkle in his eye!

The only thing sparkling in his eye last time she'd seen him were tears of pain; when the hand she'd slapped across his face had then dismissed him, cutting the fact of his existence from her life like a razor blade.

Would she even recognize him now with this happy face? Jay smiled again into the mirror.

"Mina! We're leaving for the airport in half an hour to pick up Grandma. Make sure you're ready," Jay called out down the hall as he left the bathroom.

"I know, Dad. You don't have to keep reminding me," Mina called back from behind her bedroom door.

"If only," he whispered under his breath and headed for the kitchen where he knew he'd find Adrian.

"You know Hon, I was thinking," Adrian said, glancing at Jay over his shoulder as he wiped off the counter, "if I put the mac and cheese in the oven just before we leave," he continued as he straightened the towels, "then when we get back with your mom, the delicious smell of homemade from scratch goodness will be there to delight her senses and give her the warm fuzzies about me." He glanced up with a fidgety smile, having stated his case, rearranging the flowers in the vase on the kitchen table yet again.

"No. Bad idea. We already talked about this! What if her plane's late? What if it takes a long time to collect her suitcase? We'd come home to a smoking black mess in the oven and the alarm blaring. No! We'll take her out to eat tonight and you can impress her with your phenomenal mac and cheese tomorrow night."

"Yes, you're right. I know you're right. I just want everything to be perfect."

"LOL. Everything is perfect. You've got this place looking like a bed and breakfast."

"Okay, good," Adrian replied distractedly, his eyes darting around the kitchen as if anything could possibly still be out of place. "Well, I'm going to go put on a different shirt and then I'll be all set." He paused, took a deep breath. "I'm just so nervous. I don't want her to still think I'm the devil."

"Well, just don't let your eyes glow red and make sure you keep your forked devil's tail in your pants and you'll have her fooled!" Jay laughed, reached for Adrian's hand and gave it a squeeze before pulling him into his arms and kissing the top of his head. "Seriously. Babe. That was the past. Remember, it was her that reached out. She wants to meet you now. She wants to make amends and have us back in her life. It'll be…"

Jay jumped suddenly, sucking back the rest of his sentence along with his startled breath as the doorbell's ding-dong chime jarred the mood.

"Shit. The doorbell. Always at the wrong time. I'll get it. You go change your shirt and then we're out of here.

"Mina!" He called out again, glancing down the hall on his way to answer the door, "We're leaving in fifteen minutes."

He was nearly to the door, feeling the breeze blowing through the screen, by the time he faced forward again, ready to listen to some school kid's fundraising spiel or accept a brochure from a hopeful salesman.

But there was no kid standing there with a box of chocolate bars, no salesman with a lanyard around his neck. His feet stopped moving. He stared and then blinked. He almost forgot to breathe.

"Khaki Campbell," he said softly. "All those times at Betty's Pantry. I knew it was you."

"It was me,' Khaki replied, a rueful smile tugging at her lips. "I wanted to see you. To talk to you and explain. But… You know I was always a chicken shit. "

"Chicken? You mean duck don't you?" The joke bubbled up like a hiccup Jay was unable to resist. It was something he might have said with dancing eyes and a roguish grin way back when – when they were kids, when they were friends. This time

82

it only made his eyes misty. "It's been so long, Khaki.....but I'm just getting ready to leave for the airport."

"I'm sorry...and now I've come at the wrong time."

Jay opened his mouth to say something else and then closed it again, silent. All the questions he could have asked, all the things he could have said careened through his head, fighting to be first in line. They bashed together and broke apart unaskable, unsayable. There was no time.

Instead he just stood there; breathing in and out, staring with his misty eyes as if at a ghost, afraid to say the few words there was time for - words that he knew would find him watching as she faded off his porch, wondering if there was any chance she would appear again or if this was the last time he would ever see her.

"I should go." It was Khaki herself that broke the silence, fading already as she turned to walk away.

"Khaki, wait. We can hook up later, when I've got time to talk. What's your number? I'll call you." Jay pulled out his phone, ready to tap in the numbers as Khaki rattled them off.

"Dad?"

"Wha...?" Jay jumped, startled again. "My god, Mina, I didn't even hear you coming. I'm kinda busy right now. Can you..."

"I'm ready. I just wanted to tell you I'm ready."

"Ready?" Jay looked at her blankly.

"Yeah! Ready. Are you serious? You've been nagging me all afternoon. You know, to go get Grandma."

"Right! Grandma. Oh hey, Khaki, this is my..."

"Your daughter. I know. You got married. And you had a daughter."

Something in the way Khaki said it. The look on her face. It was sadness. It was disappointment. But mostly, it was an accusation. Accusing him? Of what? Even as he asked himself this question, Jay felt the blood rise in his own face. He already knew the answer.

"Look, you're busy, Jay, and I've got to go. I'll see you next time you're at the restaurant."

"Will you? Will you still be there the next time I go?"

Khaki's answer was the hint of a sigh, the flicker of a smile, a little shrug, and a barely perceptible shake of her head. It was an answer that was no answer and all answers. It meant she didn't know. And it meant he was right. 'No' was a definite possibility.

"But anyway," Jay plowed ahead," we can't talk if you're working. Give me your number. I'll call you. Come on Khaki."

But Khaki was already off the porch, hastening to her car. She paused opposite the Mulberry, hovering, then drifted across the grass to reach up into its branches. Her eyes closed, dreamlike, as she popped the berries she had plucked into her mouth and bit down into their sweetness. She looked back at Jay and smiled.

She looked back at him again just before she got in her car. "Seven five seven four five three nine eight four seven," she called out.

Numbers. Numbers! Her phone number! It was all Jay could do to get them into his phone before they faded from his memory like the ghost from whose lips they had come.

Chapter 16
CAN I GET YOU ANOTHER MANHATTAN?

Beverly never intended to have a drink before her flight. But the bar looked so inviting with its polished wood and hanging pendant lights and green barstools; it just called out to her. And why not? She had more than enough time.

Her neighbor had tried to tell her that leaving the house at 1:00 for a 4:00 flight was overdoing it.

"It's only a fifteen minute drive to the airport, Beverly. Why don't I pick you up at quarter to two instead?"

"What if there's traffic? What if I can't figure out where I'm supposed to go? What if check-in is at one end of the airport and the gate is at the other? I'd rather be safe than sorry."

She should have listened. Even after she got waylaid at the security checkpoint, she still found herself with two full hours to kill before she could even think about making her way onto the plane.

"Step off to the side, please," the checkpoint officer had said.

Beverly paid him no mind. Surely he was taking to someone else. No one in front of her had been told to step off to the side. Why would she have to?

"Ma'am! Step off to the side!" How he had barked at her then. Something out of the norm had been detected in her bra area, he said. She had to wait for a female attendant to come pat her down, he said.

Seriously? Did they really think she looked like a terrorist?

Of course there was nothing in her bra but boobs. And they set her loose to wander the airport concourse. That was probably another reason the bar had attracted her so. Who wouldn't need a drink after that?

"I'll have a glass of white zin," she told the bartender, settling herself onto the green stool and leaning her carryon against the side of the bar.

He had the bottle in his hand, ready to twist off the cap when she stopped him. "Wait! You know, that white zinfandel's really pretty boring stuff. Instead, can you get me a Southern Comfort Manhattan? My aunt used to love those things. And put in lots of cherries. Yeah," she continued as she watched him pour and stir, "I've got two hours until my flight so I figured why not have a drink?"

"Where you headed?"

"Upstate New York to see my son." She smiled as he set down her drink. Six cherries! It could be her something to eat so the drink didn't hit her as hard. She plucked a couple of the cherries off their long stems with her teeth and started sipping her drink.

"This is good. So sweet! What's in a Manhattan anyway?"

"Not much really. Mainly, usually, it's some kind of whiskey with a dash of bitters and a dash of sweet vermouth. In your case you asked for Southern Comfort instead of whisky."

"I like it. Better than white zin." Beverly took another sip and pulled another cherry from its stem. "You know, airport security frisked me today. They thought they saw something. I don't know what. The only thing I can figure is that maybe it was the sequins on my tank top, you know, being shiny and all. Do you think that could have been it?"

"Sounds like a possibility. Makes sense to me. I say wear something different when you head home."

"Yeah! For sure! I will for sure." Beverly laughed and grinned and laughed again.

A little voice in the back of her mind piped up then; a sensible little voice telling her she was getting a tad tipsy and too talkative and that it was time she bid the bartender goodbye.

Tipsy and talkative? Really? But she'd only had one drink. And she'd eaten the six cherries. And even some snack mix from a little glass bowl. And the bartender was smiling at her, and chuckling with her, and so interested in everything she said. His eyes sparkled when he looked at her. She was just fine and she was having a great time. That little voice didn't know what it was talking about.

"Can I get you another Manhattan?"

"Yes you can! You certainly can." Beverly didn't even hesitate.

But, just like she should have listened to her neighbor, she should have listened to that little voice too. Drink number two had too big a dash of the bitters. And only one cherry. More barstools were being occupied and the bartender's time was divided and when he looked her way now, his eyes barely grazed the top of her head.

A couple of young guys walked up, passed behind her and sat on the two stools to her right. They ordered Coronas that came with little lime wedges sticking out the tops of the bottles.

There was something about the way they pushed the limes down into their beers. Something about the way they laughed. They sat with their shoulders touching and looked into each other's eyes when they talked. One of them had his hand on the other one's knee.

Beverly's eyes opened wide and then they narrowed and then she looked away, embarrassed, as if she had witnessed something she wasn't meant to see. A secret. Or a crime.

She glanced around furtively, oddly uncomfortable, and found herself shifting towards the opposite edge of her seat. As if they were tainted. As if they had cooties that might leap over and infect her. What the hell was the matter with her? She shifted back, ashamed.

"We all start out the same," she said aloud, to no one but herself. "A tiny speck of life, too small to even see. Things pull out and push in and everything gets so complicated."

Beverly cupped her hand around her glass, thinking to pick it up and take a sip but the appeal was gone. She picked up the cherry instead, held it by its long stem, and dipped it in and out of the amber liquid, watching faceted ice nuggets sparkle and swirl as the cherry nudged and displaced them.

It was like the soap bubbles in the tub when her kids were small. Parting when the girl's Barbie dolls dove in and surfaced as mermaids. Making way as Jay's bright plastic boats fought through a storm of angry bubbly bath seas. White suds glinting yellow and blue when they caught the light.

"Moova, moova..." Jay used to sing as he shoved and dunked the boats through the bubbles. From that song by Dire Straits - Money for Nothing. How Jay had loved that song. Beverly loved it too. And the video! Beverly could picture the blocky workingmen moving those color TV's even now.

"That ain't workin'," he'd sing, flying high on the swing set in the back yard. "Moova, Moova..." maneuvering his plastic boats. "Money for nothin' and your checks for free."

Except it was chicks for free that those angular workers had hankered after, not checks. Had that been a sign she should have caught but was too blind to see? A hint clueing her in when Jay was all of 6 years old that chicks were not for him? If that was a clue, if there had been other clues, Beverly had missed them all.

Or had she chosen not to see them?

What courage Jay must have had to gather. He'd probably known what she would do. And prayed that he was wrong. Six hours he had driven! Six hours to tell her in person that he was gay. And she had sent him away to drive six hours back, with the shape of her fingers glowing hot and red on the side of his face.

What kind of a mother... What kind of a mother...

Beverly sighed and shook her head slowly back and forth. She reached for her drink but the only thing in the glass was a cherryless stem in a puddle of melted ice. She didn't even remember finishing it or eating the cherry or...

Heat rose up her face, her heart started to race in her chest. "Excuse me," she said to the young man at her right, her voice shaking with urgency. "Can you tell me what time it is?"

"Three thirty six," he replied.

"Three thirty six? Oh no! I've got to get to my gate!"

Beverly hopped from the barstool and rushed towards the exit. Luckily she had already paid the bartender. Luckily the first thing she had done before landing in the bar was scout out the location of her departure gate.

"Wait!" A fervent shout in a male voice invaded Beverly's mindset, braking the determination in the speed of her steps. "Lady in the checked shirt. Hold up! You forgot your carryon."

Beverly had on a checkered shirt. She had her purse slung over her shoulder. And her carryon was…. Her carryon! She spun around to see her barstool neighbor hurrying up behind her with a turquoise carryon in tow.

"Is this yours? It was leaning up against the bar right where you were sitting."

"Oh my god. I would have gotten on the plane and then realized I didn't have it. I don't know what I would have done. Thank you so much."

"No problem."

"I've got to tell you. You remind me of my son. He's just like you," Beverly smiled, "Tall and handsome and very kind."

Spur of the moment, Beverly leaned in and lightly kissed his cheek. "Thank you again," she whispered in his ear and then she dashed away, gripping the carryon tightly by the handle like it was a high-strung terrier on a leash anxious to break away.

Her flight number was up on the screen when she arrived, the waiting area nearly empty, the line of travelers waiting to present their boarding passes dwindled down to one last couple and a small child.

Beverly darted over to join to them, fumbling and flustered. She'd gotten to the airport two and a half hours early. And she still almost missed her plane.

Chapter 17
WHAT WAS SHE SUPPOSED TO DO NOW?

Maybe it hadn't been a good idea to get a cup of coffee (regular, not decaf) every time the stewardess passed by with the beverage and snack cart. Now Beverly was fidgeting in her seat like a child, constantly checking her watch, each time sure that at least fifteen minutes must have passed and maybe even half an hour, and unable to believe when the movement of the hands claimed it had only been five.

But she had to do something to keep herself awake. The constant low drone of the engine compiled with her two manhattans kept lulling her to sleep. And then she'd awake with a start and glance to see if anyone was staring at her.

Because in her dreams they were. Staring and pointing, their shocked whispers buffeting her ears. 'She sent him away.' 'He only told her the truth.' 'Doesn't she love her own son?' 'A shameful disgrace.'

Why did she keep dreaming of her trespasses? That was all behind her now. Didn't her own brain know she was on her way to make amends? The happy reunion, the kisses and hugs – that's what she should be dreaming about. She couldn't wait to arrive.

When at last her plane touched down, Beverly's stomach took off instead; a flock of birds fluttering wild wings. By the time she got to the end of the long walkway and entered the airport concourse, those birds were jiving to the rat-a-tat-tat beat of her heart. And then they flew away, deserting her in a wash of disappointment.

Beverly had expected to see her son waiting at the gate, his eyes anxiously scanning the line of passengers as they filed out one by one, his face lighting up when he finally spotted her. But Jay was not there. It was more than disappointment. She was actually a little miffed. What was she supposed to do now?

Most of the crowd that had departed the plane along with Beverly were heading towards the escalators and riding them down to the floor below. They all seemed to know what they were doing and where they were going so she followed along, planting her feet firmly on the next ribbed metal step that appeared and gripping the worn black handrail, to find herself when the escalator deposited her on the floor below, in baggage claim.

And there, with his unmistakable football player frame and broad shoulders, leaning against a concrete pillar by the luggage retrieval conveyor belt with his legs crossed at the ankle, was Jay; not scanning the crowd for her, but with his thumbs dancing over his phone and his eyes glued to the display.

A pretty, tan-skinned young woman stood near the same pillar. She at least seemed to be on the look out for a loved one. She was craning her neck, her eyes flitting this way and that. And then her eyes landed on Beverly. A smile spread across her face. She poked Jay with her elbow and pointed. She waved.

Could it possibly be? Was this young woman her granddaughter, Mina? Beverly had still been picturing a little girl. If only Beverly had started a Facebook account. She could have at least stayed connected to Mina. Mina was a complete innocent. She had nothing to do with the absurdity of the last three years. Neither, in fact, did Jay. The only absurd thing about the last three years was Beverly.

Right beside Jay stood a slender man with thick, dark hair and dark eyes. He looked in her direction too, and smiled just like Mina. He touched Jay's shoulder and spoke into Jay's ear. He must be Adrian, the boyfriend, the partner. Adrian had on tight jeans and a blue button down shirt with the sleeves rolled up and the top buttons undone. His dark eyes were deep set and sultry. He was, god help her, so sexy!

Finally Jay looked up, and right at her too. Beverly's eyes misted over. A tentative smile skimmed over her lips and she raised her arm above her head to wave. And Jay... did nothing! His face was a blank, his eyes far away and unfocused. He really wasn't looking at her. He didn't even see her. He was still in cyberland, trapped in that damn cellphone he held in his hand.

And then there was light. His eyes unglazed and recognition dawned with a smile as bright as the sun. Jay waved back, shot a quick glance down to his phone and gave it one last dance with his thumbs before shoving it into his pocket and hurrying towards her behind Mina and Adrian, an exuberant grin spreading across his face.

"Mom! I'm so glad you're here."

Beverly forgot all about being miffed. Any uncertainties she might have had disappeared. Jay's arms were around her in a big bear hug, tears were rolling down her cheeks, and the only thing rolling around in her head were thoughts of love and absolution.

Chapter 18
HAD SHE EVEN NOTICED?

Adrian supposed he ought to give her some slack. She had, after all, never met him before. And Jay and Mina were her family. But would it have killed Beverly Hendershott to show some interest in him, to at least acknowledge his existence? He would almost have preferred that she shout obscenities at him. Better than being rejected. Better than being ignored.

She had hugged Jay with impassioned tears running down her cheeks and onto her quivering lips. She had drawn Mina into her arms and rocked joyfully back and forth. And what had she given Adrian? A perfunctory smile, an unyielding refusal to look him in the eye and a rebuff of his welcoming hug.

With the precision of a karate master she had thrust out her arm to block his embrace, offering her hand for him to shake instead. And that she had withdrawn as soon as his fingers brushed against hers.

He was still working his fingers, grasping at thin air, before he realized that her hand had disappeared. Greeting complete apparently, as least as far as Jay's mother was concerned.

At The Striped Spinnaker, even with a glass of white zinfandel to loosen her up, it was more of the same. If she wasn't looking at the menu or Jay or Mina or the waiter, her eyes were on her dinner plate. She even talked to her linguini and clam sauce, as if it was the clams that had clacked their shells together to ask about her flight or what the weather was like in Croakers Norge so far this summer instead of Adrian.

And now Jay expected him to entertain this woman while he ran off to meet an old friend?

"You're doing what? You can't be serious."
"I'll only be gone a little while, two hours tops."
"Your mother just got here. Can't you meet up with this Khaki person another time?"
"You don't know Khaki. Another time might be too late."
"You're right, I don't know Khaki. So why don't you invite her over here so I can meet this ex-girlfriend you've been talking so much about?"
"Babe… Wait, ex-girlfriend? She was never my girlfriend. Just a friend that was a girl. You sound like… Are you jealous?"
"Why would I be jealous? Girlfriend, friend friend, whatever she is, I don't care. But you shouldn't run off and leave… or… hey, you could even bring your mother with you. She knows this Khaki from when you were growing up, right? It can be another long lost persons reunion."
"I can't do that. Seriously, Adrian, you'll be fine with my mom. She…"
"She's not gonna like this either. You see how she is. Won't look at me, won't talk to me, won't get near me. She's afraid of me."
"I told you to hide your devil's tail and not let your eyes glow red, didn't I?" Jay grinned and coughed out his smoky laugh. "Listen, she's just nervous, trying to get her head around all this gay stuff. It's a lot for her to handle. "

What could Adrian do but agree? At any rate, he had been right about her not wanting Jay to leave her alone with him. She didn't protest out loud, but how she had clung to Jay as he said goodbye. And no sooner had Jay's car pulled out of the driveway, than she was hightailing it to her room in a panic, mumbling a lie about needing to unpack her suitcase that Adrian knew she had unpacked last night. Adrian heard the click as she set the lock on her bedroom door.

If he was lucky, maybe she would stay there until Jay returned or until Mina got back from soccer day camp, whichever came first. Then he wouldn't have to entertain her at all. But somehow, that thought did nothing to cheer him.

***

Thirty minutes since Jay had left. And Adrian puttered…
…Emptying wastebaskets.
…Unloading their breakfast and lunch dishes from the dishwasher - Jay's mother had never even commented on the delicious muffins he'd made for breakfast. Potato muffins they were, courtesy of the mashed potatoes leftover from dinner two nights past, and studded with Jay's beloved mulberries, courtesy of the tree in their own front yard.
…Adding fresh water to the cut glass vase on the kitchen table - Had Jay's mother even noticed the lively bouquet of gerbera daisies gracing that vase? Magenta, yellow, white and scarlet red he had selected just for her. Bold colors that had grabbed his attention the moment he stepped into Rockaway Florist yesterday morning, high on anticipation, looking forward to meeting and spending time with the mother of the man he loved. Something else that she had made no mention of.
Thirty minutes since Jay had left. Half an hour since Jay's mother had cloistered herself in the guestroom.
Nothing but complete silence emanated from that room, and actually Adrian was getting a little concerned. Was she all right? Maybe the stress of being left alone with a dangerous homosexual lurking on the other side of her door had given her a heart attack and she was sprawled on the bed unconscious.
Was she even in there at all? Maybe she'd pried open the window, slipped through and gone running to bang on a neighbor's door, desperate to find someone to protect her from Adrian and his queer and evil ways. Adrian shook his head at the thought and chuckled (a strange, dark laugh, void of mirth) and started hesitantly down the hall, stop go, stop go, ears honed in

to catch any indication that life existed behind the guestroom door.

Was that a footfall? Had he heard a breath? At the door, he leaned forward, inclined his ear, and raised a loosely held fist to knock. But there was no door to meet his knuckles, just the soft and startled face of Beverly Hendershott.

"Oh!!!!" She cried in shocked surprise, her gray/green eyes as big as the yellow centers of the gerbera daisies on the kitchen table.

"Oh!!!!" Adrian matched her cry, pulling back his hand and bringing it to rest over his wildly thumping heart. "So sorry, Mrs. Beverly! I didn't... Wasn't trying... Don't think I ..." He had to make her understand! Was she paying attention? Her own lips were flapping at him...

"Just surprised me, that's all. I don't think... My fault... I wanted to... But then I... So wrong of me..." She tried to explain but he wasn't listening!

"Please. I was worried. Just wanted to check..."

"If you could just forgive me. I see... You've been trying so hard. I should have told you how good... Biggest asshole ever born."

"Never meant... What?" Adrian stopped, gaping in disbelief, desperation morphing to anger. "What did you say? I can't believe this. Now you're calling me an asshole? I've done everything to... Did you even notice...?"

"Adrian, stop. Asshole. Is that the only word you heard me say? I'm the asshole. Not you. Can't you see I'm trying to apologize?"

"You are?"

"Yes. And there's just one thing I want to know. I've got a real hankering for another one of those muffins we had for breakfast. Please tell me there's still some left."

A few minutes later Adrian found himself sitting at the kitchen table across from Jay's mother sharing the bliss slathered with butter; the last three potato mulberry muffins that he had split, popped into the toaster and warmed till they were just beginning to brown and juices bubbled and oozed, sweet and red, from the berries.

"Mmmmmmm, so yummy!" She looked right at Adrian and smiled, a friendly smile, not a forced one, before closing her eyes to savor her one last bite of muffin as she popped it into her mouth. "Mulberries. And the tree, right in your own front yard. There was a wild mulberry tree in Croakers Norge. Jay was always stuffing his face with them. And staining all his clothes. I hated mulberry season. I never even thought to try them myself. Look what I missed out on." A touch of nerves had hijacked her voice. She warbled a little when she talked.

Adrian smiled back, a cautious smile, tied at half-mast. "Jay told me about the tree in the park. He has many fond memories."

"Does he? I hope so. Because... I always thought things were one way and then, well, apparently nothing was like I thought it was." A shadow seemed to float across her face, pinching off her smile. She stared straight ahead, at nothing that Adrian could see.

Adrian steeled himself, ready for pent-up accusations to come flying from her mouth. Instead she gave a quick shake of her head, banishing the shadows and bringing back her smile.

"So, anyway, enough of that. Show me this mulberry tree. And your gardens too. You have so many flowers. I was looking at them through the bedroom window." She hopped from her chair and headed for the front door.

Adrian sat for a moment, too dumbfounded to follow. A cold, unfriendly and taciturn bitch had locked herself in the bedroom and emerged amiable and chummy. He wiped muffin crumbs from his lips with a napkin and jumped up to trail this new and improved Beverly Hendershott out into the yard. He'd show Jay's mother (Mrs. Beverly, Beverly, Mrs. Hendershott - Adrian still wasn't sure how to address her. Perhaps... Mom? Definitely not!) the garden along the picket fence where the hydrangeas and astilbes were in full bloom. He'd show her the koi pond with its little wooden bridge and the new stone fire pit he and Jay had built. She'd see that he was not some undesirable and twisted moocher but a loving and decent partner to her son. If they could at least be on good terms with each other, that's all he wanted.

She was already under the mulberry tree when Adrian caught up to her, staring into the branches, plucking berries and tossing them into her mouth one by one. "I'll be damned, they're even better right out of the tree than baked into the muffins." She grinned at Adrian, then placed her tongue to the side of her mouth in concentration as she stretched to pluck another berry with ruby stained fingers. "These aren't going to give met he shits, are they?"

And what could Adrian do but laugh?

Chapter 19
WHERE...WHAT...WHY...?

Y ou couldn't go to Elwanger Beach Park without stopping at the Crocus Hill Creamery. Jay's favorite was Chunka Chocolate Chip. He always got two scoops. In a waffle cone.

But his favorite was lame on his tongue today. A layer of guilt and distress was coating his taste buds and instead of making him smile, the ice cream only made him cold.

His plan had been to get ice cream with Khaki. He had texted her from the airport yesterday while waiting for his mother's plane to arrive. But he had waited on the designated bench for half an hour and she still hadn't shown up. So he walked the path to the top of the slope and ordered his cone alone, hoping that when he returned, she'd be sitting on that first bench to the left of the gazebo waiting for him and he'd have good reason to feel guilty licking on a cone in front of her while she was coneless.

He shouldn't have bothered feeling guilty. Hoping had been a waste of time. The bench was empty. Jay sat back down, hunched over, staring at the dirt and sparse grass by his feet with a double dose of despair, while his Chunka Chocolate Chip got soft and drippy.

Honestly though, so what if Khaki Campbell stood him up? He lost the hunch, straightened up, tipped the waffle cone to his lips, and poured what was melted into his mouth.

What the hell did he care anyway? His life was full with Adrian and Mina, plenty of friends, a great job. And even his mother again. He took a big bite from the waffle cone and lapped up chocolate as it dribbled from the breach.

He didn't need any blast from the past coming in to screw things up. The pointy end of the cone crunched in one last bite between his teeth.

Jay leaned back, closed his eyes and lifted his face to sun. Its warmth soaked into him, soothing away whatever vestiges of chill still lay on his heart. A soft breeze skimmed over the lake, caressing his sun-warmed face, carrying scents of seaweed and coconut sunscreen, the splashing of waves and carefree laughter, and the breathy music of the carousel.

That was something else you couldn't go to Elwanger Beach Park without doing - wandering over for a ride, or to stand transfixed, or to at least snatch a passing glimpse, as a menagerie of ostriches, goats, hares, and pigs joined prancing ponies and rearing steeds and raced forever round.

He had planned to ride the carousel with Khaki too.

Jay pulled a Newport out of his shirt pocket and lit up, standing as he sucked down the smoke in one long, drawn out drag. He held his breath till he thought his lungs might burst and the trapped smoke began to escape out his nose before he exhaled, coughing as the smoke billowed out.

Like a merry-go-round himself, he did a three sixty, scanning the grounds, giving the black haired girl that he used to know one last chance to show. He sighed and shook his head, grabbed another quick hit from his cancer stick, before flicking it away and grinding it into the dirt with the toe of his sneaker.

'You'll look sweet upon the seat of a bicycle built for two' crooned the calliope on the opposite side of the gazebo from where Jay stood as he walked away from the park and towards his car.

It turned out, you could go to Elwanger Beach Park without being lured over to the carousel after all.

***

The first thing Katie did when she got to Elwanger Beach Park was hop a long striding cotton tail and let it carry her away as she gripped its ears. Round and round. Up and down. Buffalo gal won't you come out tonight and we'll dance by the light of the moon.

There was no chance of missing him. The first bench to the left of the gazebo was visible from the carousel. Her head was locked into position, insuring that each time her mount circled merrily back around there would be an immediate eye to bench connection. She'd spot him walking up or already sitting there waiting for her and she'd call out his name and wave. And smile. Hopefully she'd smile.

She'd walked up to the park from the beach, past castle builders and sunbathers and scurrying gulls, as if she hadn't a care in the world, as if the quickened beat of her heart was because her flip flops kept filling up with sand. Definitely not because she'd spotted the gazebo. Certainly not because it was getting closer and closer with each sand kicking step.

And then there was the designated bench! Even though it was empty, she couldn't catch her breath. And a little further out, the merry-go-round. Let me call you sweetheart. I'm in love with you.

Past the bench and over to the merry-go-round Katie had run, depending on the gravity of its round and round to tether her in place, the steadiness of its up and down to rock her like a child.

But where was Jay? She'd exchanged the rabbit for a plump pig, the pig for a high stepping ostrich. Could he have called and she just didn't hear her phone over the sound of the calliope? You'll look sweet upon the seat of a bicycle built for two.

Katie worked her phone out of her purse as the carousel slowed to a stop. Her eyes were glued to the screen as she dismounted her feathered steed. Zero missed calls.

Something made her look up then, past the bench, past the gazebo and up the slope to see a figure so familiar. Wide shoulders, loping stride, tall frame. Jay! Walking away, not towards. What the hell! Her finger swiped and jabbed, the phone shot to her ear.

Jay was almost out of sight now but she thought she saw him pause and then stop and then she could hear…

"Where … in her ear.

"Where are you g… from her lips

"What…"

"Why…"

"Listen…" from two mouths at once

"Khaki! Let me talk!" And the only reason Katie heard it was because she had to pause to take a breath.

"I've been waiting almost an hour," Jay continued. "Where are you?"

"You've been waiting? I've been waiting! Staring and staring and staring at that damn bench and you're no where near it."

"If you're staring at it, how could you not see me? I was there the whole time. Where are you?"

"On the merry-go-round."

"You can't see the bench from the merry-go-round. It's on the opposite side of the gazebo!"

"Didn't you say to meet at the bench on the left side of the gazebo?"

"Yeah, the left side. The merry-go-round is on the right side! Listen, just stay where you are. I'll be right there."

Katie's phone went silent and the far off figure she had held in her sights began to move again. At least his legs were moving, but was he? And was he getting closer or farther away? Maybe it wasn't even Jay at all.

But it was Jay. And he was getting closer. And Katie heard a painted pony whinny her name. She forced herself to stay put and stuffed her ears with memories and apologies and explanations.

Chapter 20
WHY WASN'T IT ME?

Right left. Left right. Right wrong. It all had to do with perspective; the direction from whence one came. If you came up from the beach, or if you came down from the main parking lot, your lefts would be on different sides.

If Jay had said 'the first bench to the west of the gazebo', confusion might have been avoided. But, east west north south, you had to know where you were to begin with to make sense of that. And knowing where she was, was something Katie had never been good at.

'I'll meet you at the merry-go-round by the ticket booth'. Now that's what Jay should have said.

At least the mix-up gave them a good laugh. Once they were done being pissed. Something to break the ice along with the hot dogs Jay suggested they get from under the yellow and white umbrella of a street vendor's cart.

"I don't know why but hot dogs at the beach always taste better than hot dogs anywhere else." Jay grinned and bit into his dog, knocking bits of chopped onion from their precarious perch to land on his knee. He grinned again as he finger flicked them to the ground.

His eyes shone, at once both green and blue, catching and reflecting the lake's seascape colors and flecks of sun that darted and bobbed from the water's rippling surface. Like they used to reflect the dancing waters of Feverfew Crick.

"I think it's the openness and the fresh breeze and the sun, just bringing you closer to nature and making you feel more alive. And therefore hungrier!" Katie had her hotdog almost to her mouth ready to take a bite. Instead she stopped, the brightness on her face becoming awe, and pointed high over the lake. "Look." The word tiptoed out; hushed, almost reverent. "See the seagulls? They look like little suns, they're so bright. Almost translucent even. The sun's shining on their wings from above and from below at the same time, when the lake reflects it back up at them. And then they reflect it back again. Like a sunlight boomerang. It's so beautiful."

How natural it felt to be sitting here with Jay; the picnic table at their backs, the sun warming her bare legs, Jay warm by her side. Comfortable and unquestioning. Like things used to be back in Croakers Norge, sitting on a different bench, in a different park. As if fifteen years hadn't passed. As if she hadn't blundered through those fifteen years and filled them with regrets. As if Jay was still her best friend.

Katie took a nibble from her hotdog and closed her eyes as she slowly chewed. When she opened them again, Jay was watching her; his eyes a dull green now, all of those fifteen stolen years hard and sad on his face.

"So, where has life taken you all these years, Khaki?"

Katie knew what he was asking. She chose to answer a different question, keeping her voice bouncy and light. "All over really - Ohio, Texas, Florida, Wisconsin, Alabama, Arizona, New York …"

"That's not the answer I'm really looking for."

"I know." Katie looked out over the lake again. A new bird flew there now; neck outstretched, its gray feathers dark beside the white of the gulls, flapping while the gulls soared. "Nowhere," she said resignedly as she drew her eyes away from the determined flight of the fast flapping duck and hung her head.

"Why Khaki? You left… and then cut me right out of your life. When you stopped at my house yesterday, you said you wanted to explain. So do it. Tell me why."

How many times had she played out this moment, rehearsing and revising her lines? How many times had she balked and run? There was no running now. Katie turned her eyes back to Jay and started to speak but it was not the stiff words she had practiced that filed out. It was the honest words she had known she would say all along.

"One day, it was morning time, I was probably thirteen or fourteen, I walked into the kitchen thinking I'd stick a couple pop-tarts into the toaster. And my dad was there in his bathrobe, standing at the stove with a spatula in his hand, frying an egg. He turned around to smile at me and say good morning and then he yawned and stretched, you know, one of those big morning time stretches, arching his back and throwing his arms up over his head, and his penis popped out from behind his bathrobe.

"I was so embarrassed. But I couldn't stop staring at it. It was only for a second. He had no idea. As soon as he stopped stretching, it slipped back behind his robe again. And I thought maybe I should tell him, just so he'd know. So that maybe he could tie his belt tighter or, or maybe… Instead I just said 'Good morning' too, hurried over to the toaster and pretended I never saw it, pretended it never happened. That's just not the kind of thing you make mention of - for everybody's sake.

"It was the first time I ever saw a penis. It made me think about my mom and dad having sex. And it made me wonder what it would feel like to have sex. To make love. To be kissed by a boy and held tight in his arms. And I dreamed… No, I wanted… the next penis I ever saw to be yours.

"You must have known. I was in love with you Jay. That's why I left. Because I was in love with you, and you didn't want me."

"That's bullshit. You were my best friend. Do you know how much I missed you when you left? How the hell could you think…"

"Think? I was a stupid, self-centered teenage girl. I didn't think. I just wanted. Wanted to be more than your friend. I wanted…"

"Khaki, you knew I was gay."

"Yes. Yes I did. But that didn't stop me. And I felt spurned and that you just didn't love me enough and I thought…

105

you know, if you really loved me you'd... And I blamed you. I blamed you for hurting me. And I wanted to hurt you too. To punish you for..."

"For what? For not being what you wanted or what my parents wanted or the neighbors or the people at church? You don't think I punished myself enough? You knew... you knew me better than I knew myself and you still..."

"I can't justify it. I was selfish and I was wrong. And I even knew it. I tried telling myself but I wouldn't listen. I was too stubborn and too defiant and too busy feeling sorry for poor wronged me." Katie paused and blinked, sending one lone teardrop trickling down her cheek.

Everything around her seemed to ripple and drift. She thought she saw a trickle on Jay's face too, thought she saw him lean towards her as if to wipe her tear away, but the only fingers that brushed her cheek were her own. It was just an illusion. A trick of the tears that still pooled and swam in her eyes.

Katie blinked and blinked again, freeing tears only to have them get trapped in her eyelashes before they could fall. Jay sat blurry but unmoving on the bench beside her, upset and wounded, wobbling as he slowly shook his head back and forth, quivering as he looked at the ground and sighed.

Almost angrily, Katie wiped at her eyes with the side of her hand. "I was mad at you for so long. But I missed you too. And then I was mad at myself because I missed you. Missing you won. Finally. It wasn't until then that I realized what it was I had done. Me. It was all on me. All the hurt and the blame I had thrown on you, you never deserved. So I picked up the phone."

Suddenly the remorse on Katie's face turned steely, explanations dried up along with her tears. Accusation stared out from her eyes now, cold and unforgiving. Was it another illusion that Jay seemed to squirm? "After all those months, I was actually going to call you. But before I could dial, it rang. I was so sure it was going to be you. Both of us with the same idea at the same time. Like somehow I had sent a telepathic message and you had caught it." Katie pressed her lips together in a grim line.

"But it wasn't you. It was my mom, so excited she couldn't get the words out fast enough. She had big news, she said. You were getting married she said. To some girl you met in college. Some girl. A girl that wasn't me."

"Khaki, there were reasons…"

"I swear my heart stopped beating. I couldn't breathe. You could fall in love with some other girl, marry some other girl, have sex with some other girl, but not me. It should have been me, Jay. Why wasn't it me?"

"Because it never would have worked out and you know it. You think I didn't notice you becoming a woman, your tight little ass, you practically throwing yourself at me? Yeah, sure, I could've done it. But it would have been a lie, just like it was with my ex-wife. Friendship, love, it all would've turned to shit. It should never have been you. And it wasn't you because I loved you too much." Jay's voice had risen steadily as he talked. It quieted now, drained almost to a whisper. "I did love you, Khaki. I'm sorry it wasn't the kind of love you wanted. I'm sorry it wasn't enough."

Katie's lips parted as if to reply, then closed again, silent. The screaming of gulls, the babble of passersby, the laughter of children splashing in the waves, the music from the calliope - all seemed muffled; sounds wrapped in layers that couldn't quite fit in her ears. She had become the accuser, put Jay on the defensive, pried apologies from his mouth when they should have come from hers.

"No." The word shot through her lips as she shook her head vehemently back and forth.

Hunched over on one end of the bench, Jay jumped at her sudden shout. He stared as she shook her head. Side by side they had started out on that bench with their hot dogs and their smiles. The intensity of their exchange had pushed them apart.

Katie sidled back over and grasped Jay's hand. He did not grasp hers back; neither did he pull it away. "I don't want you to apologize. You have no reason. You fought for our friendship. But we lost it anyway, because I let it go.

"Remember that PBS special we watched in tenth grade biology about the reproductive cycle of salmon? They were normal, fishy looking fish doing normal, fishy things at first, when they were young. But then sexual maturity strikes. After that, it was all about mating. Nothing else mattered. They didn't even eat any more. And they transformed into ugly, misshaped things. All red and horrible to see. That's me. I was like a salmon, transforming into an ugly, selfish, single-minded bitch instead of being your friend. I ignored everything I knew and deserted you. I am so sorry, Jay.

"I'm not gonna lie. Your getting married devastated me. But if I would've just spent one minute thinking about it then, I would have known why you did it. Instead I shut everything off, strapped on blinders, and ran even further. I screwed up my life! And I missed you the whole time. I just had to see you again... make sure you knew... I'm so sorry. I was such a fool." Her last words snuffled out, mired in snot and spit and salty tears.

Jay's unresponsive hand that Katie had been grasping came alive now, wrapping warm fingers around her own and squeezing reassuringly. He pressed one of the napkins that had come with the hotdogs into her other hand and pulled her close, letting her rest her head on his shoulder while she dabbed at her eyes with the scratchy paper and blew her nose.

"It's okay. Don't cry, Khaki," Jay comforted, rocking gently back and forth. "Hey, didn't you say you were a salmon? I don't think salmon can cry. Or bitches either."

"Was a salmon. I'm not a salmon anymore," Katie corrected with a snuffly chuckle that sounded more like choking than laughing.

They sat quiet now, Jay's arm still around her, rocking back and forth, back and forth, up and down, drifting round and round...

"Shhhhh." Barely there. Had she heard something? The lap of a wave? A hint of a sigh? A dream?

"Stay quiet." Yes, surely a dream. Of high-stepping horses and seagulls like white clouds and lost friends and…

"Don't move," No, not a dream. A real voice, speaking hushed words from real lips, "or you'll scare it away." It was Jay's voice. The sleep that Katie had drifted into, drifted off without her. And Jay was a solid reality right beside her.

Careful to remain still, Katie held her breath against a yawn and slowly opened her eyes. There, a mere two or three yards away, was a seagull, warily approaching, intent on a piece of hot dog bun that lay inches from the bench on which they sat.

Every few steps it stopped, eyeing its surroundings with its beady eyes, scouting for danger until, if Katie had dared to move, she could have extended her leg and almost touched the gull with her foot. The moment of its victory was at hand. It shot forward, head lowered, its pointy beak like the yellow tip of an arrow ready to spear its prize.

Suddenly the seagull was screeching; flapping against a green blur that had rushed in to attack, hopping as the green headed mallard thrust, pecking as it jabbed, finally spreading wide its white wings to glide back to the sand, screaming in defeat.

Victorious, the mallard charged over to the bit of bun, snatched the glory and waddled away. It stopped just out of their reach, turned to face back towards the point of conquest with its bounty dangling from its mouth, before slapping at the bread with its flat duckbill and swallowing it down.

"OMG. That was awesome. I can't believe it." Jay was still whispering. "I never knew ducks were so aggressive. And it's still staying so close. I can see the gleam in his eye. He's staring right at us."

No, not at them. The gleam in its stone dark eye was meant for her. Had Jay forgotten? Maybe she had been a salmon, for a short time. And maybe a bitch. But what Khaki Campbell had always been was a duck.

"Quack, quack, quacki," her cousin the mallard murmured as it ruffled and flapped its gray and black wings and took a few running steps. "Khak, khak, khaki," as it rose and flew over their heads.

And Khaki 'Katie' Campbell understood everything it was trying to say.

Chapter 21
COULDN'T SHE JUST BE MINA?

It was the largest, completely orange boring one that was the first to reach the water's edge, the round O of his mouth opening and closing. Others came scurrying behind, their tails undulating, propelling them through the seafoam water. Last came Stripes, the white one streaked with black and orange and gold. He was the most beautiful of them all, Mina's favorite, and the only one she had named.

The koi came swimming up every time someone walked over to the pond, expecting to be fed. But it was not time to sprinkle food pellets on the water now. Mina had not come for that. She had come only to sit on the bench, to gaze at the fish as they slid peacefully through the water, over the rocks and between the swaying fronds of pond grass.

"This is a reflecting bench," her father had told her when she helped him carry it over the little bridge last year to put beside the pond under the shade tree.

'What an idiot he is', she had thought. "That's dumber than dumb," she had replied. "The bench isn't even shiny. Dull stuff doesn't reflect anything."

"Reflect has two meanings. You've got the wrong one."

Of course, like an idiot, he wouldn't tell her what the other meaning was. He wanted her to look it up. She just rolled her eyes at him and walked back to the house, leaving him to sit on the bench alone.

But now it was to the reflecting bench that she had come, because although she had never told her father, she had looked up the meaning of the word, and what she needed to do more than anything right now was to 'contemplate', to loosen the confused mess that sat in her head and send her tangled thoughts diving in with the fish, hoping they would swim back in straight and clear.

It wasn't Grammy Beverly's fault that the two photo albums she'd packed in her suitcase stirred things up, squeezed Mina's brain and made it pulse against her skull. It was Miss McFee's fault. Her and her stupid question.

At first it was fun, sitting next to Grammy on the couch flipping through the pages of years long past (just like when she was a little kid and Grammy used to read her *Matilda* and *Green Eggs and Ham)*. There was her dad as a baby and as a little boy and as a teenager, her aunts and her uncles, Grammy as a newlywed and a young mother, and her grandpa that had died before Mina was old enough to remember him. But how many old photos could you look at before they started to get stale?

Mina was about to tell a little white lie about having made plans to go meet up with a girlfriend when suddenly her wandering attention was lassoed and her eyes were riveted to the page. There was her mom, so beautiful, dancing with her dad on their wedding day. There was her mom cradling a tiny newborn Mina on her lap. There was Mina toddling across the floor in nothing but a diaper. And Mina banging on pots and pans with a wooden spoon. There was Mina in a yellow polka dot sundress, giggling by her father's side, her smiling mother on his other side, her arm around his waist, her head on his shoulder.

A rare time. A happy time! The sun glowing on three smiling faces. How brown Mina looked against the yellow of her sundress. How white her mother's teeth were against her dark skin. How pale her father looked between them.

That's when the meaning behind the dumb question Miss McFee had asked at Mina's last appointment clicked and Mina's thoughts started to tie up in knots. Out came the lie to Grammy about having to meet up with her girlfriend and out to the pond instead Mina had gone to spend time with the koi.

Miss McFee, with her limp blond hair and waterlogged blue eyes, with her pinched little mouth always asking questions; she was supposed to be helping Mina sort through her issues. But all of her questions came with a fake smile and the only one Mina ever wanted to answer was her first question; the same first question she asked at every visit which was 'Would you like a cup of chamomile tea?'

Mina knew the tea was a fake too, a gimmick meant to set the mood and loosen her up. As if sharing a pot of tea would ever make her feel that Miss McFee was her friend and not just some therapist her father had to pay and they forced her to go see. But she always said 'yes' anyway because she liked the shape of the round red teapot and the arc the steaming tea made as it flowed out of the curved spout and into her mug. And she liked how nice the tea felt running warm down her throat.

'How do you identify yourself, Mina?' That was the dumb question Miss McFee had asked. What kind of a question was that? How else would she answer but 'As Mina Hendershott'? Miss McFee had just smiled, a patronizing smile that flared out the nostrils of her straight, pointy little nose and somehow made Mina feel like a fool; made her feel shrunken into a naive child holding a mug of tea that was too big for her hands; made her feel like throwing the tea in Miss McFee's face.

The photo - Mina and her mom like two chocolate cookies and her Dad the vanilla cream filing in between. Now she understood. Black or white, that's what Miss McFee was after. It had never even occurred to Mina to think about it before. Did

113

she have to think about it? Did other people think about it? What did other people see when they looked at her? Did it matter? Must she choose? Did it have to be one or the other? Couldn't she just be Mina Hendershott, plain and simple?

Black and white was another way to say plain and simple. Black and white mixed together made gray. Mina was black and white mixed together. But Mina was brown. Brown on the outside. Was she gray on the inside? Dull, slimy, wormy gray? Brown and gray. Black and white. Plain and simple. Nothing was plain and simple now.

Maybe this was something she should talk to her dad about. But what would he know about something like this? And anyway, he was busy reuniting with Grammy Beverly. The last thing he'd want to hear right now is that there was yet another issue to worry about coming from the screwed up head of his troublesome problem child.

Maybe Grammy. Grammy used to hug Mina so tight and call her the apple of her eye. Grammy used to make homemade popsicles for her and push her on the backyard swing. But that had been so long ago. Grammy seemed almost a stranger now; a stranger that she sort of knew. Besides, Grammy had issues of her own. She tried to cover it up, but Mina saw how she cringed and looked the other way when her dad and Adrian touched.

Maybe she should call her mother. If anyone would understand, it would be her. But she was living in Ireland now, with a new husband and a new family and a new life. She never thought about Mina anymore. She wouldn't want to hear about Mina's problems. She wouldn't care.

Maybe what Mina should do was lose her balance as she crossed back over the little bridge, and fall into the pond; let the seafoam water wash the tears off her face and zero out her mind, let her hair sway like the pond grass. She could glide under the water next to Stripes, opening and closing the round O of her mouth over and over again.

Chapter 22
HOW DID YOU TWO MEET ANYWAY?

Of all things that Beverly could have wondered about when Jay told her he had invited a bunch of his friends to come over on Saturday for a backyard barbeque so they could meet her and she them, the thing she wondered about first was if all the people coming to the party would be gay.

Except she hadn't just wondered. There was her mouth opening, there was her tongue pushing her thoughts out through her teeth in words that hung loud in the air. "Will everybody there be gay?"

Jay had smiled, chuckled and shook his head, amused by her innocent naivety. "Everyone I know isn't gay, Mom. But yes, some of the people there will be gay."

"How will I know which ones?"

"You'll probably be able to tell."

"But what if I can't tell?"

The brightness in his smile dimmed. "If it really matters that much to you, why don't you ask them?" And fizzled out all together as a lightening quick flash of distress passed through his eyes.

Beverly could almost see the shape of her hand flash red across his cheek too; an apparition of the past, pain with a slap like thunder.

"But really, honestly it sounds like fun!" She had jumped in, just so she could chase the dark memory from Jay's mind and see his smile return.

Honestly though, she hadn't been honest. The thought of having to hobnob with a bunch of people that she didn't even

115

know made her nervous. A bunch of people that might or might not be gay. And it wasn't because she was homophobic, because she wasn't homophobic. No! Not anymore. She really wasn't. It was just that, how was she supposed to act around them? What if she mistakenly flirted with a gay guy? What if she unintentionally led a lesbian on? She'd look like a fool.

All these thoughts swirled through Beverly's head as she walked down the hall to the bathroom. She glanced in the mirror over the sink as she passed by on her way to the commode. And there Beverly was, looking back at herself, already the biggest fool that she had ever seen. "As if," she chuckled, looking to the heavens while she undid her jeans. "Can you imagine?" she laughed, dropping her drawers to her knees.

It was hard for Beverly sometimes, doing two things at once; throwing her head back to laugh and bending her knees to lower her bottom to the duty at hand. She lost her balance, landed crooked on the seat and almost slipped off. Thank God for the sturdy toilet paper holder jutting out from the wall. She grabbed at it to right herself and then ripped off a few sheets to wipe her eyes. Oh my, she was laughing so hard.

That was Thursday and now it was Saturday and there was the doorbell and folks coming round the side of the house with lawn chairs and coolers, with potato salad, and tuna mac salad and deviled eggs, with vegetable trays, a watermelon, six-packs of beer, and a bottle of tequila with its companion lime. It was showtime.

***

"We took Jay and Adrian out for dinner a few weeks ago, and after, they took us to a gay bar!" The fiftyish woman with the pink flower in her hair was telling Beverly.

Beverly knew she was Jay's neighbor and that she was an author. And her name was...? Amy. Or Emily? Or... something like that. Beverly was so bad with names.

"I even did karaoke there," the neighbor continued, enthusiastically. "I sang Ring of Fire."

Her exuberance was contagious. Beverly couldn't help but grin and feel excited herself. "Did my son sing too? I would have loved to see that."

A tousle haired toddler in a flouncy emerald green dress sprayed with white flowers suddenly came scampering up, her face smeared bright orange, crumbly orange bits leaking from her little clenched hands as she ran.

Chasing after the toddler came a pretty young woman, honey blond curls bouncing around her head as she swooped in to scoop the tiny girl up. "Where do you think you're going little miss Michaela?" She laughed as she planted a kiss on the munchkin's powdery orange cheeks.

Beverly didn't have to tax her memory searching for this guest's name. She was Jay's co-worker, Dixie Andrews Chatelain. Almost a celebrity! Beverly had seen her on a TV morning newscast just yesterday, talking about proposals and summer weddings and love, with her face glowing as bright as the summer sun itself.

"Annie, are you talking about 140 Zander?" Dixie interjected, turning towards Jay's neighbor (Yes, Annie - that was her name!) as little miss Michaela sat in her arms, intently watching the crumbly remains of what must once have been cheese doodles spill from her open hands, fall down the front of her dress, and pool into the crook of her mother's encircling arm. "I've been there before. Did you see the drag queen show?"

"My first time at a gay bar, do you think I'd miss it? Those guys were the sexiest girls there. One of them was wearing a skintight leotard. I kept looking for some hint of a package but there wasn't even the slightest bulge. I couldn't believe it was a man. But Jay said it was. They tuck it and tape it he said. OMG." Annie grinned and took a sip from the beer she was holding stuffed into a lime green can koozie.

A man with short, salt and pepper hair came up to Annie carrying a paper plate topped with a variety of delectable looking nibbles. Annie put her arm through his and drew him close. "This one was embarrassed, I think, weren't you Honey? Hey, what do you got there on that plate? Deviled eggs! Oooooo, I love deviled eggs."

"Are you talking about the gay bar? What makes you think I was embarrassed? I wasn't embarrassed. I even gave the tall redhead with the leather miniskirt and perky knockers a five dollar bill." He smirked and winked as he wriggled his arm to untwine it from Annie's, reaching then with his newly freed hand for a saucy meatball skewered on a toothpick.

Before he popped the morsel into his mouth, he extended his arm and held his plate out to Annie. "Here, you take the deviled egg," he said considerately. Beverly couldn't help but notice how earnest his brown eyes were and how long his lashes. "You can take the whole plate if you want. I'll get more for myself later."

"No, no! You don't have to do that. That's your egg. Those are your appetizers." Annie's face shone as she smiled back at him. "I can go get my own. Is everything in the kitchen?" She took a step away, about to head off in search of the munchies when she stepped back again. "Oh, I'm sorry, maybe Jay already introduced you two, but anyway, Carl, this is Jay's mom, Beverly. And Beverly, this is my husband, Carl."

"Hello. It's nice to meet you. Carl and Annie. And you live right there, in the gray house next door? It's so wonderful that Jay has such good neighbors." Beverly smiled and took a sip from her own drink - not beer, not wine, not a Margarita in a salt rimmed clear plastic tumbler like many of the others were drinking and Adrian had offered to her at least four times now, but a nice cup of coffee - so she could keep her wits about her.

Dixie and her munchkin had already wandered off, as people tend to do at gatherings, and now Annie wandered off too heading for the kitchen. And there was Beverly alone with the long lashed, salt and pepper handsome Carl.

"So, I hear you're up here from Croakers Norge. Are you enjoying your visit so far?" Carl asked, making small talk. His arms looked so tan and muscular against the short sleeves of his white polo shirt.

"I am! Yesterday we went to the zoo. And tomorrow we're supposed to be going up to the lake for a picnic." Beverly took another sip from her Styrofoam cup, hoping the warmth of her coffee would chase away the butterflies that seemed to be fluttering in her stomach.

"Oh, you're gonna enjoy the lake. And you couldn't ask for better weather." Carl brought a swiss cheese topped cracker to his lips and took a bite. Heart shaped lips they were. And he had a dimple on his chin.

"I didn't even think to bring a swimsuit so we went to the shopping mall to get me one. So many stores! But I still couldn't find a suit that flattered my figure. I'll just tippy toe in the water and get my feet wet." What were these words coming out of her mouth, floating on a giggly flutter? And was she batting her eyes at Carl too? What was the matter with her? So much for keeping her wits about her. Even coffee couldn't stave off the raging hormones of the post-menopausal.

Carl gave a little cough and quickly looked down at his plate. Beverly kept her eyes on her coffee cup as it traveled up to her mouth. And she coughed too when she almost inhaled her next sip instead of swallowing it.

"You know, actually those appetizers do look mighty good. I think I'll go get a plate myself." Not that she was really that hungry, but she needed some kind of an excuse to wander away before she made a complete doofus out of herself.

Carl couldn't have looked more relieved. "Make sure you try the meatballs. They're really good." He called out after her, ever the gentleman, as she strode towards the steps leading onto the deck.

Out in the yard beyond the deck, she spotted a bubbly and bright Mina entertaining a couple of rambunctious tykes that squealed and danced as she tickled and chased them. One of them looked like little miss Michaela!

At the far end of the deck she saw Jay, his head thrown back in a boisterous laugh, standing behind the outdoor bar with Dixie and a thirty something guy with reddish blond hair. Beverly caught Jay's eye and he grinned at her, raising his highball glass in salute.

And there was Annie with a deviled egg in her hand, chatting with a group at the crowded picnic table. She shot Beverly a friendly wave and Beverly waved back as she turned the knob on the kitchen door.

For all the people outside, there were even more in the house; hovering around the feast of tasty morsels assembled on the kitchen table with red and white checkered plates in their hands or standing near the counter waiting to fill their plastic cups with the Margaritas that Adrian was whirring in a blender. The batch he had whipped up before had been blue. This time they were pink.

"Mrs. Beverly!" Adrian called out to her as she spread a bit of creamy liverwurst pâté on a crisp round cracker and put it on her plate next to one of the raved over meatballs and a deviled egg, "I made strawberry this time. Have one!"

"Yeah, come on, Mrs. Beverly. Are you Jay's mom? Come on Jay's mom. They are sooo good!" gushed a skinny guy holding his glass out to Adrian for a refill. His long bangs hung in his eyes, his eyes were highlighted with blue shadow and his shirt was as pink as the strawberry Margaritas.

Not that Beverly was keeping track, she had promised herself not too, but this one was obvious. Gay all the way.

"Ah, so you're Jay's mother," said a striking young black woman standing across from Beverly. Beverly was fascinated. She had shoulder length dreadlocks. "I'm Hillary," she told Beverly, her dreadlocks swaying as she reached over to dunk a broccoli floret into a bowl of French onion dip. "I work with Jay at Channel 20. Can you believe all this food? And these are only the appetizers!"

"I'm getting full just looking at it!" Beverly joked, adding an Italian dressing drizzled cherry tomato joined on a pick with a

120

leaf of basil and a cube of fresh mozzarella to the tidbits already on her plate.

Tidbits of food and tidbits of conversation.

"...at the plant store."

"He said it was a Sheltie but I think…"

"Girl, I'm telling you, you can't start …"

"...found it on Amazon and …"

"So, how did you two meet anyway?"

Beverly's ears perked up. What was this now? Her eyes followed the sound waves to zero in on a pretty, dark haired woman in a blue and tan starfish patterned shift who was over by the counter now, chatting with Adrian. Nonchalantly, Beverly moved closer.

"On the Facebook," Adrian replied, "over a misunderstanding. I took this photo of an orchid. Gorgeous. I was so proud of it and so I posted it on the Facebook but then … Hey, you know, we have it in a frame hanging on the wall. Come and see!" He put his hand on her shoulder to direct her as they started walking around the corner to the living room. "You won't believe. This is so funny. I was living in New York City and…"

And they were completely around the corner now and whatever else Adrian said, Beverly couldn't hear. She could follow them, but if she did they'd know she was eavesdropping. And what of it? It's not like this was a secret.

She stood there, hesitating between following Adrian and the starfish shift into the living room or going back outside, somehow nervous. She did want to know how Jay and Adrian had met, didn't she? All she had to do was put one foot in front of the other, walk around the corner, and she'd find out.

And one foot in front of the other she went, not around the corner, but down the hall and into her bedroom, the answer to her question crawling shame hot up her face.

No.

Chapter 23
BONHOMIE?

It was here - The July/August issue of *In Our Town Magazine*! And there she was, smiling on the front cover above the caption "Woman to Watch - Annie Vandenbunder Seizes the Glory of her Day. Page 10". Her fingers couldn't flip to page ten fast enough.

And there was the article all about her! With a picture of her novel illustrating the page. Hundreds of people could read this article, maybe even thousands. Hopefully some of them would buy her book. And hopefully, not only would they buy it, but they'd read it too.

That's what Annie wanted most, for people to read her book; to touch them with what she had written, to make them laugh and cry, to make them think. And if the bottom-line on her author income/expense report started showing up as black instead of red? Well, she certainly wouldn't complain about that.

Now, what did the article say? Annie was so excited she had to concentrate on forcing her eyes to focus on the page. *'There's an undeniable bonhomie about local author Annie Vandenbunder.'*

Wait. Bonhomie? Was that really a word? Annie had always thought it was a bit of poetic license on the part of Colin Meloy; a word he made up for that Decemberists song – Bonhomie bone drab and the war of the enzymes. She pulled out her smartphone, tapped at the screen, and up popped the definition - "Bonhomie – cheerful friendliness" - An honest word with a positive meaning.

But... If she hadn't known the definition of bonhomie, there was a good chance many others wouldn't know what it meant either. And they might not look it up. They might assume from the peculiar and unbecoming appearance of the word itself that the meaning was unbecoming too; that Annie was undeniably rude or condescending or cold.

And then they wouldn't finish the article. They wouldn't buy her book. Her author account would stagnate in the hole and never see light.

Annie closed the magazine and looked again at the cover. It was a good picture of her. She looked bright and genuine, with an energetic glow about her, and an air of... Bonhomie! Back to page ten she merrily flipped.

She was savoring the article for the second time, basking in the euphoria of perceived achievement and possible success, when Carl bustled into the kitchen, his arms loaded with grocery bags.

"You did say you wanted Devil's Food cake mix right? Cause that's what I got. And a tub of butterscotch frosting. I picked up a twelve-pack of Arrogant Bastard too. What time are we supposed to be at Jay and Adrian's party anyway?"

"Three o'clock. I've got to get those cupcakes started so they have time to cool before I put on the frosting. But guess what? The magazine with my article came! Do you want me to read it to you? Do you think I should show it off at the party?"

Carl scowled at her as if she was crazy. "Would you settle down? You always get too excited. Stay on track. The first thing you should do is start those cupcakes, like you said. And don't you think it would be kind of gauche to bring an article about yourself to a party? Listen, I gotta go shave."

"You still have to shave? I thought you did that already. Okay then, you go shave and I'll make the cupcakes and..." Annie was bouncing from cupboard to cupboard as she spoke, dragging out cupcake tins and measuring cups. "Do I need milk or water for this stuff?" She picked up the cake mix box and flipped it back and forth searching for the directions. "But anyway, you know the article's really short. And it doesn't take you that long to shave does it?" She lost her grip on the box and it fell to the floor.

It was Carl that bent down to pick it up, shaking his head in amusement, a playful half smile toying at his lips. "You're like a little kid some times, like a chicken with your head cut off. Ok, where's that magazine? I'll read the article before I go shave."

"It's right over there on the kitchen table!" Annie pointed giddily with her rubber spatula, tore open the box, ripped open the plastic bag inside and poured the Devils Food powder out.

She didn't even notice at first that only half of the chocolaty powder made it into the mixing bowl. She was too busy watching Carl's eyes twinkle and dance as he read, watching the smile spread across his face.

It didn't take Annie any time at all to push the spilled mix from the counter into the bowl. And, just as Annie thought, it really didn't take Carl that long to shave. Even still, they were a tad late getting to the party. Something else came up, spur of the moment, that they decided they wanted to do.

And they never planned on drifting off into that little catnap cuddled up together on the bed afterwards either.

***

Annie was having the most wonderful time. The flattering article and the afternoon delight had her flying high before she even set foot in Jay's back yard. Now she was enjoying spirited conversations with interesting people, shaded from the bright and glorious sun by a sage green patio umbrella, with three mouthwatering deviled eggs on her plate. The only thing she was missing was another can of that Arrogant Bastard.

She beamed and waved at Jay's mom when she spotted her making her way up onto the deck. And Beverly waved back at her before she turned to head into the house. Perhaps it was her imagination, but she thought Beverly seemed a little too hurried, a little flushed and flustered, like she was embarrassed about something.

Annie had left Beverly in the shade of the maple tree chatting with Carl when she went in to peruse the appetizers. Maybe Carl couldn't resist and had told Beverly his famous 'Italian Sausage in the Can' joke.

"I didn't know it came in a can," the broad-faced man next to her suddenly said.

"What!?" Annie sputtered and nearly choked on the piece of deviled egg she had just bitten off. Had he read her mind?

"The Arrogant Bastard beer," he said, pointing at the can visible over the top of her can koozie. "I thought it only came in bottles."

"Oh no, it..." Annie paused in her reply, sputtering even more, trying to swallow and chuckle at the same time. "... it does. It does come in a can." She could tell by the bemused look on his face that he had no idea why she couldn't seem to stop laughing.

Maybe she should explain her mirth and tell him the joke! It would be even funnier if she used his nationality to name the sausage. He didn't appear to be Italian. Maybe German or Polish.

On second thought, he might not think the joke was that funny anyway. She was almost positive the broad-faced man was gay. And that would take the punch away from the punch line. A gay man's sausage always came in a can.

Annie was still chuckling when a neon blue haired youth walked past her, brazen as could be with a lit cigarette dangling from his lips and an open bottle of beer in his hand. He was barely five feet tall. Was he even a teenager yet? Where were his parents?

Neon Blue headed over to the outdoor bar at the other end of the deck, where Jay was grinning and laughing and pouring shots from a half empty bottle of Fireball whiskey. Annie couldn't wait to see the expression on Jay's face, responsible father that he was, when he saw Neon Blue's flagrant disregard for the acceptable bounds of youth. He'd probably snatch that beer and that butt away from the kid so fast, the kid wouldn't even see it coming.

Instead, what was this? Jay grinned even wider, slapped the kid on the back, and poured an extra shot of Fireball Whiskey just for him! The whole group at the bar raised their shots in salute and then downed them in one gulp. Annie couldn't believe it. She stared in open-mouthed shock.

"Mrs. Vandenbunder!" Jay called out jovially, motioning with both hands for her to come near when he spotted her looking his way. "Come on over. Have a shot!"

He'd called her Mrs. Vandenbunder again. Mrs. Vandenbunder, instead of Annie. But Annie didn't call him out on it like she usually did. She hardly noticed. Jay had given a kid whiskey! Jay had let a kid smoke! She'd come over all right. To give both him and Neon Blue a piece of her mind. She marched across the deck, glaring. But when she got to that outdoor bar, up close and personal with Neon Blue, she smothered her glare with a sheepish smile.

Neon Blue had well built arms and a carefully tended tuft of hair between his lower lip and his chin. Short and slight as he was, it was 'man' that was written on his face; a young man to be sure, perhaps 25, but certainly no twelve-year-old boy.

A piece of her mind became only one word when she took the glass that Jay handed her and slugged that shot of Fireball down. "Whooooo!"

"Yeah! Way to go, Mrs. Vandenbunder! You slug it. No sipping allowed. Want another one?" Jay didn't wait for an answer. He was already pouring it.

"Please, no. Whooo, that's strong. One's enough for me." One was too much really. Annie wished she hadn't had the first shot.

"Claude, how about you?" Jay asked, offering the shot to Neon Blue instead, who took it without hesitation. "Mrs. Vandenbunder, did you know that Claude just came to the U.S. from Guyana about a month ago?"

"Really? Guyana. That's..... Hey Jay," Annie interrupted herself, "do you have any water behind that bar?" How badly she needed something to swish around in her mouth. Cinnamon whiskey was not a good chaser for deviled eggs.

"Water? Booze is the only thing I've got back here. How about a beer? Molson, Corona, Three Heads, Rohrbachs Scotch Ale ...."

"I'll have a Corona." Annie grabbed the bottle, guzzled some, swished some and then continued from where she had left off with Claude. "So anyway, Guyana's in South America, right?"

"Yes it is. Guyana is at the northern tip of South America." He spoke slowly, carefully enunciating each word, with only the slightest hint of an accent, yet Annie could barely understand him, he spoke so quietly. She found herself watching his mouth, concentrating on how each word shaped his lips, how his tongue moved against or over his teeth, in order to be sure of what he was saying.

Not that he said much. He was so shy. He didn't say anything unless Annie said something first. "Are you here visiting relatives?"

And half the time it was outgoing Jay that answered for him. "No, his whole family's still in Guyana. He's living with a friend and working on seeking asylum. You can't be gay in Guyana. He's got horror stories he could tell you..." Jay shook his head, visibly upset, before looking at her pointedly. "You could write a whole book about that."

"Yes," Claude said, nodding slightly in affirmation and looking embarrassed; or possibly... Was he somehow ashamed? He blinked, still nodding, and then looked Annie directly in the eye.

It was a pleading that Annie sensed in him, in that moment before he quickly looked away again. A longing to open his mouth and let his story out, to share the burden of it with someone else and thereby release its grip on him; and yet at the same time, a fear to do just that. Who was she but some stranger? A stranger he didn't know if he could trust. Telling his story was what he wanted to do most. Not telling it was what he wanted to do even more.

"How terrible," Annie said, nodding sympathetically, racking her brain for something more profound or encouraging to say and coming up blank.

"But anyway, that's enough of that. This is supposed to be a party," Jay piped up, kicking out the moment of uncomfortable silence that had fallen over them before it could settle. "Claude, you didn't drink your shot yet. Mrs. Vandenbunder, another beer?"

"I haven't finished this one yet! How many beers do you think I can drink?"

"As many as it takes, Mrs. Vandenbunder. As many as it takes." Jay spoke the words amiably, with an amiable smile. But Annie caught a glimpse of his eyes before amiable got there. It was angst she saw, throwing a cheerless light, giving a different meaning to his simple words.

As many as it takes…to do what? To have a good time? To ease your mind? To forget? To still be able to walk heel to toe along a straight line? Straight lines, fine lines, toeing the line, crossing the line.

How many lines of black letters on a white page would it take to do justice to pleading eyes and a story aching to be told?

Someone tittered and laughed loudly behind her; Annie's untethered mind came reeling back in, the party and all people milling about on the deck and in the yard shifted back into focus. In her hand was the nearly full bottle of Corona Jay had just given her moments before. Just what she needed, some nice cold beer. Her throat felt so parched and dry. She tilted back her head and took a good long, disappointing swig. The beer was warm.

How long had she been standing there in LaLa land? And who the heck was that lady in the blue and tan dress waving at her from the yard?

Chapter 24
BUT I THOUGHT...?

A nd she had thought she was being accepting. She had thought she was being supportive. What a crock. What a lie. What a failure.

Beverly abandoned her checkered paper plate of nibbles on the crocheted doily that covered the top of the dresser and snatched up her purse from the floor of the guest room closet. What she craved right now more than anything was a smoke. She rummaged around in her purse for her pack of Pall Malls and lit up.

She'd been trying to cut back. She'd even set a few rules for herself to help her do it; a schedule that allowed one before breakfast, one after dinner and one just before she turned in for the night. So what if this was not one of those times? So what if she broke her own rule? She'd broken Jay's rule too of no smoking within the four walls of his house. But she was a failure. And failures didn't care about rules.

Party chatter slipped under the bedroom door and babbled through the window screen dancing with the sounds of background hip hop; a rowdy laugh here, a giggle there, a thumping jive, a rise in pitch, a lull.

"That's unchartered territory. Don't even go there!" Adrian's laughing voice floated in, happy and carefree.

Where was he from, with that sexy accent of his and his sultry Hispanic looks? What did he do for a living when he wasn't wasting his vacation days helping to entertain her? Beverly didn't even know. Surely those topics had joined the conversation at one point or another. But Beverly had been quick to stick her fingers in her ears.

"Ooooh baby! Something for me to know and you never to find out!" Her son. His laughter skipping along with Adrian's.

How long had he known Adrian? Where did they meet? She'd seen a ring on Adrian's finger. Could they actually be married? Questions that Beverly had never asked. Every time one of those questions had lit up in her head, she'd flipped off the switch and given it a good swift kick out of her mind.

And why? Why had she plugged her ears? Why hadn't she asked the questions? Because she didn't want to know. And she didn't want to know because...shame mushroomed again, looming up from the pit of her stomach, spreading hot and red up her neck and onto her cheeks, setting fire to the tips of her ears...because details would lift a flat Adrian from a flat page and flesh him out into a real live man. Details would set things in stone and carve the abstract into vivid reality. Details would remove any chance of her waking up to discover this whole gay thing had been nothing but a bad dream.

"Hey, Sheila! You came!" Jay's voice again, brimming with happiness. "You remember my sweetheart, Adrian."

Beverly went to the window and peeked through the blinds. Jay was over by the steps greeting an older woman (Older? She was probably the same age as Beverly) wearing tan capris and white ankle socks, his cheeks glowing rose, his eyes crinkled in a grin, his arm around Adrian. Adrian, his sweetheart.

"My mom's here's too! She's around here somewhere." Jay glanced this way and that. "Where the hell did she go?" He shrugged his shoulders and continued chatting with his friend but Beverly could see his eyes were still scanning the crowd, looking for her.

She'd been hiding in here too long, sitting on the edge of the bed, puffing away. Any longer and they'd send a search party out after her. She was, after all, supposed to be the guest of 'honor'.

Beverly ground the smoking end of her butt into the glass coaster on the nightstand and spritzed some perfume into the air to cover the scent of her crime. She adjusted the lay of her shirt, smoothed the seat of her pants, and fluffed her hair.

It was hard really, trying to hide from yourself. No matter how far or fast you ran, no matter how many corners you turned, yourself always knew where you were.

She took a deep breath and opened the door.

***

Re-entry. The Party, Act Two. Act Two was going to be different. Just because you knew where you were didn't mean you had to stay there. And the coffee from Act One had done nothing to save her from herself. What Beverly craved now more than anything was one of those pink Margaritas.

First though, she'd take a look at that picture of the orchid hanging on the wall that she had never paid any attention to before. It was somehow significant in her son's life and should therefore be significant to her as well.

She made a beeline straight for it and nearly tripped on something/someone that was kneeling on the living room floor. "Ooops! Oh my, Dixie! I almost didn't see you there. I was so intent on… I'm such a ditz. So, little Michaela needed a diaper change did she?"

"Well, somebody needed a diaper change, that's for sure," Dixie laughed as she hovered over the changing pad she'd spread out, pulling off her toddler's elastic-waisted blue jeans and hiking their red t-shirt up to their shoulders to get it out of her way.

"What happened to that adorable little dress she had on earlier?"

"She still has it…" Dixie began, but at the very same moment Michaela (who somehow seemed shorter and a little stockier than she had out in the yard) squealed and twittered and pointed at somebody else passing through the living room.

It was that brown skinned teenager with the crazy head of blue hair that Beverly had spotted outside earlier. She almost wanted to point at him herself. What colors the kids these days died their hair. Blue, green, purple. If you wanted to bring attention to yourself, that was certainly the way to go.

Beverly forgot that Dixie had been saying something before Michaela's squeal drowned her out. She continued on, as if Dixie hadn't been saying anything. "I remember when my kids were small. I had four of them you know. Jay's the youngest. You'd put them in a special outfit for a nice occasion and they'd get into mischief and need a whole change of clothes. And if it wasn't that, their diaper would leak."

"Oh yes, I know how that goes!" Dixie laughed again as she unfastened the tapes that held down the diaper, and pulled it out from under Michaela's little bum. Michaela was jiggling her legs up and down on the floor, and something else was jiggling too. Something that no little girl had any business having between her legs.

"Oh!" Beverly sputtered, bewildered and perplexed. "She has a... Is that really...? But I thought... You mean Michaela's not a girl?"

"Michaela is a girl. But Beverly, this isn't Michaela. It's her twin brother, Eddie."

"Oh for heaven's sake." Beverly slapped her cheeks and cupped her chin with her two hands. "I remember now. Jay did mention that you had twins. You had me scared though. I can't tell you the thoughts that were going through my head. I kind of did think she looked a little different. Even before you took the diaper off. You know, this calls for a drink. I'm going to try one of Adrian's Margaritas. Want me to get one for you too?"

"Okay, sure, but just half a glass. I've got to keep my eye on the twins. Turn your head for just one second and you never know what they might have gotten into before you turn your head back again."

Little Eddie was running in circles, tracing the spiraled geometric pattern on the area rug, and Dixie was closing the flap on her bag of life with a toddler (or two) paraphernalia and squirting hand sanitizer, when Beverly returned. Beverly could have made small talk as she passed one drink on to Dixie and took a sip of her own. Asked Dixie about her kids, talked about the weather. But this was Act Two where she meant not to act at all, to shed her pretenses and truly become the woman she was trying so hard to be.

"You've been friends with Jay for quite a few years, haven't you?" She started light and airy. And then plunged right in. "Did you always know he was gay?"

Dixie's eyes had been on her son, who was fingering the silky tassels on a throw pillow and sucking his thumb now, her face soft with a mother's love. Her gaze shifted slowly to Beverly, not at all disconcerted but as if she had been expecting Beverly to ask just such a question. She sat down on the couch and gently patted the cushion next to her.

"Let's sit," Dixie invited warmly.

Beverly sank into the supple leather of the couch beside Dixie, her hand trembling around her plastic glass, her swallow of Margarita travelling awkwardly down her dry throat, afraid of what Dixie might be about to say yet clinging to the compassion she heard in Dixie's voice like a life preserver.

"You know," Dixie began, with a breezy chuckle and the whisper of a smile, "when I first started working at Channel 20, about six years ago, I had the biggest crush on Jay. He was so handsome! I had no idea he was gay. For years I had no idea. But when he showed up at our door that one night and told me and Mike, I wasn't even surprised. It was like an answer to something that had never been a question. So I guess the answer's really yes. I just didn't know I knew."

Her smile had waned. There was no chuckle now, just the revealing truth. "He usually called ahead if he was going to stop over but he didn't that night. There was a knock on our door and there he was, trying to act normal and pretend nothing was wrong, but he was so messed up. His eyes were open too wide and kept flitting all over the place. He'd start to say something but his voice would break in the middle of every sentence. And then he tried to laugh if off, as if it was funny. Nothing was funny about that laugh. It was a terrible thing to hear. It tore my heart right out of my chest.

"We finally got him to sit on the couch, got him a glass of water. He took one sip, got this odd look on his face that I think he meant to be a smile, and then he broke down, sobbing. He said that he'd been hiding and holding everything in for too long and he couldn't take it anymore. He said he was confused and ashamed and afraid. And we were confused and afraid too because he was so desperate and frenzied and we weren't sure what he was talking about. And then he told us he'd been sneaking onto Facebook in the evenings after Mina had gone to bed, like a criminal, reaching out to gay men. And he'd made arrangements for one of these gay men to come up from New York City to meet him. Because he thought he might be falling in love with this gay man. Because that's what he was too. A gay man.

"He got all quiet then, siting there wiping the tears off his cheeks and sighing as if the weight of the whole world had just been lifted from his chest. And we both hugged him, Mike and I, and told him it didn't matter one bit to us. He was our friend and we loved him no matter what." The whisper of a smile returned again to Dixie's lips. "And that's it. That's how I found out what I already knew."

"And that gay man from New York City was... was Adrian?" Beverly asked slowly, almost afraid to speak.

"Yes. Yes, it was." Dixie nodded.

Beverly lowered her tear moist eyes. She blinked, setting a few tears free to trickle down and dilute her Margarita. "Thank you, Dixie," she said softly, raising her head again to look Dixie directly in the eye. "Thank you for being there for my son when he needed help the most. God knows, and I'm sure you know too, he never got any support from me."

Little Eddie who, bless him, had been content fingering the pillow tassels and opening and closing the Velcro strap on the diaper bag while Dixie told her tale, was starting to get antsy

135

now. "Mom! Mom! Go. Side. Go. Side," he whined, tugging determinedly at his mother's shirt.

"Just hang on Eddie. You've been such a good boy. We'll go outside in a minute." Dixie tried to appease him while looking apologetically at Beverly. "Beverly, I'm sorry. With kids sometimes it's so hard. I…"

"Don't you worry about it. Go take care of your little one. I'm fine and I really…"

A loud laugh from the kitchen interrupted Beverly and made her jump. A hubbub of excited chatter trailed behind. Beverly had almost forgotten, so intent had she been on Dixie's words. There was a party going on. The house and yard were full of guests. She had tuned out the chitchat and background music and reduced it to the importance of buzzing crickets or the hum of neighborhood lawnmowers on a summer day.

And there came Jay, bursting into the living room, his pupils dilated and his cheeks ruddy with revelry, a baseball cap perched backwards on his head, and a smoking cigarette that he had forgotten to douse before he entered the house in his hand. "Mom, there you are. What the hell are you two doing sitting in here on the couch?" He looked from Beverly to Dixie and back again, quizzically. "Is something going on?"

"We're just talking about kids," said Dixie calmly with an almost imperceptible nod in Beverly's direction. It wasn't a lie.

"Now, Mom! Side!" whined an insistent Eddie.

"I'm having a Margarita!" said Beverly, because she couldn't think of what else to say. A strange mix was coursing through her – love for her son, joy for his current happiness, sadness for what he'd suffered through, shame for what she had done, regret for what she hadn't.

"Cool. It's about time you moved on to the harder stuff. Grab your pink drink and come on back outside. There's somebody I'd like you to meet."

"Okay, here I come." Beverly grunted as she struggled to extract herself from the couch's deep embrace, exchanging a quick look full of gratitude with Dixie as she rose to follow behind a swaggering Jay.

She'd barely gotten to her feet, when little Eddie scampered gleefully past, nearly toppling her back into the couch. He zigzagged around Jay, bumped into Adrian and dodged dreadlocked Hillary as he raced to be first in line for the door leading back 'side'. A laughing Dixie zigged and zagged behind him, trying to keep him in her sights and catch up to him before he scooted out into the warmth of a bright sun and the coolness of a gentle breeze.

Now Jay was holding the door for her but she was passing margarita central and she thought she ought to top off her glass now while she had the chance. And at the table she had to pause too. Appetizer time was running out. Adrian and Hillary were whisking away the nibbles and dips and she hadn't tasted any of them yet. Not one of the tasty bites that she'd put on her red and white checkered plate earlier had ever made it into her mouth.

It was now or never. She grabbed a handful of yellow cheddar cubes before Adrian prodded them off a tray and into a ziplock bag, popping them one by one into her mouth. She snagged one of the last remaining meatballs too, just before Hillary snapped the lid shut on the stay-fresh container.

"Mom! Are you coming? Come on! I want to introduce you to Sheila and I've got to get the grill stoked up for the burgers."

"I really should stay and help Adrian and Hillary finish putting away the appetizers and start bringing out the dishes to pass."

"Nah, they don't need any help. See how well they work together. They got an assembly line going. These two queens got it all under control!" Jay smirked and laughed out loud, the mischievous feint of a rascal gleaming in his eyes.

There was good-natured fun and the trust of friendship in the faux smoldering glares Hillary and Adrian shot back at him. Even love, as they both threw him the finger.

Chapter 25
WHAT ARE YOU GONNA DO NOW, CRY?

3 91 Cliffshore hadn't been hard to find. 'Look for a green ranch', Jay had told her. But Sheila didn't have to look for the color green or search for the number 391 above a garage door. The house with all the cars packed into its driveway and parked in front of it screamed out that this was the place to be.

Sheila drove slowly past the line of cars, parked a few houses down behind an indigo blue mini van, and pulled her keys from the ignition. Next up was to smile, get out of the car, grab her fruit salad off the back seat and step with lively anticipation towards food, drink and sociability. Instead Sheila sat unmoving, clutching her keys in her hand, looking straight ahead with lusterless eyes that saw nothing.

'Make sure you bring your husband. He's invited too.' That's something else Jay had told her. Sheila sighed and turned her head to the right, towards the passenger seat where Gordy usually sat when they went somewhere together. But the only passenger sitting on that seat was her purse.

Gordy was home. Sheila had left him there with a good-bye kiss on the cheek that she had to force herself to give him and a flat out lie. Told him that she was going to the Women Who Love to Read Book Club's annual summer gathering - a ladies only affair. And he'd believed her.

But he shouldn't have! He should have known that they were both invited; that it was to a backyard barbeque at the house of her favorite customer from when she used to work at Betty's Pantry that she was going; that she ran into him at the Ground Hog Garden Store one day and had ended up exchanging phone numbers; that it was him who had surprised her so that afternoon a few weeks ago when the phone rang and it was his voice she heard on the other end of the line, because you know how it usually goes when you exchange phone numbers with casual acquaintances. Gordy should have known all those things because he was right there when the call came in and she'd told him all about it.

But Gordy didn't know. Because Gordy didn't remember. The faceted glass had been in his hand, filled with his third round of scotch on the rocks, and Sheila's words telling him about Jay and the party invitation never soaked into his brain. They sloshed around for a couple hours in a sea of booze instead before he pissed them out and flushed them down the toilet.

It always started out innocent enough. The both of them looking to relax after spending the day mowing the lawn and trimming the bushes or washing and waxing the car, thinking how nice a few appetizers might be (some cheese and crackers, some black olives, maybe a glass of wine) to help them wind down before they started peeling potatoes, slicing up mushrooms and seasoning steaks for dinner.

They'd stand at the kitchen island, nibbling and sipping and chatting pleasantly. Sometimes Gordy might get a twinkle in his eye when he got to the bottom of his glass of wine. He'd pat her on the hand, smile as he gently squeezed her shoulder, and give a sly little wink as he headed over to the china cabinet to get his special glass – the faceted crystal Old Fashioned glass she had given him for their first anniversary. Then he'd head over to the liquor cabinet for the faceted crystal's companion, his favorite, the bottle of McClelland's Highland Single Malt Scotch Whiskey.

The glass got frosty when Gordy filled it with ice. The ice crackled and crazed when Gordy doused it with scotch. And Sheila tried not to crackle and craze like the ice had, praying that this time the innocence would continue, that Gordy would only fill the faceted glass once and their pleasant conversation would ebb and flow as the cheese and crackers made way for steak and potatoes and the sun left the sky. And they'd brush their teeth side by side at the bathroom sink and snuggle together on the bed with a kiss goodnight. And when they woke up the next morning Gordy would still be her hero, the hero he had been since the day they first met. But when he reached for that faceted glass, he rarely filled it only once.

He'd reached for it again last night. That's why she lied, why she didn't want Gordy with her today, why what she should really do was stick her key back in the ignition and leave, why where she really wanted to be right now was nowhere. But Nowhere wasn't really a place.

What was it that made his mouth suddenly become an unsmiling line on a grim face? What had made him set his fork back down on his half eaten plate to stare at her with eyes no longer soft with love but dark and unforgiving? Terrible eyes that he closed to give a long, drawn out, poisonous sigh and reopened to flash like daggers, cutting even deeper than the words that started spewing from his mouth while his lettuce wilted under its Italian dressing and his mashed potatoes got stiff and cold.

'Look around you. You see everything we got here? The nice house, the fireplace, the patio, the shed out back. It's because of me we have what we have. What have you contributed to all this? Nothing! If I had to depend on you, we'd have shit. You're worthless.'

He said that to her! His partner in all things. The one that had helped him build the shed, had even climbed up on the roof with him to pound down the nails as he placed the shingles. The one that had worked ten-hour days, seven days a week for nine months that time he was laid off, and had just now retired at sixty-eight years old. The one that had stood by him and fought for him and believed in him all these years.

'If I hadn't come along you know where you'd be? Standing on some street corner at night ready to spread your legs for every stiff dick that gawked at you through their car window, living on welfare with ten kids, each one from a different father. That's where you'd be.'

140

Is that what he saw when he looked at her, a whore? Did he really hold her in such low esteem? How could he say that to her? She'd only been intimate with three men in her whole life, two before she met Gordy and no one but Gordy after.

'There's that dumb look on your face again. Look at you. You can't even follow what I'm talking about can you? You think you're smart but you're not smart. Every word out of your mouth proves that. You know, all I ever wanted from life was some peace. Some simple peace. And I'm here stuck with a moron.'

Why? Why would he say those things to her?

'Oh boy. Here we go. What are you gonna do now, cry? And blame me for it? It's you who causes all the arguments around here. Why don't you go run off and cry at one of the kid's houses. I can hardly stand to look at you anymore.'

It was the garbage pail that enjoyed their dinners last night. It was an artic slab they laid on, their backs to each other, while Gordy snored and she tossed and turned, punching down her pillow and flipping it onto the dry side.

Sheila was staring emotionless at the stipple ceiling as the pale light of dawn seeped through the window blinds when Gordy rolled over to her side of the bed. He pasted repentant kisses on her face thick with the stink of morning breath that she turned away from and did not want. He tried to offer apologies; vague words of abstract contrition that meant nothing because he knew only that she was upset and that they had argued but not the details of what he was apologizing for.

She could have jogged his memory, tweezed his hurtful words from her bruised soul and thrown them in his face, watched them splat there and run down his cheek like spit. But she didn't have the energy and her mouth was tired of wrapping itself around useless words.

Gordy would never believe that he'd said those things. He would have just scraped those words off and flung them at her again, wondered what was the matter with her, tapped his skull like she was the crazy one, like she had made it all up, like she was a liar.

Instead she got up and made the coffee. She sat silent in the chair across from him, pushing her scrambled eggs around on her plate while Gordy ate his with gusto. And then she did lie as she scooped watermelon and cantaloupe into balls, and sliced strawberries and pineapple and grapes for the fruit salad that she wouldn't be taking to any book club event. And Gordy watched her, trying to make her smile when he snuck a few melon balls or halved grapes off the cutting board to pop into his mouth. But she had no smile to give him.

And the smile she pasted on her face now as she walked towards Jay's house with her harvest gold Tupperware container full of fruit salad was a fake.

The bouncy beat of muffled music ushered Sheila down a gray, fieldstone walkway that led from the front of the house around to the back, almost luring a spring into her step. Almost, but not quite. It was lively, to be sure, but she was not in a lively state and it was no Beach Boys or Bee Gees. Her dogged steps continued.

Just before she rounded the corner, Sheila paused to take a deep breath and reaffix her pretense of a smile and then she stopped completely, caught in a daze of visual overload. She didn't know where, what or who to look at first. There were people smiling at her from under the shade of a towering maple tree, there were people milling about on a large deck that spanned the whole back of the house, there were people sitting under the dome of a canopied gazebo, there was a brick fire pit and a stone-lined pond. And there were flowers! Flowers in pots, flowers in hanging baskets, flowers bordering the cedar fence that surrounded the entire yard.

"Hey, Sheila! Sheila, you came!" A boisterous voice throwing a lifeline. It was Jay calling out to her, as exuberant as she was depressed. He came striding from the far side of the deck to greet her, snagging a tanned and smiling guy that Sheila recognized as his partner, from a group by the picnic table to accompany him.

Jay's arms wrapped around her in a big bear hug. There was strength in his arms and Sheila wanted nothing more than to take comfort there, to rest her head on his shoulder and let him absorb all her woes. But the hug only lasted a moment, an enthusiastic greeting by a casual acquaintance. She barely had time to notice that Jay smelled like cigarettes before he was releasing her from his friendly embrace and putting his arm around his partner instead. "You remember my sweetheart, Adrian."

"How could I not remember?" Sheila summoned a zippy tone to go along with her pasted on smile. "We had such a nice conversation when we met at the garden store. Your yard is beautiful by the way. Who's the gardener?"

"We both do a little. Well, really, Jay does a little and I do a lot. I plant and water and Jay points out the weeds... So I can pull them out!" Adrian quipped. His mouth opened wide in a laugh, his eyes narrowed and crinkled at the corners. It wasn't until his mouth crinkled into a smile and his eyes opened wide instead that Sheila noticed his disparity. Only one eye opened wide. The other drooped and tilted its sights ever so slightly towards his nose.

"Well Adrian, you do a very good job. It's like a park back here. Oh, and here, I brought a fruit salad." Sheila held her bowl out in front of her, determinedly keeping her own eyes off Adrian's lazy eye when he reached in to take it from her.

"Fruit salad. Is that all? What about your husband? Is he bringing up the rear?" Jay craned his neck expecting to see her husband coming round the corner of the house just as Sheila had moments before.

Did he have to bring up Gordy, just when her heavy mood had started to lighten? "He wasn't feeling up to par today so I came alone," she said quickly and just as quickly changed the subject. "You know, I should have brought that fruit salad in a cooler. I guess I wasn't thinking. I hope you still have room in your fridge."

"We'll find some way to fit it in. Did I tell you my mother was here for a visit? She's around here somewhere." Jay glanced this way and that. "Where the hell did she go?" He shrugged his shoulders and continued. "Anyway, I wanted to introduce you. I thought you two might hit it off. She's about your age."

"Aaah, so now it comes out. I was wondering why you'd want to invite an old biddy twice your age to your party."

"You've got it all wrong Sheila. I invited you because I thought you could go around and take people's orders!"

A real smile lifted the corners of her mouth now and spread into her eyes. How she had needed this. Light hearted laughter. A spoon full of sugar to take the bad taste from her mouth. A wisp of fluff to lift her above her despair.

Chapter 26
SHOULD SHE SAY SOMETHING?

"Lynn!" Annie heard Claude call out from somewhere on the deck behind her.

"Claude!" The mystery woman on the lawn called back, waving more vigorously now. The blues and tans of her dress swayed with her, like waves on the ocean.

No need to try and figure out who she was now. It was Claude she was waving at, not Annie.

Lynn started walking, making her way across the lawn. She paused to share a smile and a quick hug with some tall, storky looking guy and then the two of them continued together onto the deck to meet up with Claude.

As Lynn got closer, the abstract hues of her ocean colored dress flowed into recognizable shapes of starfish, sand and water. And her features flowed too, into the recognizable face of someone Annie did know!

Maybe she was Claude's Lynn, but she was Annie's Lynn too! The same Lynn Annie had met just last night at a party hosted by Carl's co-worker Dave and his wife Kathy.

They'd gotten on the topic of movies, and movies that were based on books, and books that were great reads. And how could Annie possibly pass up the chance to mention her own book? Lynn had been so impressed to hear that Annie was an author, albeit a self-published one. She even bought a copy of Annie's book since Annie also couldn't help but mention that she had a few copies in the truck of her car if Lynn had any interest.

Excitedly, Annie rushed over to stand beside Claude as he and Lynn exchanged hugs and greetings. "I know you!" She blurted out, grinning, before the two had barely finished saying 'hello'.

Lynn looked at her blankly for a shocked moment and then her face exploded in a smile. "You've got to be kidding me. I know you too! What are you doing here?"

"I live right next door!"

"Seriously? It really is a small world."

"How do you know Jay and Adrian?"

"I've actually only known them a couple months. I met them through Zach here," Lynn said, patting the tall guy she had arrived with on the shoulder.

Storky Zach was standing sideways to them, conversing with Claude. Annie waited, expecting him to acknowledge Lynn's touch and turn towards them so she could make polite introductions. Instead he paid no attention to Lynn's pat, popped the top on a bottle of beer and guzzled some down. He belched loudly (Annie could almost picture his lips flapping in the burpy breeze), guzzled a little more, then passed the beer on to Claude. If she were Claude, she wouldn't have wanted anything to do with that beer. And she certainly wouldn't have put her mouth on the bottle and taken a sip, like Claude did.

"Is Zach your boyfriend?" Annie felt she had to ask, although she cringed at the thought of it.

"What? No! Zach's gay. We used to work together and now he's just a good friend. Zach's with Claude."

Zach and Claude? How mismatched could a couple be? Zach was six foot to Claude's five and looked to be at least fifteen years older. Annie was about to make a joke but decided against it. She didn't know Lynn at all well, and being that Zach and Claude were her friends, she might take offence.

"Ah, I see," she said instead, keeping it simple. "Jay was telling me Claude just came over from Guyana." Annie's eyes flitted over to see Zach wandering away from them and towards the house with Claude in tow. She gave an inward sigh of relief. "Is Zach the one he's living with then?"

"He is. Zach made all the arrangements to get Claude into the U.S., paid for his airfare and everything. I've got to tell you though, I warned him not to do it. What did he know about this guy? Nothing! He could have been a drug dealer for all Zach knew. Or a thief ready to pull the wool over his eyes and rob him blind. But Claude's really a sweetheart. The three of us have been going out for dinner together once a week. We had Ethiopian the other night! You'd be surprised how much Claude can eat, small as he is. And then Zach... Hey, is that your husband I see over there? I've got to go say hello!"

"Yes, let's go say hello to Carl!" Annie agreed enthusiastically and immediately started to head his way, more than happy to avoid a conversation that seemed headed in the Zach direction. Zach must have some good points if Lynn considered him her friend. And she guessed it was admirable that he was helping Claude. But for reasons she couldn't quite explain; long, tall, rude Zach gave her the creeps.

Another thing Annie couldn't quite explain was why, just as she was approaching the door to the kitchen, she got the sudden feeling that she should stop walking and jump back. It was like when she was driving sometimes and she just knew something was going to happen; the car ahead of her in the right hand lane was going to pull into the barely-big-enough-for-another-car spot in front of her even though they hadn't turned on their turn signal. She let up a little on the gas pedal to add a skosh more room. There was no sense talking chances. And sure enough, over the jerk came. Or like that one time when the traffic light turned green but she stayed put because she just knew that truck going in the opposite direction was going to run the red light. If she had ignored her intuition, she wouldn't have lived to tell about it!

And so Annie heeded her feeling, jumping back just as the door flew open and a tousle-haired toddler flew out followed by Dixie, her blond curls bobbing as she chasing after. Déjà vu. Except this time the toddler Dixie chased was a little boy, not the cheese puff cheeked Michaela.

Like a rabbit he hopped down the wide deck steps just out of Dixie's reach and ran towards a group gathered under the maple tree, with Dixie in his wake.

"Sorry! I hope he didn't hit you with that door," Dixie called out apologetically to Annie as she whizzed past and then, "Mike! Grab Eddie!"

And Annie and Lynn followed behind in Dixie's wake for they were headed in the same direction. Carl was in the group under the maple tree conversing with a young man holding the similarly tousle-haired Michaela in his arms. Most likely the 'Mike' that Dixie had appealed to - her husband and the twin's daddy.

"Whoa there little buddy!" Mike grunted as Eddie ran at him full speed and threw his arms around his knees. "Did Mommy get you all cleaned up?"

"Wanna see fish!" Was Eddie's response. He was tugging on his father's legs from below, as his sister Michaela strained against her fathers' arms from above, anxious to join her brother. It was all Mike could do to keep his balance and ease Michaela down without dropping her.

"Carl!" Annie called out now, as Carl stood there doing nothing but laughing at Mike's predicament. "Can't you see he could use some help with those kids?"

"What?" Carl called back, oblivious, still laughing.

"It's ok. I got it," Mike assured, finally managing to lower Michaela safely to the ground but still working not to topple over as not one, but two kids began tugging on his knees, hopping like bunnies as they tugged, and chanting "Fish! Fish!"

"Did I hear someone say fish? Shall we go see them then?" Dixie swooped in, ever exuberant and full of life. She smiled at Mike, gave him a quick kiss on the cheek, and then took little Eddie by the hand. Mike took Michaela's hand and off the happy family trotted towards the koi pond, Mike looking back to shrug and grin in Carl's direction.

"Remember those days?" Carl chuckled to Annie as she strolled up. "Hey!" He said then, seeing Lynn stroll up too.

"Weren't you at Dave and Kathy's last night? Or am I really that drunk?"

"I don't know about today, but I'm pretty sure you were drunk yesterday." Lynn joked.

"Just give me a little more time. I'll get there!"

"I sure could use another cold beer. You want one too Carl? How about you Lynn?"

Nothing goes better together at parties, than jokes and booze. It was affirmative all around.

Another woman was standing alone a few feet away from them under the tree, looking expectantly towards the house. Annie tapped her on the shoulder. "Hi there! I was heading over to the cooler to get a few beers. Can I get you one?"

She looked at Annie through thick glasses and Annie did a double take. Did she know this woman too? What was it with all these familiar faces today? She was wearing a white blouse and tan capris, but Annie couldn't help picturing her in black slacks and an apron.

"I know where I've seen you before!" She suddenly burst out. "Aren't you a waitress at Betty's Pantry?"

"No to the beer and yes to the waitress!"

Jay came loping over just then. "Here she is Sheila," he began, holding wide his arm to indicate his mother who was a few steps behind him.

Annie smiled and gave Sheila the waitress's shoulder a quick farewell-for-now pat, leaving her in Jay's good company as she made way to the cooler to complete her beer run.

***

All the booze. All the food. All the laughter. All the fun. And now daylight was fading to dusk and Annie was relaxing on a lawn chair enjoying one of her Devil's food cupcakes along with a cup of decaf coffee, thinking about broaching the subject to Carl that it might be time to head home. She knew he was probably thinking the same thing anyway. He was sitting a few lawn chairs down with his own cupcake and coffee; talking to that broad-faced guy she had spoken with earlier, and trying not to yawn.

The party was definitely winding down. Half the crowd had already left but there was still a lively group hovering by the outdoor bar whooping it up with tequila shots. And the biggest whooper, Annie was surprised to see, was Jay's mom, Beverly. 'I'm getting to be an expert!' Annie heard her laugh.

Would the whooping be winding down soon too? Annie hoped so. She was all for having a good time, but she was also all for getting a good night's sleep. Fun that never ended, ended up being no fun at all.

She finished off her cupcake, washed it down with the last of her coffee and leaned back in her chair with a stretch and a contented sigh. A sliver of moon was just visible in the waning light of the setting sun, the sky splashed with golds and pinks and reds.

It was beautiful, that sky. Romantic. The perfect backdrop for the couple Annie spotted standing together on the bridge-like section of deck that led to the gazebo. It was Claude and Zach.

Claude had his arms crossed with his elbows on the deck rail and his hands clasping his upper arms as he gazed out. Zach stood behind him, his arms around Claude as if in an embrace, his hands resting on the deck rail next to Claude's elbows.

But something about this picture felt wrong. 'Romantic' and 'perfect' left Annie's head. Claude should have looked peaceful, held as he was in his lover's arms, washed in twilight's soft glow. But his stance was stiff and defeated. And the circle of Zach's arms around him somehow seemed more like a cage than an embrace.

Annie didn't like it. She had to look the other way. Was there something she should do? Someone she should tell? It suddenly occurred to her that Claude's blue hair might not be simply a fashion statement. Maybe it was really a reflection. Or a window through which to view the despondent blue of his soul.

Maybe it was just past her bedtime.

Annie stood and walked over to stand in front of Carl. "What do you say then, Carl? Are you ready to go? Suddenly I'm just so tired. I swear, I think I'm starting to see things."

Chapter 27
LICK IT, SLAM IT, SUCK IT?

Things that can backfire: A lawn mower, a car, a truck, a joke, a conversation, good ideas, good intentions, good news.

***

In retrospect, it probably hadn't been a good idea to top off her margarita before trotting out the door to follow Jay. His stride was even longer when he swaggered and Beverly's drink kept sloshing over the sides of her cup trying to keep up with him.

"Here she is Sheila, my mom, Beverly," Jay was saying as she stumbled up behind him, attempting to sip her drink and walk at the same time. "I finally found her, downing margaritas in the kitchen."

"What kind of a way is that to introduce your mother? I was not downing margaritas. I've hardly even had one. I spilled most of it trying to catch up to you!"

Sheila laughed and patted Beverly reassuringly on the shoulder. "Don't worry about it. I know how Jay is. He's got the streak of a comedian in him."

"The streak of a comedian. Is that what you call it? I might have called it something else!" Beverly grinned over the top of her margarita.

"Anyway Mom, Sheila here is my favorite waitress at my favorite restaurant. Well, she was my favorite waitress until she left me at the alter. Now she's the only woman that ever broke my heart."

Another joke, but Beverly winced while the other two grinned. Someday she'd be used to this. If anyone were to truly break Jay's heart, it would be man, not a woman. But someday wasn't today. She hid her momentary distress in a big gulp of strawberry margarita as Jay and Sheila continued their lively banter.

"You never gave me a ring, Jay. How was I supposed to know I held the key to your heart? But don't you really mean stomach?"

"No. It's my heart. It sinks to the floor every time I go to Betty's Pantry and you're not there."

"Oh, you poor thing. But wait, I might be able to fix that for you. I've got a Band-Aid I can stick on that broken heart of yours. Betty called me a couple days ago pleading with me to come back, at least temporarily. I hemmed and hawed about it for a few minutes. And then there I was telling her I'd do it."

Had Beverly missed something in this repartee? This was good news, wasn't it? Then why did sadness crash into Jay's composure and sink his smile? What was the word he whispered that he barely had enough breath to say? News that stuttered, popped, and fizzled. News that backfired like a broken hearted joke.

All in a moment. Crash and rebirth. Jay drew in more air and rescued his smile from the depths as Sheila kept talking; unaware her Band-Aid had come with a sting.

"And so it's back to Betty's Pantry I go. I start again Monday."

"Hallelujah! An answer to my prayers. You know I'll be there. I'll bring the family for lunch. Mom, you're gonna love it. So, what..." He paused to clear his throat. "What's going on at the Pantry? Is Betty...." He paused again to fish around in his pocket for his pack of smokes. "...shorthanded or something? Did..." Another pause, this time to stick a cigarette between his lips and light up.

Beverly knew what this was - a cover up, a smoke screen! How many times had she done the same thing? Feigned disinterest to hide the truth; that the topic she couldn't care less about was at that moment the only thing she did care about and that the answer to her 'meaningless' small talk question was equal parts 'have to know' and 'don't want to know' at the same time.

"Is it the new girl?" Jay inhaled deeply and blew out smoke. "Did she..."

"Katie? Quit? You got it. Katie came into work just as scheduled on Thursday and then she told Betty it was going to be her last day. Said something about a family matter. At least she gave Betty one day's notice instead of leaving her completely in the lurch. I should have told Betty. Something in my gut told me that girl wasn't going to last. She was nice enough but she seemed, I don't know, what's the word? Feathery. I mean flighty! Or something like that."

Jay closed his eyes and lost his smile in a sigh. "Feathery. Feathery's right. Because...."

"Jay!" Adrian's shout from the deck blew in to catch Jay's words and scatter them like the wind. "What about the grill? You need to start the grill."

"Oh shit. The grill!" Jay briefly laid his hand on Sheila's shoulder, and smiled and nodded at Beverly before hurrying off to the deck and the grill and the burgers waiting to meet their destiny above the hot coals.

"Who's Katie, someone Jay knows?" Beverly asked as Jay loped away and bounded up the steps onto the deck, figuring Sheila surely would know since she had apparently worked with the girl.

But wait! Sheila was talking at the same time as Beverly; and asking the same question in reverse. "Is Katie someone Jay used to know?"

Sheila didn't know. Beverly didn't know. Did he or didn't he? Unbidden, a television commercial from when Beverly was young materialized in her mind.

"Only his hairdresser knows for sure!" She suddenly spouted.

And what was this? Sheila was talking at the same time as Beverly again. And spouting out the exact same golden oldie line from a Clairol commercial way back when! Their eyes linked in surprise, astonishment lit up their faces, laughter overtook them; two sixty-something women joined at the hip in a blast from the past.

"Oh my!" Beverly tittered, out of breath, trying to rein in her gleeful chortling. "What are the chances?"

"I'd say about a million to one. We ought to cash in on this. Run out right now and buy a lottery ticket." Sheila pulled a tissue from the pocket of her tan capris to dab at her tear-blurred eyes.

And there was Beverly, pulling a tissue from her own pocket and doing the same thing. "Oh my," she laughed again. "I can't believe it! Look at us. We're like twins!

Still tittering, Beverly peered into her plastic cup to see if anything remained to wet her laughter parched whistle. Not even a drop. "Come on twinsy," she said, linking her arm through Sheila's. "Let's get ourselves a couple of drinks!" Arm in arm they went, companions skipping down the yellow brick road towards the land of Margaritaville.

But Sheila turned the margarita down in favor of ginger ale. And not long after dinner, Sheila was bidding Beverly goodbye and making her way back to her car with an empty Tupperware bowl and a foil-covered paper plate loaded with a hamburger, potato salad, broccoli salad and baked beans held securely in her hands to bring home to her Gordy.

"Knowing my Gordy he probably hasn't even thought about getting himself something to eat," Sheila had said as she spooned out the salads. Love had hovered in her voice; a light, sweet cream spread between heavy layers of sadness.

Love, however, had not been attached to the words 'my Gordy' when Beverly brought up the husband topic earlier.

"We're both here man-free. Are you a widow too, just like me?" Beverly had asked as she and Sheila sat chatting in side-by-side lawn chairs in the shade.

Sheila's eye's had dulled. Her smile had gone flat. And Beverly wished she hadn't asked the question. What was she thinking? Maybe Sheila's husband had just passed and the ache of it was still too raw. Maybe she had never been lucky in love and this was a touchy subject. Maybe... Beverly really should have thought of this earlier, given the swing of many of the other party guests. Maybe Sheila was gay!

"No," Sheila finally said, her voice as flat as her smile. "I'm not a widow."

Beverly was searching for something to say next when Sheila had unexpectedly resumed, spurting out angry words wrapped in sarcasm and bordering on despair.

"My Gordy is alive and well and sitting home alone. He's..."

Sheila stopped talking to look away, wringing her hands and sighing. Beverly had the feeling that if Sheila had continued, her next words would have been 'an asshole.'

These were signs Beverly recognized. She had no doubt. "An argument, huh? It happens to us all. My husband and I were the perfect match. I've got my wedding ring on a chain around my neck underneath my shirt to keep it as close as possible to my heart. But we still used to argue. All the time! And always about the dumbest things."

"Yeah. The dumbest things," Sheila had agreed but the dull despair in her voice made it clear 'dumb' wasn't the description she would have used. "He never even remembers," she continued quietly, almost to herself. "If only I could forget."

Suddenly Beverly had felt a hand on her shoulder and looked up to see an effervescent Adrian bubbling at her side. "Hello Mrs. Beverly and Sheila! We're doing lick it, slam it, suck it over at the bar. Come join us."

Beverly had never been so glad to have a conversation interrupted, even though she had no idea what Adrian was talking about. "What did you say? I'm not sure I want to know. You're licking something?"

"Salt! Lick it, slam it, suck it. Tequila shots!"

"That's a big no for me." Sheila's smile, thankfully, had returned. "I don't drink when I've got to drive."

"Are you kidding? Me do a shot of tequila? I've never done a shot of anything in my whole life!" Beverly laughed.

"Maybe later?" Adrian tried again.

"Yeah, right. What a hoot that would be!" Beverly had laughed again and shaken her head.

But after Sheila left, Beverly did find out what a hoot it would be. She wandered over and joined the crowd. Life was short. Why not give it a whirl? Lick that salt, slam down that tequila, suck that lime. And Beverly gave it a whirl more than once. Whooo Hoooo! What a party! Beverly was having the greatest time. The greatest time EVER!

***

Before the porcelain god Beverly knelt. It reminded her of something; that gagging sound she made as she prepared to pray. It was that word she could barely hear. The one Jay had whispered when Sheila told him Betty wanted her back at the restaurant. Except Jay's word was soft, not covered with spit and rough edges like Beverly's. It wasn't really a word that Jay had spoken. Beverly knew now. It was a name.

She was wrong to think a woman couldn't break Jay's heart. There were all kinds of hearts, all kinds of love. Beverly had broken Jay's heart herself with a slap in the face. A hometown girl had broken it too, when she got on a plane forever ago and never came back. And somehow that same hometown girl had broken it again today, in a place far from home.

It was her name Jay had whispered. A name in the shape of a heart with black hair and blue eyes. Khaki.

Could Katie be....? Beverly's stomach lurched anew. "Khaki," she gagged again. Not the soft name Jay had whispered, but a harsh, choking sound that cut short her wondering and drove all thought from her mind as she spewed her sacrifice into the porcelain god's smooth, white bowl.

***

What you do when something backfires: You suck in your startled breath, you duck and run for cover, you learn a lesson, you change the subject, you get down on your knees and pray, "Oh god. Lord help me. Never again, never again, never again."

Chapter 28
PLEASURE OR PAIN?

Pain ripped through him. Or was it pleasure? Hot or cold, pleasure or pain, sometimes they all feel the same. He'd read that somewhere. A poem maybe.

His head swam through whispers and blurs as he cried out, gripped in agony. Or ecstasy? It was good he couldn't tell which it was. Tequila was his friend tonight.

Rock hard, he cried out again as pleasure pumped translucent white onto the mauve sheets and pain stained with red seeped from his ass to run down his thigh.

Zach's hand was on his back now, shoving him flat against the bed, reaching for a tissue to wipe up what he had left behind.

"Your asshole's bleeding again. We're going to have to get you to a doctor so he can take a look at that." Equal parts disgust and concern.

Dot, dot, dot. Too rough, too often. Even a stiff prick should be able to draw a line. Was he laughing now? Or crying? Laughing and crying, sometimes they both sound the same. Betrayal in the pleasure, pain in the pain.

Everything throbbed. And not in a good way. The window blinds were drawn, still the morning sun managed to steal between the slats. Claude winced in the glare as he opened his eyes, making the ache in his head throb even more. At least it drew his attention away from the constant dull throbbing in his ass end. And in his leg. But that throbbing was probably imagined. The scar was just a reminder. The gash the scar replaced had healed in Guyana many months ago.

Zach was sprawled out beside him, still sleeping, with one hairy butt cheek peeking out from the edge of the loosely thrown sheet. Claude eased himself out from under the covers and out of bed, holding his breath to pull a pair of sweat pants over his nakedness and tiptoe out the bedroom door, down the stairs, and to the kitchen.

Carefully he opened the fridge, lifted out the jug of cold water Zach always kept there, and slowly poured some into the glass one of them had left sitting out on the counter. There was a cellophane wrapped package on the counter too; a few cupcakes that Jay must have sent them home with after last night's party. Quietly he peeled off the wrap, thankful it was silent cellophane and not the noisy crinkle of aluminum foil. Coffee he would have to forego. Opening cupboards, running water, the beep of the microwave, the perking of the pot... Noises that would wake Zach. And Claude wasn't ready for Zach.

Claude knew exactly what Zach would do when he woke up. His loud yawn would break the morning silence along with the rush of his piss as he took a leak. After that, down the stairs he'd come, shuffling into the kitchen with another yawn and a sleepy smile; playfully slapping Claude on the butt as he passed by heading for the sink and some water to swish away his morning breath. He'd turn from the sink then and grin, put his hands on Claude's bare brown shoulders to draw him close for a kiss, and run his hands over Claude's chest to pinch his nipples, further to feel the rippling abs of his stomach, further again to slip past his elastic waistband and grab his hot cock. Nothing wrong with any of that. It was affection and the lust of the moment. What any men in love would do. And Claude knew that was how Zach saw him – as his partner and lover.

But then Zach would want more. Zach would want to slam it home. And Zach always got what he wanted when he wanted it. What Claude wanted or didn't want didn't matter. There could be no excuses.

His first night in Zach's house, Claude had been in the shower, letting the warm water wash off the stink of his long flight and the hell of his past when Zach had slipped into the shower with him. Foreplay, play-by-play, post play. Praise and glory be to the lord in heaven. And sex to men on earth.

Of course Zach had seen Claude's scar. Lying together in the bed later, he'd traced the rough, puckered line that ran from Claude's hip half way down his thigh with his finger and kissed it with his soft lips. He'd cried when he heard the story; held Claude in his arms and whispered, 'You're safe now. Safe here with me.'

And Claude had felt safe that night. He had felt joy, believing that hell had been left far behind him.

What he believed changed as the weeks passed and joy didn't find him much anymore. Not like it had found the dude he'd seen in the silver-gray car on the way to Jay and Adrian's yesterday. That dude was feeling the joy all right; rocking it on red in the left hand lane, his fingers drumming thumpita thumpita on the wheel, his head and shoulders grooving and swaying; body and soul one with the music that poured from his radio.

Claude couldn't help but point the dude out to Zach. "Look at that guy in the car over there. He's dancing in the driver's seat!" Claude smiled and started bopping himself in the passenger seat of Zach's car, caught by the beat, searching for the joy.

"Yah, must be some kind of fucking idiot. His whole car's bouncing. All I can say is he better move his ass when the light turns green." Zach had his palm on the horn, ready to blast it as soon as the light changed.

The rockin' dude beat him to the punch. Off the silver-gray car sped, the second red changed to green. Claude tried to keep it in his sights and the fading beat of its music in his ears, but Zach turned right a couple streets after the light and joy was gone.

Claude hated Zach's car. It was dark green. The same dark green as the slick mold that grew on the bathroom walls of the hovel Claude had lived in with his mother, sister and 3-year-old nephew in Guyana.

How hard his mother worked to scrub away that mold, the smell of beach so strong each breath felt like fire and he thought his air passages might dissolve. But it always grew back and she gave up on the scrubbing.

She tried the landlord next. 'Sure. Sure. No problem. I'll get someone over there to take care of it right away.' Yeah, right. Sure he would. Just like he had gotten someone over there right away to replace the cracked toilet that greeted them on the day they moved into the dump.

After a while, when their visions of sitting on the toilet and having it fall to pieces under their asses never materialized, they hardly even noticed that gray line on the white bowl. It was just something they lived with; not perfect, but it did its job and held its own.

Until the night Claude came stumbling home from the bar and his feet tangled with the throw rug in front of that cracked toilet. The crack gave way when Claude crashed down. The water let loose and the toilet reared up, slashing at him with sharp, raw edges. His piss and his blood let loose too, swirling yellow and red into the water that flooded the bathroom floor.

And he'd lain there laughing. Laughing and bleeding and soaking in piss fouled water while his frantic family cursed at him and wailed and ran to pound on the neighbor's door for help.

He didn't laugh in the emergency room. He bled on their black and gray speckled linoleum, rocking in pain, waiting his turn. Waiting for those that came in before him. Waiting for those that came in after him. Waiting while the nurses first coughed to draw his attention and then leered at him; making sure he saw the leer become a caring smile as they turned pointedly away to give their concern to someone else.

Finally his name stumbled blind into his barely conscious ears. They poured a bottle of isopropyl alcohol on the bone-deep gash in his gay boy leg to 'kill germs' while he gripped the sides of the cold metal table he was strapped to and tried not to scream. They irrigated the wound with water and picked around with gloved fingers and metal tools to tweeze out any possible shards of white porcelain while he tried not to thrash and his screams filled the room. They drew a needle in and out, in and out, tugging hard on each stitch, counting their number out loud so he'd know how many he had gotten '…nine, ten, eleven…' and making sure the gay boy knew just how many more stitches he had left to go '…twelve of forty, thirteen of forty…'

Finally they jabbed an antibiotic into his system and sent him on his gay boy way. No instructions, no appointment set for a follow-up visit, no script for a course of further antibiotics, no pain meds. They'd done the whole procedure without an anesthetic anyway. What was the purpose in giving the gay boy pain meds now?

Jay had said it to the author lady with the pink flower in her hair at the party. 'You can't be gay in Guyana.' In Guyana there were leers and threats and ambushes, there were fists and knives and pain and blood. In Guyana he'd probably wind up dead, choking on his own cock with his balls dangling from the end of the rope tied tight around his neck.

It was another world here. Sometimes maybe he'd still hear 'faggot' flung at him from behind or feel a dirty look boring into the back of his neck; maybe he'd see someone point and jeer. But most people were fine with it. They didn't care. It was okay. Okay to be gay.

There was still pain and blood, though. Hell hadn't been left behind. It was still with him. It just came with a different name now.

Chapter 29
A LEPRECHAUN?

Consciousness came to him slowly with soft light, roasted warmth, and a sharp bite – the morning sun, the smell of coffee, and the smell of cigarette smoke. Adrian didn't even remember going to bed, but in bed he was. On bed actually. It was the rough denim of his jeans he felt on his sprawled out legs, not the smooth lightness of the sheets. And the quilted lines of the coverlet were under him rather than over him.

He did remember trying to clean up – blundering about to collect bottles and cans left abandoned on the picnic table or under lawn chairs, holding them upside down to drain their dregs out onto the grass. But he kept tripping and stumbling and loosing track and the empties he'd drained kept slipping from his fingers before he could get them over to the bins meant for their disposal to drop them in.

And Mina had made such nice signs for those bins too - twelve-inch squares of sturdy cardboard, with arrows pointing the way and big block letters in permanent marker:

EMPTIES GO HERE

Why had so many empties not ended up there?

Jay had passed out on the living room chair at least an hour before the last party guest headed for home. Adrian remembered that too. And he remembered laying the chenille throw they kept on the back of the couch over Jay to warm him in his drunken slumber.

There was no evidence that Jay might have come stumbling into the bedroom in the wee hours of the morn to flop down beside Adrian. He must have spent the whole night on that chair.

Adrian rose and headed for the bathroom where another remembrance from the night before came to him as he stood streaming yellow into the toilet bowl.

'Mrs. Beverly,' he had called out with a gentle tap on the bathroom door. 'Are you okay in there? Do you need any help?'

'No,' she had croaked. 'I'm fine.'

'Thank god,' he had thought. A yes reply would have ended in a retch fest; with Adrian tossing his cookies into the bathroom sink while Mrs. Beverly tossed hers into the toilet.

He sort of remembered opening the door a crack anyway to slip in a can of ginger ale. Ginger ale always helped to ease his stomach after a bout of unpleasantries and it would have been a thoughtful thing to do. But he wasn't sure he had really done it. The bathroom door in his memory swirled like fog or steam, and the woman hunched over the bowl who was supposed to be Mrs. Beverly had spiky carrot-orange hair and didn't look like Mrs. Beverly at all.

It had to have been a dream. Hopefully her stomach had settled anyway, without his act of thoughtful gallantry, and her overindulgences wouldn't send her to hug the toilet bowl again this morning with a headache raging behind her eyes and its pounding beat escalating with each sour heave.

The warm roasted smell that Adrian had woken to called to him again as he left the bathroom and he headed for the kitchen, lured to the coffee by his nose. He wasn't sure his stomach wanted to follow his nose, though. Mrs. Beverly might not be the only one needing a ginger ale fix this morning.

Silence was the only thing he heard as he made his way down the hall - the silence of sleep from behind Mrs. Beverly's door and the silence of absence from behind Mina's. Mina had left their party early for a more to her liking sleep over event at her girlfriend's.

Silence of the absent kind also came from the living room. Adrian knew he wouldn't see Jay still sleeping in the chair where he had crashed last night. He had smelled Jay's cigarette, and of course, it must have been Jay that made the coffee. But he glanced at the chair anyway, with a soft smile. Only the chenille throw was there, looking so much like a little grey dog curled tail to nose in sleep that Adrian had to resist the urge to go over and pet it.

And now, on to the kitchen. Adrian closed his eyes, bracing for the worst; the freshly brewed pot on the granite counter amidst a chaos of spilled liquids, dried solids and un-discarded discards. He opened his eyes and there it was, the coffee pot and... Nothing! Not one speck of food or drink sullied the counter. Not one dirty dish, half filled plastic cup or soiled napkin was to be seen.

It was probably all in the garbage pail. One sweep of an arm could have gathered and dumped it all into the pail's wide maw, to be packed down with a foot and hidden, stuffed to the brim, under the self-closing lid. Adrian just had to see. Over to the pail he went, onto the step he pressed his toe, up popped the lid and inside was... Nothing again! Nothing except the clean plastic bag the pail was lined with.

Practically giddy, Adrian followed his nose back to the coffee pot. It smelled too good to resist. Warm, dark and roasty won over the cold fizz of ginger ale. He poured a big mug half full, paused and then filled it nearly to the top. Black was the way to go today, just in case his slightly queasy stomach decided to complain about the milk.

From the kitchen window, Adrian could see that the deck and yard had been cleaned up too. Every lawn chair was put away. The coolers were tipped at an angle and leaning against the fence to drain and dry; the ice they had held heaped like a pile of winter snow on the lawn, melting in the summer sun.

Grinning, he walked outside with his coffee, his nose luring him this time to the one he loved via the sharp burn of tobacco. Adrian didn't really need to follow his nose. He could see Jay smoking by the koi pond, blowing smoke rings out over the water, his white sleeveless t-shirt like a beacon against the dark wood of the bench on which he sat. The shirt he'd been wearing at the party was tossed over one of the maple tree's low-slung branches, flapping like a flag in the breeze.

"Hey Babe," Jay said, quietly subdued, as Adrian walked up. He tossed down his cigarette, ground it out with the toe of his sneaker and took up his coffee cup instead, making room on the bench for Adrian to sit beside him.

"Good morning my darling man." Adrian set his own coffee mug in the gravel at the base of the bench to take Jay's head between his hands and give him a big smoochy kiss. "I wake up to think a big mess will be waiting for me and instead I find everything all cleaned up."

"I can put it all back the way I found it if you want." No hint of a smile was on Jay's face.

"No, I don't want!" Adrian's wide eyes flitted across Jay's face looking for the tease.

"Everyone else was still zonked when I woke up and the first thing I said was 'look at all this shit Adrian's going to have to take care of.' But then I figured, I know how to clean up. I can do it. So I did. I don't want you to be disappointed though. Seriously, I can put it all back. I'm really good at making messes too." Jay took a sip of his coffee and looked Adrian right in the eye, straight faced and serious. And then the grin came. "Babe, you should see your face. You are so easy to screw with!"

Out shot Adrian's arm. Instinctively, Jay flinched and jerked back, wincing in preparation for the slap he saw coming. And the slap connected - nothing more than the gentlest of touches brushing across Jay's stubbly whiskered cheek.

"Two can play that game." Adrian smirked, his eyes sparkling playfully. "I know how to screw with you too."

Jay leaned in, pulling Adrian into his arms to whisper in his ear. "I like the way you screw, my love. Let's screw right here, right now." His hand was on Adrian's crotch, molded around the shape that grew firm under his touch. He lowered the zipper and drew Adrian forth, skin upon skin.

It took all the willpower Adrian could gather to lay his hand over Jay's, halting it as it fondled and pumped; to stop his own tongue from exploring Jay's mouth and make it form words instead. "Jay, we can't." He meant to sound firm, but his voice was breathy with longing.

"Mina's not home, remember?" Jay whispered, his warm breath mixing with Adrian's as his tongue caressed Adrian's lips.

"Your mom. Your mom's here. She might wake up and see." Adrian closed his eyes as Jay's hand tightened around him one more time before releasing him. He inhaled deeply and exhaled slowly as he readjusted and zipped back up.

"Shit." Jay stood, unsettled, pacing lust off, back and forth, back and forth by the pond's edge, stopping finally to pull the familiar green and white package of Newport 100s out of his pocket and light up. The smoke wafted over the water along with his disappointed gaze.

There was more in Jay's disappointed gaze than unrequited sex. Something in the slight sag of Jay's shoulders, in the way he flicked the ashes from the end of his smoke, told Adrian that; and also told him that whatever it was, Jay wasn't ready to talk about it.

Jay didn't gaze out over the water for long. A couple more puffs, a shuffle of the feet and a sigh and Jay was turning his head to look at Adrian again, the touch of a smile on his full lips. His smile grew wider and his eyes grew soft as he turned further to blow Adrian a kiss and mouth a hushed 'I love you.'

"I love you too," Adrian whispered back and patted the bench beside him. "Come, sit back down."

And Jay did.

"It was a great party, wasn't it?" Adrian started slowly. "I know I had a good time."

"Yeah, I did too. A great time! I think everybody did. Except maybe Mina."

"You don't think she had a good time? I saw her talking and smiling with Dixie and Mike and playing with the twins and laughing with Claude. They were both touching his blue hair."

"She was probably asking him what kind of dye he used. If she's thinking about dying her own hair some wild color, she better stop thinking about it right now. No way in hell. Anyway, she couldn't wait to get outta here when her girlfriend, Beth, called to invite her to go to a movie and out for pizza with her family and then to spend the night. She was practically pleading with me to give her the okay. I talked to Beth's goon ball dad when he came to pick her up. He's a nice guy though. He's going to drop Mina off home this afternoon."

"You know who I think had the best time? Your mom!"

"Yeah, I'll say. She caught up pretty well for someone who spent the first half of the party drinking coffee."

"Oh, she was so funny. She was laughing and living the life! Every time I looked at her she was either slurping on a margarita or refilling her glass. It's my fault. I got her started on those margaritas and created a leprechaun."

"A leprechaun? Don't you mean a monster?"

"No, a leprechaun. You know, one of those mischievous little Irish fairies."

"I thought you were the fairy." Innocence with a sly grin.

"I'll ignore that." A playful glint. "Anyway, you'll never believe what she asked me. She asked me - who does the boinking?"

"You're not serious."

"I am serious! She comes up to me and she says 'I'm on a mission. I want to know things. And the most important thing is, who does the boinking?' I thought I'd die!"

"Well, did you tell her?" Jay nearly choked on the question, tangled as it was in a fit of laughter.

"No! What am I supposed to say? Claude saved me when he came over with a round of shots. She got sidetracked with him and forgot about me. I am telling you, my face was so red."

169

Adrian fanned his face now, hot again just thinking about it. "You know your mom got sick last night. I heard her throwing up in the bathroom."

The sudden slamming of a door coming from the house had Adrian on his feet. "Oh no. I don't like the sound of that."

"Where are you going?" Jay called after him as he strode purposefully away.

"I should have done it before but I only dreamt it," he called back over his shoulder. "It'll make her feel better."

"What ever you just said makes no sense. Do you know you're not making sense?"

"It's for your mom. I'll tell you later," Adrian called over his shoulder again before he pulled open the screen door and went inside.

Mrs. Beverly's distressful moan met his ears as he fished around in the fridge for the ginger ale, her choking 'gack' as he popped the top on the can, a chunky splash and...

'Sorry Mrs. Beverly,' Adrian thought as he sprinted to the sink, trying to keep in what wanted to come out, 'this one is my ginger ale now.'

Chapter 30
WHAT HAD THEY TALKED ABOUT?

A drian was holding open the entry door as the women folk, first his mom and then Mina, went inside; looking quizzically over the top of Mina's disappearing head at Jay, still standing by the car.

"Are you coming?" he called out, his words just barely audible over the distance.

"Go on in." Jay motioned with his arm. "I'll be there in a sec." And held up his cigarette. "I've got to finish my smoke." A lame excuse for lagging behind.

Any other time Jay's half smoked Newport would have hit the pavement and been snuffed out as soon as their destination was reached. Especially if it was lunchtime and their destination was Betty's Pantry.

Betty's Pantry! And Sheila was back! Good service, a friendly smile, a witty jibe, food per his order, hold the lettuce and tomato. But there would be no mysterious black haired waitress baiting his memory and slipping into the kitchen before he could get a closer look, sending another to his table in her stead, hiding behind a new name.

Yes, Sheila was back. And that was something to be glad about, even if it was only temporary. But Sheila was back because Khaki was gone. And Jay knew that was permanent. Why had she come in the first place? It would have been better if she hadn't.

His cigarette was nearly down to the filter, its red glow extinguishing, its smoke sputtering out. There was no excuse left to take a drag on. Jay tossed it down, stomped on it for good measure and walked into Betty's Pantry to slide into the booth next to Adrian.

And there was Sheila, materializing at the end of the booth with the coffee, cola and strawberry milkshake the others had already ordered and another cola on speculation for him.

"Is cola okay for you, Jay?" Sheila asked as she set the ice filled drink before him. "Adrian and I concurred it would either be coffee or cola and since it's a hot day, we went with the cola."

"Cola is perfect." And the straw changed from clear to brown as he sucked some down.

"It's Friday, you know Jay," Sheila scolded. "I've had my eye on that door every day since Monday expecting you to show up."

"I said I was bringing the family this week. Isn't Friday still this week? I'm a man of my word, Sheila. I was just saving the best for last." Jay smiled, his spirits lifting. He wasn't even aware that his eyes were scanning the restaurant.

"The last of what?" Sheila wondered.

"My visit," his mom piped up. "I'm leaving Tuesday."

"Leaving already?"

"It's not 'already'. I've been here nearly two weeks!"

"Time flies when you're having fun, right?"

"It really does!" His mom was shaking her head in an emphatic yes.

"And that's why I wanted the experience of Betty's Pantry to be on the tail end of her visit so she'd remember it best. Now she'll rave about Betty's Pantry to all her friends back in Croakers Norge instead of The Hideaway or The Striped Spinnaker," Jay explained.

"The Striped Spinnaker? When did we go there? Is that where I got the fettuccine alfredo?"

"See!" Jay grinned as he opened his menu.

"Well now, let me tell you our specials." Sheila was grinning too with her hand on Beverly's shoulder. "New England clam chowder is our soup for today. And we have a delicious fish sandwich that comes with one side. We also have Cincinnati spaghetti. It's very popular. Homemade chili on top of spaghetti instead of the usual tomato sauce. And Beverly, you've never been here so you probably don't know, but we offer breakfast all day. We're famous for our biscuits and sausage gravy. I think you'd love it. Let me give you a few minutes to decide and then I'll be right back."

Jay's eyes followed Sheila as she walked away. But when she stopped at the next occupied booth, his eyes did not stop with her. He spotted Rayanne coming out of the kitchen with two plates loaded with something red and steaming, probably the spaghetti special. And was that actually a smile on her face? He saw two middle-aged women laughing together by the register as they paid their bill.

And farther down? He craned his neck. Maybe he'd spot her coming out of the adjoining room. Maybe she was... She who? It was then Jay realized what he had been doing since he walked in the door, like a bad habit, searching and still hoping for a glimpse of Khaki. A girl he'd probably never see again.

"I'm torn," his mother was saying as Jay shook his head to chase Khaki out of it and turned his attention back to the table and the people he was with, "between the Cincinnati spaghetti and the biscuits and sausage gravy. What are you getting Jay?"

"Not the Cincinnati spaghetti! I don't like the beans. I'm going with the fish sandwich. And a side of fries."

"What about you Adrian?"

"That's what I'm getting too. The fish sandwich. And the chowder. I love the New England."

"Everybody's getting the fish! Are you getting the fish Mina?"

"I think a hamburger and onion rings. Or maybe a hamburger and mac and cheese. Can I get both sides Dad? Dad?"

"What? Both sides? I think that's a song."

"What are you talking about? I'm talking about mac and cheese and onion rings. Can I order both of 'em?"

"Sure, go ahead." *'Focus, Jay. Focus.'* "But I've got first dibs on the leftovers."

There were no leftovers. Every bite of Mina's rings and pasta disappeared from her plate. She only ate half the burger but Jay scarfed the rest of that down after his golden brown fish - crunchy on the outside, moist and flaky on the inside – went down his hatch. Adrian spooned up every drop of thick and creamy chowder. And 'yum' was his mother's pronouncement with each and every mouthful of biscuits and sausage gravy.

And Sheila's excellent service was beyond compare. Moments after they had all savored their last bites, Sheila was back to clear away the empty plates. "Looks like we've got a table full of happy campers here. Did anyone save room for dessert? We've got a lemon…"

"Don't even tell me!" his mom interrupted. "I might be tempted to say yes and I am so full!"

"Anybody else interested? I can whisper the choices in your ear so Beverly doesn't hear."

"Nooo. I couldn't eat another bite." Adrian patted his stomach.

And nobody else could either.

"Well, you all just sit here and relax and I'll be right back with your check." And Sheila was off again.

"That was so good!" His mother wiped her mouth one more time and laid her napkin on the table. "You know, I just remembered, something reminded me of her the other day."

'Her' his mother had said. And Jay automatically tensed. The 'her' to whom his mother referred was going to be Khaki. Somehow he knew. And he was right.

"Khaki Campbell! Whatever happened to that girl? I used to ask her mother about her now and then but she always seemed to change the subject. I got the impression Khaki moves around a lot. Have you ever heard anything from her Jay? The two of you used to be so close."

Jay felt Adrian's eyes on him. He hadn't even told Adrian yet how his meet up with Khaki had gone. And he was glad Adrian hadn't pressed him about it. But if he had, what would Jay have told him?

How had the meet up gone? Good? Bad?   The answer was 'both' and 'neither' and the exchange had left him depressed and bruised; feeling like a healed over wound ripped wide open again, raw and tender to the touch. And Khaki had taken wing again and slipped through his fingers. And Jay didn't want to talk about it. But he guessed he had to. Or, he could just tell his mother 'no'. But Jay didn't like to lie. And in his thirty-four years, he'd already lied way too many times.

"I… She… Actually I saw her last week. She happened to be in town and stopped…"

"Oh! Is that the lady who came to the door when we were leaving for the airport to get Grammy?" Mina butted in. "She seemed weird, but kind of pretty though."

"Well, did you get a chance to talk to her? How is she?"

"She's good. Fine. Been busy." Skim the surface. The less said the better.

"Busy doing what? You haven't seen each other in ages. Didn't you talk about anything?"

Jay pushed the ice around in his glass with the straw, stirring the cola that still remained into a whirlpool, watching the ice spin round in its wake. What had they talked about? Confused directions and seagull's wings, penis's and sex crazed teenage girls, old regrets and gristled excuses and friendship lost.

Had she thought to rekindle that friendship? Leaving again was a funny way to do it.

Had she thought her disjointed explanations would be a catharsis? He felt emptier now than he had when she first left fifteen years ago. Not empty really. How could he feel empty when he had Adrian? Upended. Upside down. That's how he felt.

And what had they talked about? Nothing.

"She likes to travel and see new things so she never stays in one place too long. She's been all over, to almost every state in the U.S." Jay paused, wondering if that was enough Khaki feed to satisfy his mother. Apparently one of the folds in his cerebrum decided it wasn't, because there was his mouth opening and he was saying more. "I told her you were in town and I even invited her to the barbeque we had last Saturday."

"Really! I would have loved to see her. But I guess she couldn't come, huh?"

"No. She was going to be gone already."

And then there was Sheila to drop off the check and turn the tide.

"Oh, hey! Jay, I wanted to tell you, Betty did hire another new girl but not to fear, I'm going to stay on. Only part time though, starting in two weeks. Thursdays and Fridays from seven to three."

"That's great Sheila! Those will be the days for me. I'll engrave it on my brain. Thursdays and Fridays only." Jay stood up then and kissed Sheila on the cheek. Kissing waitresses in restaurants wasn't something he normally did, even if the waitress was Sheila, but he felt it was something he really needed to do today.

Life was always shifting. People came and went. Habits, likes and dislikes had a tendency to change from time to time.

Jay used to like to chew gum. But he didn't like to chew gum anymore.

It used to be his habit to have a cup of hot chocolate after shoveling snow on a cold winter's day. Hot chocolate gave him a stomachache now.

Used to be that he would shave religiously every single morning before he went to work. Now, he only shaved twice a week. And never down to the bare skin.

It used to be his habit to go to Betty's Pantry for lunch too. At least two or three times a week. But it would be along time before Jay went to Betty's Pantry again now.

Habits change. He hoped Sheila would understand.

Chapter 31
WHO WOULD EVER HAVE THOUGHT?

Flowerless though they were, Beverly's favorite garden occupants were the lamb's ears. The leaves were furry and velvety soft, exactly like their namesake Beverly imagined, and, as she could never resist doing every time she perused the garden, she bent low now to rub the grey/green leaves between her thumb and forefinger.

Behind the lamb's ears grew the lavender. Beverly ran her hands over the tall spires and then stuck her fingers under her nose for a good whiff of the lovely scent.

What the other flowers and plants in the garden were called, Beverly couldn't say, even though Adrian had pointed out and named each one for her when he gave her a tour on her second day there, after the mulberry muffins they'd snacked on had moderated a tentative peace between them.

"That tall yellow one in the back is yarrow."

"Did you say yellow?" Beverly had to ask him to repeat. She was no gardener. The names were unfamiliar to her. And with Adrian's accent complicating things, she couldn't even guesstimate.

"No. Is called yarrow." He'd enunciated so carefully. It still sounded like yellow to Beverly. "And this pink one is phlox."

"Fox? Like foxglove? I think I've heard of that one!"

"I don't think it's the same. This one is phlox."

After a while she'd just followed along, pointing with her mulberry stained fingers and oohing and aahing in admiration. What did it matter? Short and pink or tall and red, fluffy or flat, yellow or yarrow. Which was which and what was what would

177

never stick in her head anyway. And, except for the easy to remember lamb's ears and lavender, all the other names had gone in one ear and out the other.

Beverly continued down the garden past the yellows, purples, pinks and whites to stop in front of a section that was separated from the rest by a filigreed metalwork border fence and ended at the gazebo. Seashells, resin cherubs, and colorful wire and glass butterflies on copper stakes decorated the spaces between the plants here. Attached to the stockade fence at the garden's back was a large black metal plaque - words in raised letters, gold upon the black:

You May Have Left
My Life
But You Will Never Leave
My Heart

"What's this garden?" Beverly had asked on that first tour, wiping away a muffin crumb that was tickling the corner of her mouth. "It looks special."

"This is for my mother." Adrian's voice had cracked. "To honor and remember her. I loved her very much."

"It's beautiful." That was all she said. And then she'd moved on down to the next section.

Why hadn't she put her arm around his shoulder and given him a little squeeze of comfort or at least shown some interest by asking what his mother had been like or when she had passed? That she hadn't done any of those things stuck in her craw now. She had been so nervous and uncomfortable around him then, though.

How she had changed over the last two weeks.

Beverly held her lavender scented fingers under her nose again as she walked up onto the deck and into the house. Jay was lugging her suitcase and her carry-on, one in each hand, out the front door while Mina held it open for him. And Adrian was doing a last minute room-by-room sweep to make sure nothing 'Beverly' had missed her own previous sweeps. Tears welled up in her eyes.

And those two weeks ended today.

Truthfully, after two weeks of being away from home, it would be good to get back to normal. Beverly was looking forward to pushing open her newly painted elderberry front door and walking into her wicker colored house; to snuggling up with her own pillow in her own bed.

Yesterday she had been almost gleeful as she went about in search of her far flung belongings - her sweater from the front closet, her sneakers from the mat by the back door, her book of Sudoku puzzles from the coffee table – to lay beside all the other items waiting to be organized for flight and packed into her suitcase.

But now that the time for good-byes had actually come? All Beverly wanted to do was stay.

What a wonderful two weeks it had been.

And Beverly had a flash drive loaded with photos, and an extra ten pounds, to prove it. She had a Facebook page too! Mina had gotten her all set up and showed her how to share her vacation photos with her friends. Beverly had three friends already – Mina, Jay and Adrian.

Jay had taken lots of pictures. He was, after all, a photographer. Board game night, the zoo, the beach, the amusement park, goofy faces, head thrown back and snoring faces, and Beverly pouring syrup on a stack of Adrian's peanut butter pancakes. There were no pictures of drunken Beverly though. No lick it, slam it, suck it. Thank the lord.

Breakfast - that's where the extra ten pounds came in. Back home in Croakers Norge, morning meant a bowl of Multigrain Cheerios and skim milk. Not so here. Every day began with Adrian (Maura was his last name and Bogotá was the city in Colombia that he had come from. Beverly had asked) cooking a big breakfast – mulberry muffins or peanut butter pancakes, eggs in a frame or bacon, ham, and sausage scrambled eggs. And, of course, after breakfast came lunch. And after lunch, dinner.

Not that Beverly was complaining.

Of all the photos Jay had taken, the most beautiful was the one of the peacock at the zoo. Had it gotten out of its cage or was it supposed to be running loose? Beverly wasn't sure, but regardless, it had been standing, tall and iridescent blue, next to the path they were following on their way to the elephant enclosure. Adrian (New York City. That's where he had been living before he moved upstate to be with Jay. Beverly had listened) had clucked at it as they passed and it had started following them.

It watched the elephants munch on hay with them. It followed as Adrian clucked to watch the llamas amble and the timber wolves prowl with them. And when Adrian lingered to watch the wolves a little longer as the rest of them headed for the mountain goats, the peacock stayed behind with him.

Beverly turned to look back when she heard Adrian talking to the peacock between smiles and clucks. The peacock bobbed and flapped and clucked in return. And then it happened! She clutched at Jay's arm, knocked Mina on the shoulder, and tried to hold her voice into a whisper so as not to disturb the amazing sight that was unfolding before them. Her whisper failed. 'Jay! Mina! Look!' She squealed excitedly.

Luckily the peacock paid her squeal no mind. Out fanned his tail feathers and the already spectacular bird grew more spectacular still; beauty bejeweled - eyes of turquoise and indigo ringed by gold and orange floating in plumes of feathery black and charcoal gray; a glorious display to be captured perfectly by Jay and his camera.

Captured too was the peacock's courtship dance as it strutted before Adrian; professing its love, proving its virility, persuading that it was the one Adrian should pick above all others to make an egg with.

Mina couldn't keep her wide eyes off the bird. Jay couldn't stop laughing. And Beverly couldn't wait to see how the love story would progress. What would the peacock do when Adrian turned down its advances? But Adrian (Orchard View Assisted Living. That's where he worked. Adrian was the activities director. Beverly had learned) couldn't wait to high tail it out of there. He was afraid to find out!

The four of them all scooted away undercover of the crowd that had gathered to snap pictures of the stunning, boastful bird, leaving it to bask in its moment of fame for a while before it realized its love was unrequited.

What a happening day it had been at that zoo. Beverly had to say though, that her number one favorite had been the day they'd spent at Elwanger Beach Park. The bright sun, the fluffy white clouds, the cool breeze off the lake, her scoop of maple walnut with chocolate sprinkles. (Jay had turned down the ice cream. And he'd steered clear of the carousel too. Beverly wasn't sure why). And the sand castle contest! Seventeen teams of two - armed with shovels, cans, boxes and pails - had ninety minutes to build the best sand castle ever.

'Winterfell!' Mina had shouted with her fist in the air when the whistle blew signaling the countdown had started.

'Winterfell? What kind of name is that? Shouldn't we call it Summerfell?'

'Yeah, right. Funny, Grammy!' How Mina had laughed as she dug in with her bare hands and started mounding sand up around her.

What was so funny? Summerfell made a lot more sense.

Whatever, their castle was a masterpiece in sand - two-feet tall with towers, parapets, turrets and drawbridges. Beverly thought for sure she and Mina would win. Until the whole thing toppled over before the judges had a chance to see it. Luckily Jay snapped a picture before Winterfell/Summerfell fell.

There was no chance of Jay and Adrian's entry toppling over. Their castle was long, low and cylindrical with one end rounded and the other end flanked by two identical globes. Jay told the judges it was a grand banquet hall, with one of the globes housing the huge ovens for baking bread and roasting meats and the other globe being the kitchen. They didn't notice the mischief in Jay's eyes or Adrian's impish grin.

It truly was an elaborate affair; the grounds around it landscaped with seaweed ponds and pine needle bushes, and a pebble walkway that led to the ridged dome of the one-eyed entryway in the rounded front. Beach glass gem windows embellished the ridge itself and ran along the grand banquet hall's sides, and pinecone smoke stacks sat atop the twin orbs at its back.

The judges were fooled. But not Beverly. And she tried not to laugh too hard when the judges awarded the blue ribbon to a fine specimen of the male anatomy.

That sand castle penis was very photogenic. Beverly had Mina put it up as the cover photo on her Facebook page.

Another photo Beverly loved was the one Mina had taken of Jay and Adrian (Radiation treatments. His lazy eye was a side effect. He was a lung cancer survivor. Beverly had learned this too), their arms around each other as they stood on the beach at the waters edge in the day's fading light; the sun a glowing orange ball behind them.

Jay's face was aglow too, with love and happiness and peace. He was where and with whom he had always been meant to be. How could Beverly ever have wished more for him? More? That's the word she would have used before. Less was the word she would use now. How could she ever have wished for him anything less?

And now her suitcases were in the trunk of Jay's car. Tomorrow she'd wake up in Croakers Norge and she wouldn't see her son!

Her son! He had grown inside her. She used to read him bedtime stories. She had helped him fill out his college applications.

Or her granddaughter! How Mina used to giggle when she was a baby. Beverly used to push her on the swing. Now she was a teenager. Soon she'd be a woman. She was growing up so fast.

Maybe they'd looked at the calendar wrong. Maybe today really wasn't the day. Beverly should make Jay take her suitcase back to her room. How could she possibly leave? She was going to miss Jay and Mina so much.

And Adrian? Well...

It had been on Beverly's mind for days but the time never seemed right. But two days ago she had done it. Jay and Mina were out at the store and Adrian was sitting at the kitchen table opening the mail.

She sat down beside him, her face awash with affection, took his hand in hers... And then she had modified the wrong noun, dropped a clause and left half of her thoughts unspoken in her head. No wonder his face had fallen instead of lighting in a smile.

"Well, this is sure not what I expected. I thought we'd grown close." Beverly's eyes flitted across Adrian's face in confusion, trying to fathom his unexpected reaction. "I thought you'd be touched that I want you to call me mom."

"You say 'I'm going to regret asking you this but call me mom'. Regretting doesn't show having grown close. Regretting doesn't make me happy. Regretting takes the happy away."

"I didn't say I was going to regret you calling me mom. Well, if I did that's not what I meant. Why would I ask you to call me mom if I didn't want you to?"

"I don't know, but I'm hurt. I'm hurt, Mrs. Beverly."

"See, right there. Mrs. Beverly. The way you say it. That's what I meant!" Beverly beamed, sure it would all make sense to Adrian now.

He stared at her blankly, if anything his face fell even more, and then he pushed away from the table, coughing a little into the crook of his elbow as he stood and started to walk away.

"Now just hold on there one minute!" Beverly jumped up to stand in front of Adrian with her hand on her hip. "This isn't going at all the way I planned. I know I was a bitch when I first got here and I know I didn't treat you very well but then you were so nice to me and I got to know you and... Listen, let me start over." Beverly grabbed for Adrian's hand again. "Adrian, I have grown very fond of you and I would like it very much if you would call me Mom. What I'm going to regret is that when you call me Mom, you won't call me Mrs. Beverly anymore. And I love the way you say Mrs. Beverly. It kind of dances on your tongue. 'Mrs. Beverly'" Beverly adopted a lilting flutter, trying to mimic Adrian. "Makes me sound like someone young and beautiful. Instead of dumpy old me."

There was the tear. There was the happy smile she had expected. "Oh, Mrs. Beverly, don't think you aren't beautiful. You are beautiful. Mom will sound nice too. I will love calling you Mom."

The airport wasn't as confusing as it had seemed to be on the day of Beverly's arrival. She signed in, checked her suitcase and stood outside the security checkpoint with her family. There was nothing else to be done. They couldn't follow her through to the gate and wave from behind the large glass windows as her plane took off like they might have done before the days of 9/11. Nothing left now but good-byes.

It was a quick embrace she shared with Mina. A teenager's denial. But her granddaughter's eyes were as moist with tears as Beverly's.

Jay. He had been a helpless infant in her arms. Now his strong arms were wrapped around her. She felt warmth there, and love, and forgiveness. And she felt an ache in her breast and tears run down her cheek as he kissed the top of her head and whispered 'I love you, Mom' into her hair.

And then there was Adrian, with his accent and his gardens and his margaritas, with his caring and his thoughtfulness. She could hardly bear for the hug to end.

Who would ever have thought? The biggest surprise. It was Adrian she would miss most of all.

Chapter 32
BABE, ARE YOU ALL RIGHT?

Spring had become summer and now summer was heading towards fall and the constant tension of indifference and disdain was wearing Adrian down.

Ignoring Mina's aloofness and the disrespect she continued to throw at him without ignoring her. Engaging her in conversation even though he knew she would rather that he kept his mouth shut and left her alone. Pretending things between them were still the same as they used to be. These were all becoming burdens. Burdens increasingly difficult for Adrian to handle.

But handle them he must because there was Mina, already in the kitchen that Adrian was just entering. He was heading for a glass of water to help suppress a cough being egged on by the tight feeling in his chest and the dry tickle in his throat. She was putting a slice of left over pizza into the microwave and closing the door; three times it beeped as she pressed the controls for her desired warming time.

Adrian managed a quick smile in Mina's direction before the coughs erupted; three, just like the microwave, only in barks instead of beeps. He reached into the cupboard for a glass and filled it with tap water, coughed once more to clear his throat and then drank some down, putting the cough to rest.

When he turned back around, Mina was looking right at him. He smiled again, hopeful. Despite everything, he was always hopeful. "So, school starts again in two weeks. Are you excited?"

And, just because he was hopeful, Adrian considered the slight upturn of Mina's lips to be a smile in response, but there was no shine in her guarded look and it held no warmth. Neither did her voice. "I guess."

"And next week is your birthday! Sweet fourteen!"

"Sweet goes to sixteen." The microwave beeped again, a momentary invasion into the dull scorn of Mina's tone, and she popped open the door to retrieve her pizza. "Fourteen is nothing."

"What do you mean fourteen is nothing? It is too something!" Adrian clung to upbeat and the chance that his bubbly might win over her scorn. "It's a special…"

"It's a saying. Sweet sixteen is a saying." Mina sneered over her shoulder as she walked away with her plate. "Nobody says sweet fourteen. Except you." Her bedroom door closed hard behind her.

Adrian flinched at the sound. And that's how it went. How it had been going every day since spring when Mina had slapped him in the face.

It's not that Mina was never happy or didn't laugh at all any more. It's not that she never smiled at him. But if her smile did dazzle and her face glowed, it was only because exhilaration hadn't worn off yet when she happened to turn towards him or because she was tired and she forgot who she was smiling at. As soon as she realized it was him she was gracing, her warmth froze over and her smile disappeared. Her times of laughter and smiles were never meant for Adrian.

And when Mina dragged and slumped and sighed? Adrian saw, but he knew those times weren't meant for him either. They were meant only for Mina, when she thought no one else was looking.

Spring to summer. Summer to fall. How many visits to the therapist for Mina did that make? Too many if they weren't helping. And Adrian couldn't see any sign that they were.

***

"Did Mina tell you she wanted to drop out of soccer?" Jay was standing by the dresser pulling his t-shirt over his head. The dim light of the bedside lamp cast shadows that rolled over his newly bared torso as he lifted and stretched, rippling over and accentuating his muscles; and hiding the thin layer of flab that was starting to blur their detail.

Adrian liked the view. He smiled to himself from the bed, propped sideways on his elbow, his eyes rolling over Jay like the shadows.

"Well, did she?"

"Oh, sorry, I was thinking about something else." His eyes sparkled playfully before he switched modes from sexy to serious. "Do you really need me to answer that? You know Mina doesn't tell me anything anymore."

Jay sighed in dismay as he unzipped his pants, worked them down over his hips and off his legs. A green and gold tartan print in one hundred percent cotton was all that covered his fine specimen now. "Yeah, well Mina's been after me to let her drop out. What do you think? Should I let her?"

"She's always loved soccer. I think you should make her stick with it. She needs to learn not to be a quitter. And besides, it's good for her. You know, the exercise and the camaraderie and the team spirit. Did you ask her why she wanted to quit?"

"I'm thinking it's soccer overload." Jay dropped his drawers to climb naked into bed, propping himself up sideways on his elbow to face Adrian. "Maybe summer day camp wasn't a good idea after all. Too much of a good thing."

"But remember, the reason you signed her up for day camp in the first place was to keep her occupied. And it..." Adrian paused suddenly; turning hurriedly away from Jay to reach for the glass of water he'd taken to keeping on his nightstand. He coughed before he got the glass to his lips. And he coughed again after the water had gone down. "...and it did that, so..." And once more to clear his throat, "...so, it was a good idea."

"Babe, are you all right? I notice you've been coughing an awful lot lately."

"I'm fine. It's just allergies." Yes, certainly allergies. He'd been telling himself the same thing for weeks. And the increasing tightness in his chest was all in his imagination. He'd been telling himself that too. "Anyways, I always felt like Mina looked forward to those soccer day camp days. Seems odd to me that she would want to drop out now that school's started. You really need to ask her why… she wants to… quit. I think …" Adrian fought the urge to cough, his face turning red with the strain. Again he reached for the water (As if it would help. As if it ever did), almost spilling it when the cough won against his efforts and his hand jerked.

"Babe, seriously, you need to go see the doctor. And don't give me any bullshit about allergies. Promise me you'll call in the morning."

Adrian was sitting on the edge of the bed now, sipping as he tried not to cough, sipping and trying, sipping and trying. All he could do was shake his head in the affirmative while his chest ached and the single note of unease he'd been blocking out for weeks grew into a discordant song.

Jay was out of the bed. "I'm going to go get you some cough medicine." Pulling on his boxers. "And if you don't call," he added, "I will."

***

This was the truth:

A sorrowful wailing filled his ears, and a droning prayer, but he could hear nothing.

He was a feather and he was a stone.

Per istam sanctan unctionem et suam piissimam misericordiam, indulgeat tibi Dominus quidquid …

He was a bright spark and he was lightless.

Por esta santa unción o aceite, y por la gran bondad de su misericordia, que Dios te perdone los pecados que hayas cometido ...

He existed and he had never existed.

Through this Holy Unction of oil, and through the great goodness of His mercy, may God pardon thee whatever sins thou hast committed…

And Adrian had knocked on Heaven's door; only twenty-three years old, his lungs betraying him, locked up with cancer, shoving his desperate breaths away unused.

The door had opened at his knock and God had answered, but Adrian could not say what Heaven looked like. He had been too weak to peer around God's wide spread arms to see what glory might lie behind.

Love had shone upon him from God's smile. He encircled Adrian in tenderness. He kissed him gently on the cheek. And then He had stepped away, blowing softly. God's warm breath caressed Adrian's face, ruffled his hair, lifted him high…

And Adrian was floating and falling. Back into the hospital bed he fell, color rushing into his death-pale face as the air rushed into his lungs; as 'A Miracle!' replaced the last rites on the priest's lips; as grief lost its grip on his mother's fragile heart and joy ran wet down her cheeks.

This also was the truth:

Heaven was the marvel of a day; watching the arc of the sun as it traced the sky from the pink promise of morning to twilight's gentle peace, leaving the night to the moon and the stars to embroider in white and gold.

Heaven was biting into the ripest, sweetest peach and feeling the juice flow down his throat and dribble down his chin.

Heaven was the contentment and the security in belonging.

Heaven was the love song in his heart when he looked into Jay's green eyes and Jay looked into his.

Heaven was when there was lift off and passion rocketed him to the stars.

This was the heaven on Earth; the heaven that Adrian already had; the heaven that, at this moment in time, was the only heaven Adrian wanted.

It was a cough that had been cancer's harbinger when he was twenty-three. Pray that this cough, sixteen years later, was not a harbinger of the cancer's return. Pray that, if it were, God would help him again to beat it. Thirty-nine was still too young for God to let him see what majesty might lay behind Heaven's golden door.

Chapter 33
WHAT DID THE DOCTOR SAY?

'Get in'

What Jay wanted to do was pace. What he wanted to do even more was step out into the bright September day and have a smoke. What he was doing instead was staying put; sitting in a sickly green, straight-backed waiting room chair, waiting. Each time he heard the faint click of a doorknob and the movement of hinges, each time he felt a slight pressure change in the room, he looked up from the glossy pages he was flipping to stare with tractor beam concentration at the white door kitty-corner to the check-in window, willing it to be Adrian that he would see walking through when the white door swung open. So far, he had been disappointed every time.

What could the doctor possibly be doing that was taking so long? It seemed forever ago that Adrian had disappeared behind that white door to follow the nurse that had called his name.

There was the click of the doorknob again. There was the change in pressure. There were Jay's eyes on the door. And there, again, was no Adrian. Jay sighed and returned his eyes to the magazine he was looking at and the page he had just flipped it to.

The page certainly was colorful but what was it he was looking at? He squinted and cocked his head; and then surreptitiously turned what he had been holding upside down right side up to reveal a large black dog racing across a wildflower-strewn field. He must have set the magazine on his lap to stare at the white door and then picked it back up upside down by mistake. What article had he been reading? He leafed through the pages, a few forward and a few back, but nothing clicked. What magazine was this anyway? He looked at the cover. Field & Stream. He'd probably been holding it upside down the whole time! Zero interest. No article. Just something to occupy his hands while he waited. And worried.

What was the doctor doing? What was the doctor saying? Was Adrian all right? Come on through that door Adrian so you can let me know.

Jay rose from his seat and walked over to the magazine rack on the wall. He deposited Field & Stream in one of the empty compartments and scanned the rack for a more suitable replacement. The Field & Stream he'd been (not) looking at was the April issue. June and July were there too. Also the May and July issues of Outdoor Life, several issues of Woman's Day and the popcorn and cranberry garlanded Christmas tree cover of last December's Country Living. Jay shook his head and tried not to groan. What about Newsweek or The New Yorker? And couldn't they at least be current? It was September for god's sake. If only he hadn't forgotten to charge his smart phone last night. Infinite possibilities to occupy his time and his mind could have been a simple finger stroke away but at only twenty two percent, he had to save the remaining charge in case of emergency.

He stood at the rack a moment longer, fingering the magazines and feigning interest, just to loosen up his legs and get the blood flowing in his butt cheeks again. And then, feeling somewhat obligated after having stood there for so long, he picked one of the poor choices from the rack and turned with it in his hand to glance around the waiting room. He took the long way back to his seat; passing by the check-in window and the wastebasket he'd spotted there to let the loosely held Christmas issue of Country Living slip (oops!) from his hand. It tumbled readily into the basket. Even the magazine knew that's where it belonged.

The sickly green chair Jay had been calling home for the last hour was occupied by a matronly woman engrossed in her cellphone when he returned from perusing the past and culling the herd so he settled himself instead into an equally uncomfortable sickly blue one, leaving a respectable pair of empty seats between himself and the newcomer so as not to invade her privacy. Hopefully he wouldn't be sitting here much longer. Hopefully...

And the white door was opening. And this time it was Adrian that was walking through! Jay jumped up, scanning Adrian's face for clues. Was he smiling or frowning? Nervous or relieved? Jay couldn't tell. It was a face of mixed reviews.

Their eyes caught as Adrian crossed the room and made his way over to Jay. An unmistakable smile formed then, on both their faces, because they were glad to see each other and because, no matter what was to come next, at least this part of the mission was over.

"What did the doctor say?" Jay asked as soon as they left the anemic atmosphere of the doctor's office behind for the bright hope of a sunny afternoon. He couldn't get the words out of his mouth fast enough.

He couldn't get the pack of Newport 100's out of his pocket fast enough either. He was about to light up when Adrian coughed. He stuffed the cigarette back into the pack and shoved the pack back into his pocket as they walked across the parking lot, heading for his car.

"He said everything points to bronchitis. I've got this prescription to fill for an antibiotic." Adrian rifled anxiously through several sheets of white paper he held in his hand as he spoke.

"Thank god! That's great news."

"But it's not for sure." They'd reached the car by now and Adrian stood by the passenger door, rifling again through the papers he held, separating one from the rest and scanning the page. "I've got to go for some blood work and get a chest x-ray

at the hospital. Then he'll know if it's really the bronchitis or..."
Adrian paused nervously, "or if it's the cancer again."

"Well, lets go. Let's get you to the hospital." Jay had the
driver's side door open, ready to climb in.

"Why don't you take me home first so I can get my own car."

"Why the hell would I want to do that?"

"You really don't have to come with me. I can drive myself.
You'll be wasting your whole day, sitting in waiting rooms.
Instead you could be doing other things."

"You're making me mad now, Adrian. What makes you think
I'd rather do anything else besides going with you and making
sure you're ok? You're the only thing I care about right now. The
only thing that's important. Don't you know that?"

"Yes. No. I don't know. I just don't want to be a burden on
you."

"Babe, I love you. You could never be a burden. Now get
in. We're going together. I'm taking you to the hospital for those
tests."

'Get out'

Usually raring to go, despite what Claude himself thought,
even his one track minded little head had learned that the pain
always grew worse when Zach called it out to play. His pecker
cowered in the company of his ball sack and Claude had to coax
it out with lies, and help it rise to attention with his own teasing
strokes and erotic fantasies involving rock-hard studs that
glistened and rippled and throbbed. And looked nothing like
Zach.

Claude and his tortured nether regions had been given a
reprieve this morning though. His second visit with the colorectal
specialist was scheduled for ten a.m. and Zach wanted him
clean.

Zach was waiting for Claude by the front door, looking out
the window at the September sun and neighborhood goings on

with this hands in his pockets. He pulled his car keys from his pocket along with his hands when Claude walked up beside him.

"Here you are, finally. Took you long enough. You didn't get any blood on the towel did you?"

"Relax, I used a tissue. Why do I need to go to the doctor again anyway? It's a waste of time."

"Because what he prescribed the first time should have worked and it didn't! You're still bleeding. And I hear you moaning in the bathroom when you're taking a shit."

"Are you really that..." ...fucking dumb? Those were the two words on the tip of Claude's tongue ready to complete his sentence. "...concerned?", was the word he chickened out and used instead.

"Of course I'm concerned. You're my lover aren't you? And I want you well. Now let's go. I took off from work to get you to this appointment and I don't want you to be late."

Zach backed into a spot within sight of the doctor's office door, put the car in park and took the keys from the ignition.

"Go on in. I'll wait here. It might look funny if another guy comes in with you." Zach had said the same thing when he'd brought Claude to the first visit. As if the doctor wouldn't be able to tell that the rectum he was examining welcomed stiff cocks and that Claude was gay.

Claude walked to the building, feeling Zach's eyes on him. What would Zach do if he suddenly cut and ran? What was the doctor going to say when he saw that, after four weeks, the sorry state of Claude's colorectal area was no better? Was probably, in fact, worse? Claude's heart was pounding as he opened the door and went inside.

When Claude had returned to the car after his first visit with the specialist, Zach had bolted upright from his slouch in the front seat, anxious to hear the diagnosis.

"So, what did the doctor say?" Concern sat heavy in his voice.

"He said I'm all inflamed up there. I've got hemorrhoids and tears and fissures. He gave me some prescriptions. One's for a stool softener and one's for an anesthetic cream. There's even one for some kind of nitroglycerin ointment. He said I should eat high fiber foods and he wants me to soak my rear in a warm bath at least once a day." Claude hesitated, suddenly nervous, not sure how Zach would take the last instruction the doctor had given him. "And no anal sex."

But Zach had made no comment. He'd only listened intently, shaking his head up and down as he took 'no sex' in along with the rest of the doctor's recommendations. Right to the pharmacy they had gone to drop off the scripts. And they shopped for fresh fruits and vegetables, prune juice, granola bars and high fiber bran flakes while they waited for the scripts to be filled.

And back at home that afternoon, it was Zach that had filled the tub with warm water and made Claude get in. He'd sat on the edge of the tub to chat while Claude soaked, reaching in now and then to swirl the water so he could watch Claude's cock float and bob in the undulating waves.

Claude had followed the doctor's orders. For four weeks he'd been taking the stool softener, eating the high fiber diet and soaking his ass. The creams and ointments sat on the little table next to the toilet so they would be within easy reach when he needed them. He needed and used them everyday. But the hemorrhoids and fissures and inflammation and constant deep ache hadn't improved.

Oh, the fires that could be stoked, the pleasures that could rip through a body using four hands, two mouths and tongues and throats, a couple of penis', and one bunghole. But Zach was never completely satisfied if he couldn't come in Claude's back door.

"Extra Vaseline. That's all we need. Spread it on me thick. Oh yeah, like that. Oh yeah. Oh god! And now I'll ease it in."

The lube job didn't help. And there was nothing easing about Zach's pounding thrusts.

"So what did the doctor say this time?" Zach asked as he pulled out of the doctor's office parking lot and into lunch hour traffic.

"He said he couldn't help me if I didn't follow his orders."

"What the fuck. You did follow his orders. Did you tell him that?"

Claude didn't reply.

"Did you? Did you tell him you soaked your ass and stuffed your crack with those worthless creams he prescribed every day and it made no difference?"

Claude stared out the passenger side window, silent.

"What the fuck's the matter with you now? Do you have a bug up your ass or something? If you…"

"You dumb fuck." Quiet, measured; the words came slowly from where they had been stewing. And then boiled over. "What's the matter with me is you! Can't you fucking see that? No sex means keeping your fucking prick out of me. But you can't do that, can you? I'm just your fucking sex slave! You…"

"What did you say to me?" Zach's eyes bulged with fury. "You fucking ungrateful bitch. Get the fuck out of my car." He was screaming, spitting the words, wrenching a hard right on the steering wheel as he shot to the curb. "Get out. Get the fuck out!"

Claude yanked on the handle, threw open the door, and flung himself from the car; nearly tripping on the curb as he jumped, only just making it to the safety of the sidewalk before Zach sped away amidst the startled squealing of tires and the angry honking of horns.

Chapter 34
ARE YOU HUNGRY?

The blaring horns, the squealing tires, the screamed words. Get out. The cage door had opened. Get out. His heart pumped the words through his veins.

What should he do now? Adrenalin kept Claude afloat as he strode down the sidewalk towards a coffee shop he spotted on the corner. Where the hell was he? The street sign ahead at the crossroads said Damask. He peered around the sign pole. In the other direction it said Graves. And the sign above the coffee shop said Howl The Moon.

He walked into the shop, ordered a small coffee that he barely had enough money to pay for, and sat down with it at a round wood-topped café table by the large storefront window. With shaking hands, he pulled his cell phone from his pocket.

"Lynn?" She had become a good friend. "It's me, Claude." Even if she was friends with Zach too. "I need help." Adrenalin had left him. He was crying into the phone.

"Wait right there," Lynn said. "I'm coming to get you."

The watched pot never boils. Watched time never flies. And a cup of coffee only lasts so long, no matter how small the sips and how far apart you took them. Where the hell was Lynn?

The girl behind the counter had taken to staring and frowning at him every five minutes, then looking down at her wrist, then looking up again to glare and scowl. Her telepathic message was loud and clear – Tables are for customers only. Your customer status has been revoked. Purchase or leave.

There's nothing Claude would have liked more than another cup of hot coffee; to order one of those cinnamon rolls, like the grandmotherly woman at the next table over, and let his teeth sink into its gooey sweetness. Or even better, a savory grilled sandwich with melted cheese oozing out from its toasted and buttery edges like the one that passed by in the hands of a business suit heading for an empty table. But all he had was pocket change. Not even a dollar. He couldn't make a purchase. Customer status revoked. He had to leave.

Reluctantly, Claude got up and walked to the door, pausing by the waste bin intending to deposit his empty cup. Instead he exited Howl the Moon with the cup still in his hands. He'd need it to act as a prop; something to make it appear to other coffee shop patrons that he had a right to sit at one of the outside tables.

Luckily there was still one unoccupied table that he could sit at. And luckily it was behind a large poster that had been taped up in the storefront window. The jerk of a clerk wouldn't be able to see nonpaying table-stealing Claude sit there.

Claude pulled the black metal chair out from the black metal table, reaching into his pocket for his cell phone as he lowered his butt into the seat. Six minutes later than the last time he'd checked. Almost an hour since he'd called Lynn. She hadn't called or texted him. Should he call her again? No. Lynn said she was coming. She'd be here soon. He didn't want to pester her. He slipped the phone back into his pocket, and ran his hands nervously through his hair. They were shaking again.

He picked up his cup to give his hands something to do and raised it to his lips, forgetting it was empty. He glanced up and down the sidewalk, peered into the distance, ran his hands through his hair again, and folded his arms across the cold metal of the table. He rested his head, facedown, on his arms.

The watched pot never boils. Watched time never flies. And waiting was such hard work.

***

"Continue straight. In one mile, your destination will be on the right," Martin advised, his directions firm and easy to follow.

Yes, Lynn had named the business-like male voice she'd selected from the variety of guide options. And so what? She probably wasn't the only one who had named their GPS. When she first got this phone she'd gone with a smooth British accent. Daniel. But that didn't work out too well. She found herself spending more time visualizing her sexy travel companion and imagining him tall, dark and handsome on the seat next to her than following his directions. She'd missed turns and had to double back so many times.

"In five hundred feet, your destination will be on the right," Martin advised. And Lynn squinted intently through her windshield looking for signage emblazoned with 'Howl The Moon'.

The traffic moving down the street, the people bustling on the sidewalk, the businesses and shops bordering the way – all of it suddenly seemed to fade into the background, existing only in shades of black and white; a bright blue beacon on the sidewalk near the corner of Damask and Graves had flared to grab her attention; dismissing everything else as moot, pointing the way, guiding her to her mark. Claude. That had to be him.

Lynn had actually expected to find Claude waiting inside the coffee shop. Even though the day was bright, it was still rather cool. But it was better this way. Now, as long as she could make her way to the curb and get his attention, she wouldn't have to park.

And she was in luck! A white car in the parking spot directly in front of the building and the blue-haired person who sat there, pulled out just as she approached, and Lynn pulled in. She lowered her passenger side window, peered out through it from the driver's side and tapped her horn lightly.

"Claude!" she called out.

His head was resting on his arms on the tabletop. Was he sleeping? She tapped the horn and called his name again, louder this time. He raised his blue-topped head and looked groggily in her direction. A youthful, brown face and a small, slight build accompanied the blue hair. It was definitely Claude, looking ever so much like the little boy that he wasn't.

Recognition erased the grogginess; relief melted the tight anxious lines she could see on Claude's face even from ten feet away. Claude jumped up, ran to her car, hopped in and turned to face her; his eyes wide and white, so many emotions crowded onto his face that his face was emotionless.

Time stood still as they stared at each other uncertainly. Neither one of them seemed to know what to do, what to say, how to act. It was only for an instant. The next instant time unfroze. As bizarre as this situation was, it was simple really. Claude needed help and she had come to help him.

Lynn reached over to pat Claude on the knee with a reassuring smile. "I'm really sorry it took me so long to get here, Claude." She turned then to look out her drivers' side window, watching for an opening in the traffic as she continued, "I was just about to tell my boss that I had to leave, when she came running over with an issue on some important lab results..." The way was clear. Lynn pulled out and rejoined the queue at thirty miles per hour. "...and I had to make a bunch of phone calls to get it straightened out before I could go." She looked back at Claude then, "Are you hungry?" The best way to anyone's heart, no matter how deep and dark the situation, was through their stomach.

"Yes." Claude had been staring straight ahead. He looked at her now, and attempted a smile. "I am. I'm starved." His smile wavered on his face, but didn't completely disappear.

"That Ethiopian place we went to a couple weeks ago isn't far from here. Wanna go there?"

Her eyes were on the road when she asked. When she turned to glance at Claude for his response, the distraught look on his face made her wish she hadn't suggested it. The 'we' she had made mention of that had gone there a couple of weeks ago had included Zach. Sultan Ethiopian was, in fact, one of Zach's favorite restaurants.

"What if... I don't want... Maybe another place. Just a hamburger would be good. McDonald's?"

Filling in Claude's stuttered blanks was easy - What if (Zach was somehow there). I don't want (any chance of seeing Zach).

"I know the place to go! There's a nice family-style restaurant near where I work. They've got great soups and really fresh salads. And, I've never tasted one of their burgers, but I've heard they're good."

"That's right. I forgot. You're vegetarian. Really, any place, whatever you think is fine. Except the Ethiopian because..." Claude trailed off, leaving another easy blank to fill in. His eyes trailed off too, moving away from her to stare straight ahead at whatever lay behind his eyelids.

Lynn sighed and smiled sympathetically at the side of Claude's head before facing the front herself; her own eyes on the road, her own head full of blanks that she couldn't fill in - except to lead them off with the name Zach.

The restaurant was relaxed; the lunch crowd thinning out, the height of the lunch hour over. They were seated in a quiet booth, one easily lent to deep conversation, but Claude wasn't opening up and Lynn thought it would be best to at least get something in their stomachs before she began prodding him with questions. She leaned for support on small talk.

And what better thing to small talk about than the weather? "It certainly is a beautiful day. I love September. The sun can be so bright and warm but there's this little touch of coolness in the air that makes everything seem crisp and fresh. You know, I don't think I've ever asked you before, is the weather in Guyana the same as here, Claude? Do you have a change of seasons?"

"Nothing at all the same. We have two rainy seasons and the rest of the time it's dry. But always it's warm. Here it will snow in winter. There is never snow in Guyana."

"So you've never seen snow?"

"Never. I'm looking forward to it though. I want to build a snowman!" Claude's brown eyes sparkled playfully, his adult troubles forgotten in a moment of childlike innocence, making him look again like the little boy that he wasn't.

And then there was the waitress! Lynn's Cobb salad was layered with crisp micro-greens, avocados, tomatoes, a variety of sprouts, and slices of hardboiled egg. And Claude's rare, half-pound burger leaked red-tinged juices that made his eyes open wide with delight; and made her avert her eyes so she wouldn't have to look at it. Each to their own. She wouldn't hold it against him.

Bite, chew, swallow.

Crunch, crunch, crunch.

Bite, chew, swallow. And Claude looked at her.

Crunch, crunch, crunch. And Lynn looked back.

Bite... chew... swallow... And Claude filled in the empty blanks, with carefully chosen words.

Crunch... crunch... crunch... And Lynn listened, appalled, fighting the desire to fly from the table so she wouldn't have to hear.

Was this really Zach that Claude was talking about? Zach had never been anything but kind to her. They usually got together two or three times a month - for dinner at one of the many ethnic places around town or to go to a jazz concert or bar hopping. And if she had car trouble or needed help putting up curtain rods, Zach was there in an instant. Zach was her guy. He watched her back. He made her laugh.

But... There was another side to Zach. Lynn had seen it. And then put on blinders and looked the other way. She'd seen a shade seem to pass over his eyes and malice darken his face. She'd seen him deliberately cut people off in traffic; and then throw them the finger. She'd seen him kick a dog precariously balanced in its bandy-legged poop stance with its duty half done; and then laugh. And she knew that the reason he was no longer her co-worker wasn't because he had left of his own accord.

Too many irate customers had complained about Zach - the disrespectful, rude, belligerent non-professional in customer service that had been no help to them at all.

And so – Could this really be Zach that Claude was talking about? Yes, it could and it was. The blinders she had put on had been ripped off now.

"I can't believe... I don't want to believe... I knew Zach had a dark side but... but this is just..." Distress filled in the blanks now, and built in her chest. She waged war against the last few bits of romaine still standing on her otherwise empty plate, forcing them back and forth with the angry thrusts of her fork. The rest of her salad sat in her stomach, heavy and hard to hold. How did it even get there? She must have eaten it on autopilot. And now she was afraid her stomach might give up on trying to keep its load down and toss it up and out instead.

Lynn stopped shoving around the lettuce and put down her fork. She closed her eyes and took a deep breath. She lifted her glass for a sip of water and told her stomach that she was the boss. And then she looked across the table at Claude; hunched low in his seat, dragging a stiff, overdone French fry through a blob of ketchup to paint slashes of red across his plate. He looked up when he felt her eyes on him and straightened in his seat.

"So, you've got medicines at Zach's that you need for your...issue, right? And clothes and stuff?" Lynn was in control again. If she was going to help Claude, she had to be.

"What are you thinking? I don't care about my stuff. It doesn't matter. I'm not going back there. Zach can," Claude's voice had been rising. He lowered it now, out of respect for his friend and his surroundings, to spit out two fierce but whispered words, "fuck himself," before leveling off to continue, "with my stuff."

"You need your stuff. It does matter." Lynn grabbed her purse and her jacket from the seat beside her as she spoke and started to make her way to the door, with Claude beside her.

"But you're right, you're not going back there. I'm taking you to my house. And then I'm going to Zach's to retrieve your things."

"Are you sure that's a good idea? What if Zach turns on you?"

"On me? I'll be fine. Zach wouldn't hurt me." And she truly believed that, until the words had made it out of her mouth. That's when uncertainty began to buzz. It crawled up her spine, as she got back in her car, to gnaw at her faith that what she'd just said was true.

And Claude's skeptical frown from the passenger seat did nothing to waylay her growing doubt. "I'll call him first to feel him out and tell him I'm coming. And I want you to make me a list of the stuff I need to make sure I get. If anything gets left behind, I don't want it to be anything you really need. I don't want to have to go to Zach's more than once."

"Lynn, really, I don't need..."

"I'll get your stuff and then, I've only got the one bedroom, but my couch opens up into a bed, so you can sleep there. You're going to be fine. Everything will be fine." She smiled in Claude's direction and patted his knee reassuringly again.

How brave she sounded. How confident and assured. So much braver and confident and assured than she felt - especially as each rotation of her wheels against the road brought her closer to the time of plan implementation and possible confrontation. How would Zach sound? What would Zach say? Was this really happening? Had Zach always been this way? Did she really have a reason to be worried? Could Zach be trusted? Could Claude be trusted? Was Zach still her friend? Too many questions. And she didn't have the answers for any of them.

Chapter 35
CLAUDE?

'Everyone needed a place...'

Home. There was no place like it. It was the silky edge on the blanket, the warm shower rinsing stress away and leaving peace. It was every perfection known, and every imperfection perfect.

It was what Lynn smiled now to think of and couldn't wait to see as she turned her key in the lock and pushed opened the door - Tigsy and Star running into the kitchen, their tails like curved canes held high in warm greeting, their padded feet quiet on the faux gray/brown slate of the linoleum floor. Her two tabby babies, hurrying over to weave love in and around her legs.

And trailing behind, as always, came haughty Scarlet, sauntering into the kitchen well behind her younger siblings, displaying her disdain for their overly obvious affections before giving in to rub her own head against Lynn's knee and do some love weaving herself.

Lynn loosed herself in their affections; a moment stress free, a bit of comfort that she knew wouldn't last. Her babies were not fond of strangers. And, as she knew they would, all three cats flew from the kitchen to scatter and hide when Claude suddenly stepped over the threshold and into the kitchen behind her.

"Your cats are afraid of me." Claude sounded disappointed.

"They'll warm to you. Just give them a couple of hours."

Claude tiptoed quietly across the linoleum, following the cats' path of flight into the living room. He crouched down to hold out his hand and snap his fingers when he saw a black and white feline face peeking out at him from behind a chair. "Here kitty, kitty," he said before glancing over his shoulder to ask Lynn, "What's his name?"

"Her name is Scarlet." Big emphasis on 'her'.

"Here Scarlet. Here kitty, kitty."

And, what do you know? Scarlet did make a move in Claude's direction - to shoot past him like lightening and hightail it into the bedroom down the hall.

Lynn laughed, "The other two are actually the friendlier ones. Star is the orange tabby. He's a boy. And the brown tiger is Tigsy, another girl. Star and Tigsy were littermates. Brother and sister. I already had Scarlet before I got the two of them. Anyway, like I said, give them a couple of hours and then you won't be able to get rid of them!"

"I won't mind. I love cats." Claude's voice was flat now, his previous cat talk enthusiasm gone. It was just something for his mouth to say as the unthinkable situation he was in reasserted its chokehold. He stuffed his hands in his pockets and looked awkwardly around the room.

The stress free moment had poofed away; the time to act had arrived. And now Lynn felt awkward too, suddenly aware of the embarrassingly untidy state of the room they were standing in. She hadn't been expecting visitors. How was she going to make Claude feel welcome and at ease in a mess like this?

"Well," She kicked a couple catnip mice to the wall and also several colorful plastic balls that tinkled merrily as they rolled. "We should get down to business." She picked up several magazines that were strewn on the couch and placed them on the end table instead, brushed the cat hairs from a few throw pillows and plumped and straightened them. "Why don't you make me that list of everything I need to make sure I get at Zach's and..." The thing she was dreading, "...I'll give him a call."

"Can I use your bathroom first?"

"Of course! Just down the hall there, on your left."

Lynn waited till she heard Claude close the bathroom door and then went into the kitchen to grab her purse off the table and extract her phone. Maybe it was silly, but she was glad Claude wouldn't be listening in on her end of the conversation. It wasn't that she planned to say anything she didn't want Claude to hear, but every story did have two sides and she had only heard one of them. She owed it to Zach to hear his.

She took a breath, vowed to remain calm and unaccusing, rehearsed her simple opening line, and touched Zach's picture on her screen to connect.

Zach picked up on the second ring, no hello, just the fury of a bullet exploding from a loaded gun, "The bitch is with you, isn't he?"

The force caught Lynn off guard, cinching her stomach into a knot and driving it into her chest, ramming her heart then into her throat, its rapid beating threatening to cut off her air supply. Quickly she lowered her phone to her side so Zach wouldn't hear her heart's loud pounding, her sharp gasp as she took air in, or her shaky breath as she let it back it. Slowly now, in and out, in and out. One more deep breath in…

…And, phone back to ear, one more slow breath out. "If you mean Claude, yes, he is with me." Her voice was unflustered and level, giving no clue that he had fazed her. "What happened Zach?" Calm, sympathetic and unaccusing, just like she wanted. Hopefully she could get under his rage and lift it away.

It didn't work. Zach was still a loaded gun. "What happened? You're asking me what happened? As if you don't already know. As if the bitch didn't already tell you. Whatever he told you is a fucking lie. But you believe him, don't you. He's a fucking lying whore and you still fucking believe him."

She had expected Zach to be upset, but nothing like this. "Zach," she tried again, soothing and nonjudgmental, "I only wanted…"

"Did he tug on your heart strings? Did he tell you that he came here an innocent fucking virgin and I'm the monster that took advantage of him? He probably fucked every queer in

Guyana up the fucking ass. Sucked all their cocks to prime 'em up. Got 'em rock hard and quivering, ready to explode in his own fucking asshole." Zach's malice rose with each venomous word.

Lynn's calm was eroding, her heart pounding so loudly in her ears she could barely hear the words that struggled from her own mouth, "Zach, if you would just…"

"Why don't you ask him? Yeah, go ahead and ask him. Maybe he'll let you suck his brown, gay-boy cock too. I knew you'd side with him. You're both a couple of fucking bitc…"

Lynn's finger stabbed the display to end the call; her heart hammering in her chest, her eyes wide with shock. She had thought of Zach as her friend! She stormed across the kitchen, from the table to the refrigerator.

She had intended to be reasonable, but he had never given her the chance! Her feet pounded the linoleum, refrigerator to table.

She had intended to be non-accusatory. And he had accused her! She stomped again, back and forth; her hand clenched so tight around her cellphone that her knuckles turned white.

He had turned on her! Like a snake, like a wolf, like a monster! If her phone hadn't been locked into her fist, she would have hurled it, watched it hit and shatter against the wall; an innocent third party obligated to represent another, to relay their words as if they were its own; bound together by invisible waves undulating through space.

A monster! He was being sarcastic when he called himself that, as if it wasn't true. But it was true! And she would call him that herself now. She would scream it! Back and forth, back and forth she paced.

How could she not have seen what he was? Her frenzied travels were losing steam. How could she have been so blind? She stopped her pacing to put her elbows on the counter and her head in her hands. How could she ever have called Zach her friend?

"Lynn?" Claude was walking into the kitchen, concern drawing his eyebrows together into one bushy line. (Had he really been in the bathroom all this time?) "Is everything okay?" His hand was a gentle touch on her shoulder.

"I called Zach. He was… Not good. There's no way I'm going over there. I can't. Not alone anyway."

"I'm sorry. Now I've caused you problems. I didn't mean for this to happen."

"Claude, there's nothing for you to be sorry about. None of this is your fault. I'm your friend and if a friend can't call another friend for help, what good are they? I'm glad to help. I want to help. But I don't think I'm going to be able to help you on my own. We need someone else. Someone strong that can go over to Zach's for your things or at that can at least be my bodyguard."

Lynn stopped there. No purpose would be served in mentioning this now – except to add another layer of distress to task Claude – but there was something else that was going to be needed. Claude would be sleeping at her place on the couch tonight; she wouldn't have it any other way. And for the next couple of nights too, if it came to that. But longer? She only had the one bedroom. And being a single woman? She wouldn't feel comfortable. Other arrangements, something more permanent, were going to have to be made.

Everyone needed a place where they could feel secure, unburdened and understood. Everyone needed a place they could call home.

"I'm calling Jay," she said.

'… they could call home.'

The dogs were barking. "Woof, woof, woof!" So loudly that Jay could hardly think. "Woof, woof, woof!" They were at his front door, scratching and clawing. "Woof, woof, woof!" How did they get there? Who let them out? He couldn't rise from his seat

211

to let them in. The cymbals were in his way. Did this make any sense?

Suddenly Bandit was there, jumping up to put his white paws on Jay's shoulder. But Bandit had died when Jay was a teenager! "Dad!" Bandit barked. His bark sounded like cymbals. No, not cymbals. Bandit sounded just like Mina.

Mina! His phone! Bye Bandit. It was nice seeing you again. Jay's mind dove from the muddled heights of dreamland to re-anchor in reality as his eyes shot open to a sunny afternoon. And there indeed was Mina in front of the couch on which he sat, leaning over him and shaking his shoulder. Adrian was there too, on the couch right beside him, sound asleep.

"Your phone's ringing!" Mina informed, straightening up now that she saw he was awake.

"Woof, woof, woof. Who let the dogs out?" sang his ringtone in confirmation.

"Seriously, you know its not night time right? What are you doing sleeping on the couch anyway?"

For half a second, Jay couldn't answer. Before the second was over, the events of the day (the doctor's office, the hospital, the Christmas issue of Country Living) had caught up with him and reasserted themselves in his time and space.

And why were they sleeping on the couch on a Friday afternoon? Because they had sat down there. Because the couch had embraced them in soft, supple leather. Because after an anxiety filled day, a hug was just what they needed. Because there was no place like home.

"Stress," he replied reaching for his phone to see Lynn's picture on the display. Lynn? She rarely called. He couldn't ignore and save for later. He had to take it. "I'll tell you about it after this call," he said to Mina as he swiped right, silencing the woofs to answer the phone. "Lynn, what's up?"

"I'm really sorry to bother you Jay, but I've got a predicament here and I thought maybe you could help." Was her voice really shaking or was it his ears? Maybe it was just a bad connection.

"Sure, if I can. What's going on?"

"It's about Claude."

"Claude? Shouldn't you be calling Zach?"

"That's just it. I can't call Zach. Well I did call Zach, but Zach's the problem. Zach...."

It wasn't a bad connection. Hanging up and starting over would do nothing to smooth Lynn's trembling words or spin them into a more pleasing pattern that his ears wouldn't rebel against or struggle to un-hear.

"I can't believe this. This is unreal." Jay was running his free hand through this hair, shifting his weight from foot to foot. He didn't even remember getting up off the couch.

"Maybe I'm overreacting. He's still Zach. I've known him for years. Maybe I should just go..."

"No! Don't even think about it. Do not go over there by yourself. Wait for me. Just give me an hour. I'll be there."

Jay tapped the screen, disconnecting the call; feeling disconnected himself. Reality didn't feel real; the comfort of his own living room wasn't comforting. Two people shared the room with him, their faces living question marks looking to him for an answer. An answer to what? What was the question? He knew these people, didn't he? Yes – Adrian (the love of his life, awake now and rising from the couch) and Mina (his beloved child). For one moment, they had seemed like strangers. It was the senselessness of a dream with a fiendish plot. Only this time he wasn't dreaming.

"What's happening Jay?" Adrian was by his side now, full of concern.

"What's going on Dad?" Mina was all eyes and ears, full of curiosity.

"An emergency. A nightmare. As if we didn't already have enough stress today. You won't believe it. Claude's at Lynn's. Him and Zach are finished. Everyone and Zach are finished."

Adrian raised his eyebrows at Jay quizzically and Jay gave him a pointed look in return, shaking his head almost imperceptibly and inclining it slightly in Mina's direction. Adrian raised his eyebrows again; he got the picture - subject matter inappropriate for a teenage girl.

"I told Lynn I'd go to Zach's with her so we can get Claude's stuff," Jay continued verbally, ending their silent exchange.

"I'll come too. Claude will need moral support."

"Are you sure you're up to it? I think you should stay here and relax."

"I already relaxed with a nice nap, and if I stay behind all I'll do is worry. We'll just be sitting and talking. I'll be fine."

"What about me? Can I come too? I like Claude." Mina smiled eagerly, as if she was asking to join them on a picnic. "And, oh yeah, that reminds me, what were you doing sleeping on the couch like a couple of old people in the middle of the afternoon?"

Jay sighed, vexed. Was Mina really that shallow? Couldn't she feel the dismay hanging heavy all around her? He chose not to call her out on it. What would be the point? "Adrian had a doctor's appointment this morning. Remember I told you? And then he had to go to the hospital for some tests. It was just a long, exhausting day Mina." Jay's voice trailed off to add in a whisper, "And it's getting even longer."

"Oh yeah." Memory dawned on Mina's face, "Because of his cough."

"But he's fine, its just bronchitis." Jay left out the word 'probably'. They wouldn't have the test results until after the weekend. "Nothing to worry about," he added, in case Mina's mind needed easing. But that vexed him too. Worry was not an emotion he saw on Mina's face. If anything, she looked bored, ready to move on to topics more stimulating. "And no, you can't come with us. This is an adult situation we've got to deal with. We're not going over there for a good time." He didn't have to search Mina's face for a reaction to this. Disappointment was all over it, followed by insolence.

"You always treat me like I'm a kid. Fourteen's not a kid anymore Dad. I…" Her phone chirped then, stopping her in mid-sentence. Her eyes glazed over as her surroundings lost substance and her attention shifted away from Jay and down to the small, all-important, rectangular object suddenly in her hand. Her eyes refocused, became riveted to the screen, as her thumbs began to dance.

Another thing for him to be upset with her about. It didn't matter that he himself had been guilty of this particular infraction before. He was still vexed. Vexed and concerned. He'd been meaning to have another one of those good, sit down, father to daughter talks with her. So, when was he going to do it? Why did he always come up with feeble, internal excuses as to why 'later' would be better than 'now'? There was nothing feeble about his excuse for this 'now' though, and Jay's attention shifted too, away from Mina and back to the immediacy of disaster and the assistance he had been called upon to provide.

"We gotta go," he said, turning to Adrian. "Are you sure you wanna come?"

"Yes. I'm coming."

"Okay then." He turned again to Mina. "We'll be back Mina," he said, laying his hand on her shoulder and quickly kissing her cheek. "I love you," he added, even though he knew she wasn't listening. Back again to Adrian. "Let me just take a quick piss and then we're out of here."

Jay couldn't leave Adrian in the dark, even though repeating the distressing news that Lynn had relayed was the last thing he wanted to do. Sex slave. Homeless. That pretty much summed it up. And now, that said, his mouth wasn't willing to say anything more. He drove, staring straight ahead at the road, with Adrian in silent shock beside him.

The only sound was of the tires hitting the pavement at forty miles per hour, spinning on their axels, revolving round and round, as they carried them to Lynn's. Their thoughts spun in time with the tires, revolving round and round, trying to grasp and absorb and sort and formulate. Eventually they overflowed and spilled out in bits and pieces that made no sense and perfect sense at the same time.

"What will he do? Where will he go?"

"Lynn doesn't have room."

"He needs someplace to stay."

"Is this a good idea?"

"We have to do something."

"Mina is my top priority. How might this affect her?"

"The guestroom!"

"There would have to be rules."

"If it doesn't work out, we'll just tell him he has to make other plans."

Simultaneously they both turned to look in each other's direction. Their eyes caught. Their thoughts connected. Conclusion reached. Decision made.

"Everyone needs a place they can call home," they both said, nodding, reaching across the seat to take each other's hand.

Chapter 36
HAS ANYONE EVER HEARD...?

"So, you know there was an issue with Lynn and Claude and Zach yesterday and I had to go help them, right? And you know Claude and Zach were a couple and Claude was living with Zach." Her father was looking her right in the eye as he spoke. Mina knew what that meant. He always looked her in the eye when he was only telling her part of the story and holding another part back. And usually that meant that the part he was holding back had something to do with sex.

"Well, Claude and Zach had a huge argument and broke up," he continued, still staring her in the eye. Mina was only half listening now. The X-rated part of her brain had taken hold of this sex idea and started rolling with it. "And since Claude only just recently came to the states from Guyana and doesn't have any family here or anything, that leaves him with nowhere else to live. So, it'll be quite a bit different around here after this morning." Different? Mina's ears perked up. What was it her father was saying? Her thoughts of sex and how it might relate to Claude and Zach and breaking up shifted to the background. "Lynn's going to be bringing Claude and his stuff over here in a little bit and Claude's going to be moving in with us."

"What?" Outrage erupted, burying all else under a ranting tirade. "Who decided this, you and Adrian? What about me? Doesn't my opinion count? I live here too you know. Don't you think you should have asked me first what I thought before you just went ahead and told Claude he could live here? This is going to change everything!"

217

With every shouted word she knew she was acting like a child; like Michaela and Eddie when their time at the playground was over - screaming 'No!' and holding their legs stiff as boards so she couldn't maneuver them back into their stroller. If she really wanted to act like the adult that she purported herself to be, she would just shut up. But the momentum of her terrible twos tantrum was behind her and she couldn't stop.

And then her father made her feel the totality of her jerkdom when he kept his cool and actually agreed with her. "Yes, Mina, your opinion does count. But Claude was in trouble and needed help and you can't tell a friend they'll just have to wait for your help until the time suits you. You should never turn your back on a friend."

Like an adult, she almost apologized. Almost. But like a child, she held the apology in. She couldn't admit that she was wrong. She had to save face, even if it was the face of a jerk. "You should have asked me anyway. It's just not fair!" One last childish blurt before she stomped into her room and slammed the door.

She'd only just flopped down on her bed when she heard the rumble of a car pulling into the driveway. She heard the knock on the front door. She heard Adrian's and her father's purposeful steps. She heard the commotion of greetings and salutations and people making their way inside. She heard Lynn's self-conscience laugh.

And then there was her father outside her door telling her what she already knew, "Mina, Claude and Lynn are here. Come on out and say hello."

The scowl she came out of her room with was intended for her father; a follow up to make sure he knew she hadn't forgiven his disregard for her. She never meant for it to still be on her face when she greeted Claude, but Claude turned to look at her before she wiped it off. It was her scowl that met his smile. And her scowl blew the smile right off Claude's face. Shame then blew the scowl off hers.

Why was she acting this way, anyway? Her father was helping a friend. He was honorable and right and she was wrong. What was the matter with her? And she even liked Claude. Now she had made him feel unwanted.

She grabbed Claude's hand then and put her other arm around his shoulder to draw him close, hoping a hug might fix her bungled welcome. She kissed his cheek too. It seemed to work. His smile did come back, but it wasn't one that looked very sure of itself.

Later, while the adults (of which she couldn't even purport to be right now) sat unwinding at the kitchen table with beers and a plate of nachos that Adrian had concocted, Mina discreetly took a small glass vase from the cupboard and slipped out to the back yard. She picked a few bright yellow, long stemmed flowers from the garden, put them in the vase with some water from the hose and then slipped back in to set the bouquet on the dresser in the guestroom, which was really Claude's room now. Flowers made a lovey welcoming statement. That's what Adrian said way back in June when he'd put flowers in this same room for Grammy.

Monday morning her scowl came back as she pounded on the bathroom door. "Dad, what are you doing in there? You know I've got to catch the bus. I need to brush my teeth!"

"I'm sorry, Mina." It was Claude hogging the bathroom, not her dad. "I didn't know. I'll be out in a few minutes."

She didn't care if it was Claude. "A few minutes is too long! I'll miss the bus!"

"I'm sorry."

"I've got to leave. I've got to leave right now! I ate cereal and now I'm going to have curdled milk breath all day!"

"I'm really sorry. Tomorrow I'll remember to stay out until you leave the house."

Three times he'd apologized now, but she wasn't going to give him the satisfaction of accepting any of them. "That's just great. But it doesn't do me any good for today!" She clomped through the house, grabbed her book bag and launched herself out the front door.

She was not proud of herself over it.

And even less proud when she came home (knowing Claude was going to be there and wishing he wasn't, lamenting the loss of her 'home alone' time and the disruption of her 'just got home from school' routine) and he greeted her with a big smile.

"Hi Mina!" He was looking up at her from where he was crouched in front the kitchen cabinet that held the pots and pans, rummaging around. "I was thinking I'd cook. I hope it's okay that I took chicken out of your freezer. What time do your parents get home?" He rose from his crouch with a large skillet in his hand.

"You mean my Dad and Adrian?"

"Yeah, who else would I mean?"

"Adrian's not my parent."

"Well, he's as good as one. He cares for you a lot. Do you like fried chicken? Do they like fried chicken?"

"I guess."

"In Guyana when I made fried chicken for my family, they loved it. So I'm going to make it for you too. You can help. I'll show you how I do it."

She wasn't too enthused, but Claude was, and he roped her in. It turned out to be fun! Who knew? And the chicken turned out awesome! Well, maybe a little too much cumin, but still awesome.

***

Things changing versus things staying the same. That was the topic of discussion her teacher, Mr. Rohrburg, introduced beginning the first Monday back to school after the Christmas/New Years break.

"Has anyone ever heard the saying 'variety is the spice of life'?" Mr. Rohrburg scanned the room for raised hands while Mina scanned Mr. Rohrburg. The reddish highlights in his close-cropped, brown hair glinted under the ceiling florescents when he moved just so and Mina couldn't help but wonder - would his hair be soft like the fuzz on a peach or rough like her father's stubbly beard? Probably soft. His lips looked soft too. Just how soft was something she would never know, but something she would love to find out.

His scanning gaze moved to the left now, sweeping in her direction, and Mina quickly averted her eyes, looking back again just in time to see the sky blue sky of Mr. Rohrburg's eyes light up behind his glasses when he spotted several raised hands.

"Joe," Mr. Rohrburg smiled and pointed, singling out one of the kids nerdy enough to admit knowledge, "what do you think it means, that variety is the spice of life?"

"It means that variety makes life more interesting and more exciting."

"Exactly! I see that pizza is on the menu for lunch today. Who likes pizza?" More than half the class either shot their hands into the air or at least nodded in the affirmative and Mr. Rohrburg smiled and nodded too. "But what about if it was pizza on the menu every day. And you had pizza for supper everyday too. Would you still like pizza?"

'No way', 'Not me', 'No', 'It wouldn't be special anymore', 'Boring'. Murmurs erupted around the room.

"Yes, definitely boring. After a week, I'd be dying for a hamburger or some spaghetti. If it was longer than a week, I might even enjoy a plate of liver and onions!" Mr. Rohrburg smiled over the room, bright as the sun, as sounds of culinary distress groaned through his students' lips. He had the class. He owned it. "So that must mean then that change and variety are good things, right? We like excitement. We like things to be interesting."

He had Mina too. Even she was groaning and chuckling and nodding 'yes' by now. No student could hang onto teen indifference for long in the engrossing presence of Mr. Rohrburg.

"Well, in an effort to add some spice to your lives, I'm going to change things up around here. Starting tomorrow there will be no assigned seating. You can sit wherever you want. Every day in a new seat!"

Excited chatter began to buzz. Mina caught her friend Beth's eye three rows over and grinned. No more sitting behind stuck-up bitch Rachel and next to blobby dumbass William. She'd be sitting with her besties tomorrow. And if she got to class early enough she might be able to nab them seats in the row next to the windows!

On Tuesday Mina did get a seat by the window - the last seat in the last row in the far corner of the room - with Beth in front of her and Clare on her right. All the nerds sat up front so they could be close to the action. And stuck-up bitch Rachel sat up front too so Mr. Rohrburg would be sure to notice her long lashes when she batted her eyes at him.

And each day for the rest of that week? Every single person sat in the exact same seats they had decided to plop their rears down in on Tuesday.

Monday again. Kids heading for their seats. Mr. Rohrburg fiddling with papers on his desk. And then there was the bell signaling the start of class and Mr. Rohrburg moving away from his desk to stand at the front of the room. He seemed different somehow, stiff and overly serious, but at the same time... Maybe Mina was just imagining it... Were his sky blue eyes really dancing?

"Has anyone ever heard the saying 'variety is the spice of life'?" Mr. Rohrburg scanned the room and everyone else turned in their seats to scan the room too, exchanging confused looks, shaking their heads and shrugging their shoulders, finally looking to the front again to stare at Mr. Rohrburg. Had Mr. Rohrburg lost it over the weekend? Was he crazy? Or were they crazy? What was going on here?

"Um, Mr. Rohrburg?" It was Joe the nerd. "You asked that same question last week." Joe the brave.

"Did I? I thought so, but then I wasn't sure because, well, I also thought I said that there was no assigned seating. Am I right? Did I say that too?"

"Yeah, you said both those things."

"Okay. Good. My memory still works then. And I also seem to remember everyone agreeing that change was a good thing and everyone liking the idea of no assigned seating. Isn't that right?" Mr. Rohrburg was nodding his head, answering his own question. "So then, why isn't anyone changing their seats? Why are you all sitting in the same place, next to the same people day after day when you don't have to?"

Mina knew why. So much had changed in her life over the last three months, she didn't even have to think about it. Nerves sent impulses across her synapses; tingling in the muscles of her arm, readying it to raise her hand above her head; tingling around her mouth, readying it to open and speak the answer.

But Mina had never been one to raise her hand in class and answer questions. Her arm stayed down, her answer remained unspoken. And her answer explained, not only why she and the rest of the class had claimed a seat and invisibly etched their names into it, but also why she couldn't gather enough courage to break her mold of non-participation - There was comfort in routine. Change stripped routine away. Change buried the comfort of the known under the fright of the unknown.

Maybe she hadn't been brave enough to verbally answer the question but she had no problem with the written word. Their assignment, due the next day, was to write an essay explaining why variety might be the spice of life but sometimes bland was better.

Mina wrote her essay about Claude:

I like change. Updating to the latest & smartest smart phone, getting trendy new clothes, adding a streak of wild color to my hair. A new place, a new taste, a new song, a new color. Change keeps life fresh. Change is exciting. Change is the road to the future.

But also I am a creature of habit. Every school morning my alarm clock rings at six a.m. I hit the snooze button. I fall back asleep. I jump out of bed when it rings again 9 minutes later to hurry into the bathroom. I wash my face. I get dressed. I grab some toast & some juice & rush out the door to catch the bus. On the bus I always sit in the fifth seat down on the right hand side next to Heather Witt. I like sitting in the same seat. I call this seat mine. If someone else is sitting in my seat, I get mad.

I like having a place because it makes me feel safe. I like having a routine because when too many things change at the same time, when the world spins too fast for me to follow & in directions I'm not ready to go I like it that some things don't change. Routine is my security blanket.

Last September a friend of ours named Claude suddenly didn't have anywhere to live & my father told him he could live with us. Everything changed. I lost my security blanket.

Claude got in my way. He occupied the bathroom when I needed to get ready for school. I didn't get to wash my face. I didn't get to brush my teeth.

Claude intruded on my alone time. He was there when I got home from school. I didn't get to walk in the door & not have to talk to anyone. I didn't get to grab a snack & eat it on the couch with my music blaring as loud as I wanted.

Claude changed the rhythm of the house. He was the guest that never left. I lay awake into the night waiting to hear the sound of his leaving so I could sleep to the normal beat of 3 hearts under our roof. I would finally drift off to sleep unfulfilled to the not normal beat of 4.

But things changed again. Claude learned our schedules & stayed out of the bathroom when we had to get ready for school or work. I got used to Claude being there when I got home from school. I even started to look forward to seeing him. Claude was interested & interesting. Claude was fun & funny. He taught me how to make fried chicken. He convinced my father to let him put pink streaks in my hair. He made me feel proud of myself & of my family. And he was like me because he was black too.

Only his black was 100% & from India & my black was 50% & from Africa.

4 hearts beating under our roof became normal & now Claude is like my big brother. Things still change. Claude got a job at the grocery store in October & I was alone again when I came home from school like I was before only this time it was being alone that seemed strange. I got used to it.

I like change. Sometimes.

I am a creature of habit. When my routine is messed with I feel messed with too.

I am adaptable. I don't like it when I lose my security blanket but if I do lose it I always find it again or else I make a new one.

Change can be scary at first. But the thing about change is that after a while what has changed becomes normal. Until that happens we all need a security blanket to cling to. A little something we can count on to stay the same.

Pride swelled in Mina's chest when she got her paper back. 'A+' and 'Excellent!' were scrawled across the top of the page. A blush swelled in her cheeks too because, also at the top of the page was a hand-drawn smiley-face with peach fuzz hair.

Later that day, before she put the essay in her top dresser drawer for safekeeping, a blush again swelled in her cheeks when she closed her eyes, pressed the paper to her lips, and kissed Mr. Rohrburg's silly and sweet, cartoonish self-image. He'd captured himself perfectly with those few simple pen strokes. It was the closest Mina would ever get to kissing the real thing.

Chapter 37
AND WHO ELSE?

He didn't want to startle them. But he didn't want to deny himself the pleasure of pressing his nose into a purple cluster for a lilac-scented whiff of heaven either. How slowly he had opened the screen door. How quietly he'd tippy-toed over the deck and out into the yard. They startled anyway, scattering cracked corn, sunflower seeds and millet from the feeder as they scattered themselves – chickadees and sparrows, starlings and cardinals - jittery and devoid of trust.

Earlier that morning, just like he'd done every other morning for hundreds of mornings, he'd gone from the deck to the birdfeeder to lift its green lid and fill it with seed. You'd think the birds would recognize the hand that fed them. And maybe they did!

"Adrian," they chattered and squawked as they flew to safety in the branches of the winterberry and the maple. "Adrian!"

Lilac fulfilled, awash with amazement and aglow with the wonders of the bird world, Adrian was about to head back up onto the deck when a movement at the periphery of his vision stopped him. It was a flapping, to be sure, but not the wings of any starling or sparrow returning to the feeder at the sight of his retreating back. It was something larger. Perhaps a hawk! But hadn't there been a hint of red in the flapping? Maybe it was a pileated woodpecker. In slow motion he turned, hoping for at least a moment's clear glimpse of the bird before it too startled and flew. And there it was!

"Adrian!" it called out from the far side of the picket fence, staying put as it waved an arm sleeved in a grey and red patterned blouse.

Adrian laughed as he walked over to chat with Annie Vandenbunder, amazed now at his gullibility. "I thought you were a bird!"

"A bird? Are you trying to tell me my voice is like a song? Somebody else told me once that I have a sing-songy voice but they didn't mean it as a compliment." A disgruntled frown passed quickly across Annie's face, like a wisp of dark cloud over a bright sun. "Anyway... So, next Saturday's the day! Carl's been tweaking his recipe all week. Who ever thought of such a great idea? A chicken wing challenge! It must have been Jay."

"Sort of Jay. But more Claude and Mina. It all started because Claude showed Mina how to make fried chicken and she somehow took off with the idea of cooking. She adjusted his recipe to suit her taste and each one bragged that theirs was best. They did the same thing with chicken wings and different sauces. And they kept bugging me and Jay to tell them whose we liked the most. But how could we take sides? So Claude said we needed to get people who weren't in the family to judge. And Jay suggested we have a contest party with other people entering too and not do fried chicken but only chicken wings because they would be easier for lots of people to take a taste."

"Cool! So I guess Carl will be going up against Mina and Claude and who else?"

"All together there's seven. Also me, Dixie Chatelain, Hillary, I think you met her at the barbeque last July, and another friend of ours that I don't think you ever met - Big Lou. And everybody else who comes are the judges. Even the cooks are judges. But they are forbidden to vote for their own."

"Well I'll tell you, Carl thinks he's gonna win. And his wings are pretty good! He adds... No, I shouldn't even tell you. It's something special that he adds to his wing sauce. A surprise ingredient!"

"I can't wait to taste it. But I'll tell you; I think it's going to be me that's the winner. My wings are… Well, soon you will see."

Annie laughed and then turned thoughtful. "I've got to say, it really seems like Mina's settled into herself again. Cooking and entering the chicken wing challenge.   Remember last summer? We were standing right here in this same spot and you were telling me about all the problems you were having with her. You were so…"

And like a flashback, the sting of Mina's unexpected slap was fresh on Adrian's face. His eyes zoned out and last summer zoomed in like the roller coaster it had been. Not the sleek and modern, locked firmly in your seat kind streaking down tracks laid over a monstrous steel framework. But the rickety kind that careened down tracks suspended in air by fir and pine, that creaked as it climbed and shook as it plummeted and tipped you to the left and the right behind your support bar as it barreled and cornered.

Adrian had buckled in, buckled down and buckled under. He'd prepared on the straight ways, braced as it climbed, prayed as it fell. He'd laughed and cried and whooped as it twisted and spiraled and wound. And he'd danced in the dark as it shot through the tunnel of love.

And then came September and the hairpin turn where Adrian had gripped the bar till his knuckles turned white and thought for sure he would crash and burn. He'd sucked in his breath, ready to scream, and laughed instead as the brakes caught, jolting him backward and pitching him forward, to rise on wobbly legs and retake firm ground with cancer's empty threat behind him.

October had raced him down the tracks again, giddy in the lead car, arms held high above his head, fearless and joyful; to breath in and breath out and gladly climb then into the saddle of a spirited yet predictable carousel steed.

Through winter and spring he'd ridden, hands light on the reins, smiling to a breezy, toe-tapping beat. Up and down and round and round and here was summer again, coming up just around the bend, and he was still smiling and…

The rising lilt of Annie's voice pulled him back from his musings. She was asking a question, "...with Mina should be better this summer, huh?" And was eyeing him with her head cocked, waiting for a response.

"Oh yes. Mina is doing so much better." Adrian began cautiously, scanning Annie's face, not completely sure he was answering the question that Annie had asked, since he'd been lapse in his listening. "She smiles more," But the absorbed look and understanding nod that Annie was giving him told him he was on target and he continued in earnest, "which makes me so happy to see. And even happier that she talks to me again. Not the same like she did before, but I'll take it. It's since Claude moved in. Something about him, I don't know, but he's been good for her."

"That's wonderful, Adrian."

"And, I should have her show you, she wrote this report. So good, it made me cry. All about life and change. Her teacher gave her an A. She was so proud. And Jay and I, we were so proud of her too."

"I'd love to see it! Maybe she can show it to me at the cook-off." Annie shifted on her feet. "I've got something I'd like to show you too."

"What is it?" Adrian asked, but the sparkle in Annie's eye gave him the answer before the question was even out of his mouth. "Your new book?"

"Yes! It's finally done. It took me forever, but it's finally done. I was wondering if you'd read it for me and let me know what you think. You're in it, you know. Only I changed your name to Gomez and he's not really you, just loosely based on you."

"Oh my god. I feel embarrassed. Should I be embarrassed? I have to read it now just to see what I do! But even if I wasn't in it, I'd read it. I love the way you write."

"Thanks! I hope you like it. It's different than the last book, but at the same time, it's the same. You'll see what I mean when you read it. I'll bring it over next Saturday if I don't stop over with it sooner. Listen, I better run. Carl's probably wondering where I am. We were supposed to be going for a walk. I'll see you again soon!" She turned and headed for her house, lifting her arm to wave a backwards goodbye as she walked away.

And Adrian turned too - towards his own house, waving his own backwards goodbye, even though he knew Annie couldn't see him. It was just something people did. When someone waved at you, you waved back. Just like the birds, Adrian figured - when something came towards them, they flew away; even if they did recognize the one who always came bearing seeds. But then again, was it really the same - people waving and birds taking flight?

Both seemed to be instinctive, but waving was simply a greeting, a social and neighborly thing to do. Whether you waved or not, it held no lasting consequence. Flying away, on the other hand, was survival; a safety measure embedded in a bird's DNA in an attempt to secure a longer life for a fragile creature in a danger filled world. Not flying away could mean the difference between life and death.

So then, why was waving instinctive? There had to be a reason. Instinct. Something imbued in us to ensure our survival, perhaps since the beginning of time. A band of cavemen appeared in Adrian's mind, wandering a desolate landscape. Suddenly they stopped. Another group was approaching. Apprehension gripped their hearts as they tightened their hands around the weapons they carried. And then they saw the wave. They waved back, relief flowing between them as they continued on their way.

Adrian had been right all along. The wave - now a social grace, then a matter of survival, a sign of peace and good intentions so the oncoming tribe didn't put arrow to bow or club to head.

Smiling to himself at the image, Adrian opened the screen door and stepped into the kitchen. Déjà vu and flashback again. Like last summer, he'd stood in the exact same spot at the picket fence chatting with Annie Vandenbunder. And like last summer he'd then come into the house to find Mina in the exact same spot that he found her in now, her back towards him as she stood bent in front of the open refrigerator perusing its chilled contents. Last summer this was when the slap had come. Instinctively, like the caveman and like the birds, Adrian stiffened; ready to fly.

But this summer was not last summer. And there was no need for flight. Even from the back of Mina's head, Adrian could tell that she was smiling.

She straightened and turned towards him with a plastic jug in her hand. "You got the lemonade I asked for! Have you tried it yet? Is it as good as the commercials make it sound?"

"I hope, but I don't know. Let's find out. Pour me some too."

Adrian eyed the drink suspiciously as Mina twisted open the cap and liquid as yellow as a traffic YIELD sign glugged from the jug. YIELD – a warning; only a step away from a full-blown STOP. And yield Adrian did. "Just half a glass for me!" As much a matter of self-preservation as any wave of old. "What do you think of it?" he asked, letting Mina be the guinea pig as she took the first sip.

"It's pretty good! I like it!" She finished her drink with gusto, looking over the top of her glass questioningly at Adrian, as she drank it down. "Aren't you going to try it?" She was already pouring herself a second round.

"Sure I am! Here goes." He smiled at Mina as he brought the glass to his lips. And he forced the smile to stay there as the chemical concoction the jug proclaimed to be lemonade ran slick across his tongue and slid, overly sweet, down his throat. "It is good. I like it too." How hard it was to sound convincing as he struggled not to gag.

The lemonade may have been an imposter and an affront to lemons everywhere. And Adrian saying he liked the lemonade was a falsehood that might cost him having to drink more of the foul imitation in the future. But the happiness he felt in strengthening a bond that had once been broken was real. And there was nothing false about the kindred moment he had shared with Mina. Bring on the genuine artificial imitation lemon flavor. Time spent with Mina was well worth the cost.

Chapter 38
DO YOU WANT THE EDAMAME?

Claude struck a pose in front of his dresser mirror, shirtless and chest forward, smiling at the way the late afternoon sun gleamed off the tiny diamond-look balls of cut glass that sat on either side of his hard, dark nipples; anchored in place by the gold bar that pierced them.

A new pose – He turned sideways for the mirror now and looked suggestively over his shoulder, cupping one hand under his distinct pec and placing his index finger lightly on his erect nipple.

And full frontal again, with a sultry smile, his barbell adorned nipples bold on his chiseled chest, his thumbs hooked over the top of his sweat pants; pulling them down as low as they could go and still provide cover for the one-eyed snake laying in wait just below the elastic waistband.

"You know you want it," Claude whispered, low and provocative, "Come get a piece of this." He was thinking of Ken.

Ken was the sandy-blond, blue-eyed Adonis that had done his piercings. Deep was his voice, full were his lips, broad and built his arms and when he moved, the black cobra that climbed his right arm rippled with his muscles; ready to strike from Ken's shoulder where sat its wide red mouth, fangs bared.

Claude's own snake had struggled within the confines of his bikini briefs just at the sight of him. And, hallelujah, the Adonis had a gay vibe abut him. Or was that just wishful thinking? Claude could usually pick them out, but with some men it was hard to tell. To be practical, Claude put the chances of Ken being gay at eighty percent. Seventy-five, eighty percent. But he could still dream!

Just such a dream, with the chances at one hundred percent, was beginning to dance in Claude's head when Ken, in preparation for the piercing, gripped his nipple with the metal forceps - not cold, but warmed (like two fingers) to make Claude more comfortable. Claude's hard-on had been immediate. And his little head joined forces with his dreaming head to formulate a plan for stealing into the back room with Ken when the piercing was over to fuck each other's brains out.

"Are you ready?" Ken had asked then, meaning for the piercing, as he positioned the needle at the point of entry.

"I am," Claude had replied, meaning for sex.

"You'll feel a prick and then some pain. But it will be over in seconds." The piercing.

"Yes. Let's do it." The sex.

And needle penetrated nipple. His hard-on had deflated like a stuck balloon. Thoughts of sex blasted away as pain blasted in. He'd almost chickened out on nipple number two.

The pain was behind him now, forgotten, as he stood posing in front of his mirror. But his fantasies of Ken lived on. The one-eyed snake lying just below his waistband swelled, raising its head above the elastic to strike. Claude caught it with one hand, wrestled it into submission and sent it back to its lair, spent and satisfied.

He wiped up, cleaned off and threw on a T-shirt, wincing as the shirt passed over the sensitive nubs of his nipples on the way down; wincing even more as the fabric continued to rub; catching and tugging on the barbells each time he moved.

Ken had put a crisscross of surgical tape over each nipple to protect them before he sent Claude off with his new adornments. But Claude had pulled the tape off when he got home to admire himself in the mirror and forgotten to replace it. Now he paid the price. He lifted his shirt to see a little drop of blood oozing from the left side of the barbell on the right, smearing the glass ball with red.

Claude removed his shirt, dabbed at the blood with the corner of a tissue, unlocked his bedroom door to peak down the hall and make sure no one was watching, and then slipped quietly from his room to the bathroom. A sheet of instructions fluttered in his hand against the bag of nipple care supplies Ken had sent him home with.

Nipple care hurt like hell. And, according to 'What to Expect After Your Piercing', they'd probably be sensitive for at least six weeks. Hadn't he had enough pain in his life? He should have done more research. Maybe this was a big mistake. He turned his uncertain and slightly distressed face to the mirror and posed before it once more. Damn he looked fine! He was smiling as he cut the surgical tape and carefully positioned it over his gold and glass embellishments.

And still smiling as he pulled his t-shirt back over his head and began collecting the tape and the sterile saline solution, the cotton swabs and scissors to put them away until next time.

"Hey Claude, what the hell are you doing in there?" Jay's sudden voice on the other side of the bathroom door startled the smile off Claude's face and sent his arm sweeping across the vanity. Only his quick reflexes in sweeping his arm back again saved the nipple care products from falling over the edge and clattering to the floor.

"I've never seen anyone take so long to take a shit," Jay continued. "I've been waiting for you to get out of there for fifteen minutes. I'm going to order Chinese from Asia House. Do you want the edamame?"

"Hang on, let me think. I'll be out in a minute. I just need to wash my hands." He flushed the toilet, even though the bowl was empty. If Jay thought he'd been taking a dump, he had to make it sound realistic.

Jay would find out about the piercings soon enough. May was making way for June, the weather was warming up, Claude would be walking around shirtless and chest exposed; and then, Claude knew, Jay would be pissed.

He could hear him now 'It's pure vanity. A complete waste of money. Money you could have put in a savings account. You have to start thinking about your future, Claude. You have to wise up. You can't always let your little head do the thinking.' But Jay was not his father, and as long as he handed him the $300 room and board payment on the first of every month, what Claude did with the rest of his money was none of Jay's business.

True, Jay had helped him in more ways than he could count. Not only had he given him a place to stay for a bargain price, he'd helped him maneuver his way through the forms and layers of bureaucracy in his continued quest for asylum. He'd helped him get his green card and gotten him a job at Economy Grocery. He'd opened his arms and made Claude feel like one of the family.

But being a member of the family household also came with rules:

#1 – A curfew – 11:00 on weekdays and 2:00 A.M. on weekends.

#2 – An order – No over night guests or, in other words, no sex under Jay's roof.

Claude understood Jay's reasons for imposing these rules. It was because of Mina. She was an impressionable teenage girl and Jay didn't want his daughter exposed to promiscuity and debauchery. But, just because he understood the rules, and even agreed with them in relation to Mina, that didn't mean he had to like them. And like them, he did not.

Claude stashed his bag of supplies in the cabinet under the vanity and left the bathroom, fighting the urge to jiggle his shoulders and tug at his shirt. The tape was pulling on his skin but it wouldn't do to have anyone take note that he was fidgeting and ask him why. He struck a pose again, one of nonchalance he hoped, and assumed a stride of normalcy as he walked over to the others congregated around the kitchen table.

"Finally. Did everything come out all right?" Jay smirked. "So, is it yes for the edamame? And what else do you want?"

"What are you all getting?"

"I'm getting a quart of pork fried rice to go along with the plain white rice that they always give you. That's for everybody. And for me I'm getting beef skewers, beef with broccoli and beef with snow peas."

"All that?" Claude was rolling his eyes and shaking his head. "For just one person?"

"I'm a big eater!"

"No." Adrian was rolling his eyes too, and smiling as he shook his head. "Well, yes, he is a big eater but beef is what he's getting. Just beef. Who do you think will eat those veggies? The broccoli and snow peas will be on my plate. And shrimp lo mein."

"Yuck to the shrimp." Mina made a face. "I'm getting sweet and sour chicken, like always but this time with double the pineapple. That's my favorite part."

"Well then, yeah, the edamame for me and maybe..." Claude paused, seemingly trying to decide which Chinese delight he was in the mood for, but what he was really doing was trying to work around the feeling of guilt that had suddenly grabbed his gut. He was letting Jay order and pay for food for him, taking advantage of Jay's kindness and generosity; and all the while he was also doing things behind Jay's back. Like the piercings. And like something else too.

Claude cracked his knuckles and jiggled his shoulders. The tape over his left nipple slipped a bit, freeing a fold of skin that was pinched too tight and trapped under the adhesive. It was such a relief, that his guilt was freed as well. It slid away from his gut to let the rumblings of hunger slide in. "I think I'll have the moo shoo pork. And have them throw on a few extra pancakes!"

But guilt returned to gnaw again as the waxed paperboard boxes with wire handles delivered from Asia House emptied and Claude's stomach filled with rice and pancakes and pork and cabbage and mushrooms. Happiness and gaiety shared the table with the four of them as they chewed and joked and laughed. It was a wonderful feeling, a beautiful picture; a picture that would soon be changing.

This was the something else that Claude was hiding. The plans were already in the works but he couldn't bring himself to tell them. Not yet. Besides, Jay would be pissed about this too. And why rock the boat now anyway? August was more than two months out. But he'd have to tell them soon, maybe next week after he won the chicken wing challenge. He'd tell Jay and Adrian, and his little sister Mina, and he'd tell angel Lynn too – On August first he was going to be bailing from the Hendershott household and moving to New Jersey with Juan, his friend from the grocery store.

Juan was a straight dude, but he didn't care that Claude was gay. They shared jokes and conquests, aspirations and woes with each other while they stacked cans of peaches and jars of jelly on shelves and smoked pot behind the building on breaks. Juan had family in New Jersey and a great new job all lined up working on the assembly line at the plastics manufacturing plant where his brother-in-law was manager. And he had a great new apartment all lined up too – an apartment he wasn't quite sure he could afford on his own.

"Come with me, man! My brother-in-law can get you a job at the plant too. You can be my roommate and help with the rent and utilities. I got the two-bedroom. I can fuck who ever I want in my room and you can fuck who ever you want in yours. Are you interested?" he'd asked Claude.

And without a moment's hesitation, Claude had replied "Hell yes!"

Mina was breaking open a fortune cookie and unrolling the strip of white paper enclosed in its golden brown folds. She held it before her, serious eyes morphing to effervescence as she silently read. "This sounds like how Adrian talks! It makes no sense." Bright was her face as she read the fortune out loud. "Do it now! Today will be yesterday tomorrow."

"Do it now!" Jay repeated, grinning. "That does sound just like Adrian. But it makes perfect sense."

"I mean the other part, Dad! The today and tomorrow part."

Mock affront sprung up on Adrian's face and immediately dissolved in a laughing smile. "I always make sense and I can tell a better fortune than that - If you don't learn the meaning of fortune you'll be looking for another job. But you know the sentence in the cookie does make sense. Think about it. If you talk about today tomorrow, you will call it yesterday."

"What?" Mina cocked her head. "Wait a minute. Today is today. And tomorrow... Oh! Now I get it!"

A warm, fuzzy feeling enveloped Claude. This was called having a good time. This was called being together, being a family. How could he leave all this behind? Was he making a mistake in planning to move away? Maybe he hadn't really given it enough thought. Maybe tomorrow at work he should tell Juan he'd changed his mind and decided not to go to New Jersey after all.

One last piece of edamame still sat on Claude's plate. He brought it to his lips, placed it on his tongue and then drew the warm, salty pod threw his teeth. Out popped the beans, right from the pod and into his mouth. And he thought again of Adonis Ken and something else shooting, warm and salty, into this mouth.

To Jay, Adrian and Mina, and to Lynn, he would be forever grateful. They had gone above and beyond to help him in his time of need. But Jay did say he should think about his future. And that's exactly what he was doing. It was like looking into a crystal ball. There he was in New Jersey with his own apartment and his own rules, which were no rules. There he was with a jewel piercing his tongue and desire roaring within him, like the lion tat that roared from his shoulder; wooed by hand and tongue and teeth till his eyes rolled back in his head and he exploded in euphoria.

Sex. Lots of sex. That's what Claude saw in his future. Claude liked it when his little head did the thinking.

Chapter 39
THE TRUTH …

'Telling the truth'

To write a good book, you had to start with a passion, a unique perspective and an interesting storyline. You had to pay attention to detail and populate your story with layered, three-dimensional characters and believable dialogue. You had to draw your reader in, make them see and hear and feel, make them care. You had to tell the truth.

The truth was the sun was bright, but it was not yellow. It was white.

The truth was the best comedies had a touch of drama and the best dramas had a touch of comedy.

The truth was Annie may have looked like she was in her mid-fifties but she was really sixty-three. The middle finger on her right hand often ached with arthritis and had the unfortunate tendency to get stuck in the fuck-you position.

The truth was, even though she was not overweight, her skin was starting to sag and wrinkle, especially on her upper arms and between her breasts.

And the truth was that Annie had lied. Only a little lie, but a lie just the same. 'It took me forever but it's finally done. I finished my new book!'

She'd only told the fib, standing there by the picket fence last Saturday as she chatted with Adrian, because she wanted so badly for it to be true. And it was, after all, almost true. An ending was all she needed. One or two more chapters. The whipped cream and the cherry. A ribbon to wrap round and tie at the top in a jaunty bow.

But then she'd followed that little lie with another. 'Do you think you could read it over and let me know what you think? I'll drop it off next Saturday at the chicken wing challenge.' And she'd only said that because she thought giving herself a deadline might force her writer's blocked brain into creativity.

She'd thought wrong. Here it was, Thursday already, and her brain was still a blank blob. She only had two and a half more days! Two and a half more days to snare the vague shadows in her head and lead them to the light at the end of the tunnel; to whisk a lie and dissolve it into the truth; to turn herself again into an honest woman.

'The moment of truth'

Taking a good photo was something that Jay Hendershott excelled at. And he had a wall in the basement dedicated to the photography awards that had been bestowed upon him to prove it.

He knew that it took a keen sense of observation and a strong attention to detail; noting the position of the sun - the way it sparkled in the eye, from the dewy tips of field grass, off the ripples on the water. Noticing the fold of the fabric, the tilt of the head, the bent of the tree, the rise of the land.

It took a breath held in and a breath let out; no holds barred - strength and vulnerability, honesty and deception, shadow and light; captured with a click at the moment of truth.

But taking a good photo was, at this moment of truth, something Jay could not seem to do. He stood before the mulberry tree in his front yard with the warmth of the morning sun barely noticed on his back, his camera like a foreign object hanging from an unsteady hand on the end of a limp arm, his eyes sending images to his brain that his brain flailed at and tried to send back.

He had come out to the tree to photograph the fluffy white clusters that peeked out like shy children from under mother mulberry's leafy green skirt; clusters that would ripen by mid-June into assertive, ruby-red fruits. But the immature clusters had implored him, frightened instead of shy, to look not up at them, but down at what it was they were frightened of.

A visitor had come in the night and left his mark behind to mar the mulberry's grey/brown trunk. A word, like a bloody wound, painted with a hostile hand in drippy red. FAGGOT.

For seven years he'd lived in this house, as one with his neighbors. Who would have done this? And why today, when his spirits were high with anticipation, ready to welcome friends and eat mountains of chicken wings? Why? Why now? Why today? Why any day?

He reached inside himself for his mantra. 'Fuck 'em. God bless and have a nice day.' It was probably just some teenagers high on a dare and who knew what else. 'Fuck 'em. God bless and have a nice day.' Just a one-time, thoughtless prank, not worth worrying about or feeling violated over. 'Fuck 'em. God bless and have a nice day.' If it escalated into something more, he'd worry about it then. 'God bless everyone, and have a nice day.'

Have a nice day. A smile worked its way onto Jay's face then. He left the tree, walked into the house and returned a few minutes later with a quart size can and a paintbrush.

Jay breathed in. With careful strokes, he surrounded the offence and filled in the heart-shaped outline he had drawn with red paint of his own. When he was done, he stood back, raised his camera to his eye, and breathed out.

Click at the moment of truth; the promise of summer in bright blue and vibrant green, the promise of sweetness in fluffy white clusters of fruit yet to come, the promise of a red heart on a grey/brown trunk that love could block out hate.

'The truth of the matter'

Taste was a matter first of the eyes and the nose, and next of the imagination. But finally, and most importantly, taste was a matter of the tongue.

And the truth of the matter, as per Adrian's tongue, was that his sauce melding tangy tomato, malt vinegar, melted butter, sea salt and chopped jalapenos was perfection. That sauce, bubbling hot and poured then over crisply grilled, meaty chicken wings became a mouthwatering match made in culinary heaven. How could he not win?

There was another truth, however, to this matter of the tongue. Taste was subjective and not all tongues came to the same conclusions. Adrian had no doubt that every single person busy at this moment putting the finishing touches on their own culinary creations was thinking the same as him – that they would be the one crowned king or queen of the chicken wing.

Mina certainly did, glowing with assurance and pride as she pan-fried her wings to a rich, golden brown and carefully poured over them a smooth sauce redolent with honey and rosemary. And Claude surely did, radiating confidence as he reached with his tongs into the deep fryer and brought forth a crispy, batter-dipped treasure of southern fried gold.

Seven chafing dishes, to assure that each entry stayed warm and at the peak of flavor, had been lined up on the speckled black granite of the kitchen island. Adrian nudged his perfectly charred chicken wings off the platter he had placed them on and into one of the chafing dishes now, ladled his sauce over the top and lit the little fuel can underneath.

He looked over at Mina, standing beside him as she poured her chicken from the sauté pan into another of the chafing dishes and put his hands lightly on her shoulders. "Good luck!" He kissed her on the cheek and then stole a bit of her honey-sweet sauce with the tip of an index finger. "Yum," he said, licking the sauce from his finger and smacking his lips.

Over to Claude he went then to pat him on the back and snatch a crumb of crispy coating that fell from a chicken wing and landed on the counter instead of in the dish. "Delicious," he said, popping the morsel into his mouth and biting down on it's crunchy goodness. "But not as delicious as mine!" Adrian broke out into a grin. "I am wishing luck to you both. Luck to us all. May the best man or woman win. And mostly I'm wishing that that man or woman will be me!"

Claude threw Adrian the finger and laughed. "In your dreams, Adrian. It will be me who wins. Your wings are too spicy."

"No. My wings are…"

A muffled but excited scream coming from the direction of the Vandenbunder house next door wafted in through an open window, caught the rest of Adrian's' words and whisked them away unsaid. What was going on over there? Adrian's cheeks reddened, just a bit, and then he smiled.

He'd heard this meant-to-be-private sound before, most times accompanied, for and aft, by adrenalized cries of 'Oh Baby! Honey Baby!' escaping from the Vandenbunder house. No way would he ever ask them (How embarrassed they would be!), but he wasn't innocent enough not to recognize the sounds of making a little whoopee. The Vandenbunders were a wonderful couple, his role models actually. To be still so much in love, still enjoying each other even after all their years together; it was a rare and special thing. He could only wish the same for himself and Jay as their relationship moved through the years.

But wait! Maybe he had been wrong thinking Annie's energized squeal was one of intimacy. This time anyway. Jay was greeting someone at the front door, and it was none other than Carl Vandenbunder, apparently sans his wife. "Here's my winning entry!" Adrian could hear Carl quip jovially. "I didn't want my wings to get cold waiting for Annie. You know how she is sometimes. She gets so excited. Some kind of a revelation about the ending of her new book. Did you hear her scream?"

Adrian heard Jay stifle a laugh then, covering it up with a little cough. He had heard Annie's scream and had jumped to the same usually correct but this time incorrect assumption that Adrian had! Adrian smiled and stifled his own laugh, picturing the wicked, knowing smile he was sure he'd find twitching at the corners of Jay's mouth now.

The next thing Adrian heard was the bubbling gurgle deep in Jay's chest that his little cough had stirred up. That damn, upsetting gurgle. How many times had Adrian pleaded? Couldn't Jay at least try to quit smoking? Jay had to cough again to clear his chest. And Adrian had to shake his head to clear his mind of the worry and frustration that was trying to lodge there.

"Hopefully she'll be here before the contest is over." Carl was still talking. "I want her to see me get the blue ribbon!"

But wait again! What was this revelation about Annie's new book? Hadn't she already told Adrian that it was finished? He must have misunderstood her. Or maybe he had misunderstood Carl, listening in from afar, as he was, to a conversation he wasn't part of.

"Adrian. Adrian!" Mina's voice interrupted his concentration. She was calling his name from the kitchen sink; the water running, her hands lathered with soap.

"What? What is it?"

"You need to answer the door! Didn't you hear the knock? I think it's the Chatelains. And I can't let them in right now!" She lifted her soapy hands to emphasize.

His thoughts dissolved like sea salt in a tomato sauce bath as he hurried to the door. The others were all starting to arrive now – hopeful entrants and hungry judges alike; all ready to lick their fingers and smack their lips.

The truth of the matter, as per the tongues of nineteen people Adrian knew and loved, was upon them. The Hendershott Chicken Wing Challenge had begun.

Chapter 40
DID YOU VOTE FOR ME?

The moon was a white disk mottled with gray, a bright beacon to light the night sky, and Jay stared up at it, entranced. Or at least he pretended to be entranced so that he could also pretend he hadn't heard Adrian's question.

"Did you vote for me?" Adrian's head had been resting, peaceful and dreamy, on Jay's shoulder as they relaxed side by side on the slat-backed glider bench at the far side of the deck. He raised his head to look at Jay when he asked the question and Jay could feel his eyes on the him; like a tractor beam boring into the side of his face to pull forth an answer.

Why not make it simple for himself? He could submit to the tractor beam and let it pull forth an answer of 'yes'. But it would not be the truth, and in good conscience, Jay just couldn't do it.

Not that he hadn't wanted to vote for Adrian, in support of the love of his life, but also in good conscience, he just couldn't do that either. Adrian's chicken wings, even though he did like them, had not been his favorite at the Hendershott Chicken Wing Challenge.

Besides, the contest was supposed to be blind. Each of the entries warming in their chafing dishes (courtesy of Mike Chatelain's Channel 20 advertising connection, Grove House Catering) were identified by number only. He wasn't supposed to know that Adrian was number six. Or that Mina was number two and Claude number three. It wasn't his fault that he could pick out the chicken belonging to members of his household on sight alone. And even blindfolded he'd know Adrian's peppery hot, Mina's honey sweet, or Claude's southern fried; he'd supped on

246

them and snacked on them and, good lord, he'd even had them for breakfast!

And so, as the honest person he was, Jay had tasted all seven entries with an open and unbiased mind and had voted for the chicken wings he truly liked the best - the soy glazed, sesame crusted boneless wings with the wasabi dipping sauce basking in chafing dish number seven.

Entry number seven had garnered six votes to claim first prize. And honestly, he'd already known whose wings these were too. He'd eaten them before - as an appetizer at Mike and Dixie's when they invited them over last November to celebrate Jay's thirty-fifth birthday. Mike had mish mashed several recipes together from his old standby cookbook Elementary Asian.

"Well, did you?" The question again - Adrian wouldn't leave it alone.

"Did you?" He countered instead.

"Did I what, vote for myself? I was forbidden!"

"So? It was a stupid rule anyway. If I had cooked chicken wings and I really thought my wings were the best, I would have voted for myself anyway. I think Big Lou voted for his own wings. He was his own only vote."

"Oh my god. His wings were terrible! What did he have in that sauce? But no, I did not vote for my own wings. I voted for Mike's 'Enter the Dragon' sesame ones. I loved the crunch. And that wasabi dip!"

"Me too."

"You too that you loved them or you too that you voted for them."

"Both."

"Traitor!" Adrian slapped Jay's hand, hard enough to make him wince. He reached up then and Jay instinctively tensed for an accompanying slap to his face; a playful slap hopefully. Instead it was a kiss to the lips that Adrian delivered as he gently squeezed Jay's face between his palms. "But I love you anyway."

"Kiss my ass."

"Oh I will," Adrian promised, snuggling again into Jay's shoulder. "Later, in bed."

Jay firmed his arm up around Adrian and drew him even closer to kiss the top of his head and whisper into his hair. "Why wait till later?"

Adrian just smiled. "I was so happy for Mina that she got second place. She was proud like a strutting rooster with her four votes. Four votes! And I only got two."

"Your wings were my second favorite. And Mina's my third. All the wings were good really. Except Big Lou's. Claude only got two votes too. He was pissed about it, or pissed about something anyway. He seemed a little off all night, didn't you think?"

"Maybe. I don't know. I didn't really notice."

"Well, something's going on with him."

"Hmmm." It was a content purr, locked in love and moonlight, immune to hints of anything problematic. "Everyone was mentioning the heart you painted on the tree." Adrian was mumbling now, half asleep.

The heart. Some had ribbed him about it. Some had complimented his creativity. Some had even ooohed and aaahed over it. But everyone had smiled. And he had smiled too as he stuffed himself with chicken wings and downed long island iced teas, willingly embracing the happiness the heart brought out and shoving away the violation that had brought out the heart.

"Is like… Is like…" Adrian's mumblings were fading out, on a countdown to dreamland. "…to guard us. That word…"

The word. Violation shoved itself back in, chasing away the sleep that Jay himself was starting to drift into like a bucket of ice water poured over his head; or like a dripping brush slopping cold, wet paint to form a hot, red word.

Jay had decided not to tell anyone about that hot, red word. Innocence still existed and it deserved to be protected. But could it be that Adrian had somehow seen the word before Jay painted it over? Had his innocence already been compromised?

His serenity broken, Jay shifted on the bench, suddenly uncomfortable. And in shifting he disturbed Adrian as well.

"Mmmm... What? Was I talking? A dream maybe... No, I remember, it was the heart. I wanted a word to describe. Guardian is the word I want. The mulberry tree is like our guardian now. I love that you painted the heart!" Adrian's eyes flickered softly in the moonlight.

"I had to protect your innocence."

"You think I am innocent? What have you been smoking? Besides cigarettes."

"I've been smoking your essence. Are you ready to kiss my ass now?"

"Come on." Adrian stood, taking Jay's hand to pull him up beside him and lead him into the house.

They only got as far as the living room before Adrian got sidetracked. "Hang on, what's this?" He let go of Jay's hand and reached instead for a blue binder that was sitting on the end table next to the couch. "Oh! It's Annie Vandenbunder's new book! She said she was going to bring it over." He flipped a few pages. "Answers. Answers with a question mark after it." A few more pages leafed through his fingers. "That must be the title."

"I have a question for you that you might be able to answer. Are you going to kiss my ass or not?"

Adrian set the binder back on the end table and reached for Jay's crotch, wrapping his fingers around what had sprouted under the blue denim at his touch. "Because I am so innocent," he unzipped Jay's jeans and slipped his hand inside, "how about I start kissing here," his fingers fumbled for access through the opening in Jay's boxer shorts, "and then work my way round back."

"Yes. Good idea." Desire whispered from the words and burned in Jay's loins.

Foot on the throttle, hand tightened firmly around the stick shift, Adrian pulled Jay along, down the hall and into the bedroom.

Not that Jay had to be lead. His motor was revved. And he already knew the way.

Chapter 41
WAS THIS REALLY THE END?

Oh, the glory of the morning! Especially when it followed, as it did this morning, a night with a particular kind of glory all its own. Summer dawned and fresh was the breeze, warm the sun on her face, warm the cup of coffee in her hand, warm the paver stones under her bare feet, and warm was Beverly's heart as she sat at the tile-topped café-style table on Herb's backyard patio; the bustling sounds and enticing smells of Herb cooking breakfast for them wafting from the open kitchen window behind her.

Breakfast would be buttermilk pancakes again this especially glorious morning, Beverly knew. After whipping up countless batches year after year for their church's annual pancake suppers to the rave reviews of the dining parishioners, buttermilk pancakes were Herb's point of pride.

A few strips of bacon or a couple sausage links would have been a tasty accompaniment to the pancakes, but there would be none of those; Beverly knew that too. Herb didn't eat pork.

What there would be was plenty of butter and maple syrup and a bowl of fruit. And there would be Herb sitting across from her with a smile as they ate the meal he had prepared with a loving hand. No sausage link was worth more than that.

"Do you need any help in there?" Beverly called out, turning her head so her mouth was aimed towards the house and her voice had a better chance of making it into Herb's hearing-aid powered ears. She always asked, even though she knew how Herb would reply.

"Not a bit! You stay right out there and enjoy the sun. I've got everything under control."

Beverly could see Herb through the window, his shoulders moving as he reached for things on the counter and ran water in the sink. She smiled and shook her head, affection soft on her face.

As she turned back to look out into the yard again, the sash on her housecoat loosened and the light cotton fabric shifted, exposing her bare leg from ankle to crotch. Her panties would have shown - if she were wearing panties.

Like a vision, the essence of the glories she had shared last night with Herb cavorted into her mind. Her nipples became points to poke against her flowered robe; heat pulsed in her suddenly moist nether regions.

The night held no ownership over the pleasures of the body, did it? Was there any reason Beverly had to wait until then? Like a vision herself, Beverly rose from her seat; she let her housecoat loosen completely and fall from her shoulders; she stood, willing Herb to glance out and see her there alluring in her nakedness, to glide then, a seductress, into the house where desire would consume them... Right there on the kitchen counter, next to the bowl of pancake batter.

As if! The vision poofed away with a chuckle of reality as Beverly drew the housecoat back over herself and knotted the sash. Herb would never go in for that. He was far too conservative and traditional to appreciate the risqué. He'd be mortified just to know that Beverly had come out to sit on his patio with nothing on under her housecoat but her birthday suit.

Years ago, she probably would have been mortified herself! But age had made her bolder. The racy, the naughty, and the unconventional titillated her these days. Not that the past had ever seen her as a prude. Her husband had never had any complaints.

"Bev?" It was Herb, calling her.

"Yes?" Beverly turned towards the window with her reply, careful this time to hold her housecoat in place so it didn't slip off her leg.

"Did you want to eat breakfast outside?"

"That would be wonderful! It's so gorgeous out here. I'll come in and help you carry stuff out." She jumped up, holding her robe closed to hurry into the house.

Beverly had to admit, as eager as she had been for some male companionship and to rekindle her sex life, the stronger of the emotions that had pounded in her heart at the thought was nerves, and even downright fear. She'd read the articles:

Sexual inactivity in combination with the hormonal changes of the post menopausal woman often leads to vaginal atrophy and consequently, to difficult and painful sexual intercourse

In other words, use it or loose it. And Beverly hadn't used it in ten years! Luckily, 'often' was not 'always', and her fears had been for naught. Beverly's vagina had worked just fine. And so had Herb's similarly inactive penis.

The first time they'd done the deed (It was on the third date. Beverly didn't want to give Herb the impression that she was easy. Honestly though, Herb hadn't even attempted to get physical until then anyway, but, whatever), it hadn't gone that smoothly. Herb's manhood lived under the large shelf and constant shadow of his Santa Clause like belly and getting from point A to point B had required a bit of creative maneuvering. But they'd managed, and to everyone's extreme satisfaction too.

Navigating each other's hills and valleys never posed a problem for them anymore. Practice makes perfect they say. And they'd been practicing at least once a week for six months now.

"Earth to Beverly, Earth to Beverly."

"What?" Beverly had been smiling dreamily, staring absently off into space with her coffee cup halfway between the table and her lips, stalled in midair. She focused her eyes on Herb now and brought the forgotten cup to her lips for a sip. "I'm sorry, were you saying something?" The imp still danced in her smile.

253

"I was just asking how you liked the pancakes. What were you thinking about?"

"About how good the pancakes are. And about how beautiful the morning is and about how glad I am that I'm sitting here eating these delicious pancakes and sharing this beautiful morning with you."

Herb smiled broadly and reached for her hand across the table to give it a squeeze.

Beverly wondered sometimes, and even found it a bit odd, that she liked Herb so much. She would have thought that if she ever fell in love again (Did she say love? Were her feelings for Herb really that strong?), it would be with someone similar to her husband, Clark. But, except for the fact that Herb had a penis, he wasn't very much like Clark at all.

Before Clark got sick, he had always been muscular and athletic. Herb was rotund. She and Clark had enjoyed sharing a bottle of wine together from time to time. Herb was a teetotaler. Clark would dance around the house with her to the lively beats of rock and roll. Herb liked the very un-danceable grooves of smooth jazz. Romantic comedies and love stories had been Clark's movies of choice, as they were hers. Herb gravitated to war movies and historical dramas.

But Herb had the bluest eyes and the warmest smile, and he spread the warmth of his smile over everyone he met. If he saw someone in need, he was at their side in an instant, ready to offer help to friend or stranger alike. He attended church every Sunday and had a deep faith in God that resonated in Beverly's soul. And, well, back to the sex again, Herb was an expert in the ways of the tongue. He ate her up like candy. He made her scream.

"Hey, look at this!" Herb had been perusing the newspaper he had spread open to the right of his plate. He picked it up excitedly now to bring it closer to his face for a better look. "There's a jazz fest coming up next month in Hendrix!"

"Is there? Hendrix is only about an hour's drive from Croakers Norge. Wanna go?"

"I sure was thinking about it!" Herb eyes were as wide as a kid's at Christmas. Then he lost the glow. "But, it's jazz. I know you're not that much into it. Would you really want to go?"

"I would, because you know what? Jazz is actually starting to grow on me." Herb's blue eyes lit up excitedly again. "And besides, Becky Campbell says there's some great antique shops in Dauphin." Only to fall once more into disenchantment. Beverly almost laughed. Apparently Herb was not into antique shops. "Maybe we could spend the whole weekend? Listen to jazz and check out the shops. We could book a couple nights in some nice B & B."

"Maybe." Herb's head bobbed up and down as the word inched out of his mouth, slow and unconvincing. But then the bobbing sped up, excitement returned to his eyes, and a livelier word sprang forth. "Yeah!" The idea had caught fire. "Yeah, maybe we could!"

It was Beverly's turn to reach across the table now and take Herb's hand, soft and warm, in her own. "It'll be so much fun. I can't wait! I'll go online and find out about tickets and check out B & B's and stuff."

"Sounds like a plan. Hey, do you need more coffee, Bev?" Herb was starting to rise, ready to head in for the pot. "I should get one of those insulated coffee carafe things so the coffee doesn't have to stay plugged in to stay warm."

"You don't have to wait on me hand and foot, you know Herb. I'm a big girl. You stay here and I'll get the coffee." Into the house she went to retrieve the coffee pot, practically skipping, her head in the clouds, gliding on air.

She returned the same way, happiness radiating from the hand she placed on Herb's shoulder as she refilled his cup. Her hand came away cold.

"Look at this article." Angry was the finger that Herb jabbed into the newsprint. "These two queers are all sad and sobby because some baker refused to make them a wedding cake. And they expect me to get all sad and sobby too? They shouldn't even be allowed to get married! It goes against all the

255

laws of God." Disgust boiled in the voice that spewed from Herb's mouth. "It says it right in the bible, marriage is meant to be between a man and a woman." Vulnerable and defenseless felt the body that cowered now under Beverly's lightweight housecoat, longing for the security of her panties and nighty. "Gay marriage and gay rights. What about the baker's rights? Why should he be forced to do something he doesn't believe in? It would be like joining hands with the devil and spitting in God's face." Herb slapped the paper closed with an agitated hand and gave it an irate shove.

Slap. A sound too close to home. Beverly startled as a memory jarred loose; a memory of a different slap delivered by the hand of a different Beverly; a Beverly that had held the same hate filled opinion as Herb, a Beverly that no longer existed.

The newspaper slid with Herb's shove across the mosaic-patterned tiles and toppled over the table's edge, catching the breeze as it fell to skitter across the patio and take nest in the rosebush beside the sliding glass door. "It can stay there," Herb muttered.

Instead Beverly went to rescue it, careful not to rip the thin sheets as she freed them from the thorny branches. She folded the newspaper neatly and laid it, offensive article side up, on the empty chair next to Herb.

Herb barely noticed. He was grabbing, still agitated, for his coffee cup. Coffee sloshed out at his rough touch and ran down his hand. "Damn that's hot." He winced as he wiped the spill from his hand and off the table with a napkin. "I guess I wasn't paying attention that you refilled my cup." He smiled at Beverly apologetically, almost surprised to see her there, so absorbed had he been in his protestations. "Sorry about ranting like that. I'm a pretty easygoing guy but there's some things that just go completely against my grain. And perverts are one of them. Gay rights. Them and their ideas disgust me."

How much of love was sex? And how much of sex was love? Beverly took her seat again next to Herb, deliberately letting one leg slip out from the folds of her robe to lay liberated and proud above the other as she crossed her legs. "We all begin the same, you know." She spoke quietly, bringing her coffee cup to her lips and looking pointedly over the top of the cup at Herb as she took a sip. "Tiny specks of life too small to even see."

Herb wasn't paying attention. His eyes were on her leg.

"Did I tell you that my son was coming for a visit next week?"

Herb's eyes (they were bright and lively now; no longer stormy and dark) left her leg and looked up at her face. "You did. I'm looking forward to meeting him. Actually I think I remember your son from when he played high school football. My daughter was a cheerleader. I'm pretty sure she had a crush on him." Herb chuckled at the memory.

"Jay's bringing his whole family. He's anxious for his daughter to see where her roots came from. My granddaughter was born in Croakers Norge but she doesn't really remember anything about it. Mina was only seven or eight when they moved to New York. She's fourteen now. And he's excited to show Adrian around too. The quaint village he grew up in and all the places he used to frequent.

"Is Adrian Jay's wife?"

"No. But they've been living together for several years now. I smell marriage in their future, which makes me very happy. I just love Adrian."

"Well, I'll be looking very much forward to meeting your granddaughter and future daughter-in-law too."

"Son-in-law."

Herb looked confused. "What was that again? I missed what you said."

"No, you probably didn't. Son-in-law is what I said. Adrian will be my son-in-law. And he won't be Jay's wife. He'll be Jay's husband."

Herb stared at Beverly, his eyes blinking fast, like a directionless turn signal.

"In case you haven't quite figured it out, my son's gay." Beverly paused, giving Herb's brain a chance to catch up with her words. "I'm proud of my son, Herb, of what he has accomplished, of the man that he has become. He and his family are very important to me and we come as a package deal. Like soup and sandwich or like pancakes and syrup. If you can't accept him, then you don't get me either."

Would Herb be around to shake Jay's hand when he came for his visit next week? Would there ever be a jazzy trip to Hendrix where Beverly would cozy up beside Herb in a bed and breakfast's canopy bed at the end of a delightful day? Would she ever find out what was in that tiny velvet box she had mistakenly glimpsed tucked in Herb's underwear drawer under his size fifty-two boxer shorts?

Blink once for 'yes' and twice for 'no'. Blink constantly for 'muddled uncertainty'. Wordlessly open and close your mouth for 'answer in murky water and sinking fast'.

Beverly rose from her seat. Silently she stood in the murky water and reached across the muddled uncertainty to collect the breakfast dishes and stack them up. She picked up the stack and started to carry it towards the house.

Finally the opening and closing of Herb's mouth produced words. "Just leave those on the counter. There's no need for you to stay. I can clean up by myself."

And Beverly guessed that was her answer.

Except to pull a pair of panties over her vulnerability and tie on her sneakers, Beverly didn't even bother to dress. She stuffed her belongings into a paper grocery bag and swept out of Herb's house, her housecoat flapping around her legs as she threw the bag onto the passenger seat and got behind the wheel.

She sat there, staring at the controls, her head suddenly in a fog. Was this really the end? What should she do now? Where was her key? And why was the radio playing when she hadn't even started the car yet? It was her favorite song!

Awareness dawned and Beverly fished in her purse for her cellphone.

"Hello?" It was out of habit that she answered the phone this way. Modern technology had already informed her it was Adrian.

Notes of earnest excitement and sincerity flowed into her ear. "Hello Mom! I have something to ask you. I've gotten a ring. I want to ask Jay to marry me. You know I love him with all my heart. But first, I am hoping for your blessing."

The blessing that rose from her own heart washed off her tongue before she could give it, with a quiet sob and a stream of tears.

"Mom? Mrs. Beverly? What is it? Why are you crying?"

"They're happy tears, Adrian. I'm overjoyed. Yes, certainly you have my blessing." It was both the truth and a lie, splashed with tears that were both joy and despair.

A simple question and an answer that was anything but, pushed and pulled in all directions, just like life and the tiny speck it began with.

ABOUT THE AUTHOR

Diane Rivoli lives in beautiful upstate New York with her husband of forty plus years, Joseph. She enjoys the changing of the seasons, singing karaoke, puttering in the garden, and visits to the now empty nest by the two grown sons that vacated years ago and the daughter-in-law of her dreams.

In addition to *Push And Pull*, Diane is also the author of the 2015 novel *License* and a poetry collection, *Every Moment is a Poem, Every Poem a Song*.

License, a sequel of sorts to *Push And Pull,* ends four years before *Push And Pull* begins. Jay Hendershott, the central character in *Push And Pull*, is introduced as a minor character in *License*. Dixie Andrews Chatelain, Jay's friend and co-worker and a minor character in *Push And Pull*, takes center stage in *License*.

www.dianerivoli.com

dianerivoli@gmail.com

17462949R00163

Made in the USA
Middletown, DE
03 December 2018